Highla...

Convenient mar...

Neighboring Scottish clans must form alliances to defeat a dangerous common enemy. New clan leader Ross MacMillan is prepared to enter into a marriage contract to safeguard his people. His brother and sister are under orders to marry strategically as well. Is there a way for love to flourish amid the battle for land and castles in the Highlands?

Read Ross's story from Terri Brisbin in
The Highlander's Substitute Wife
Available now

Fergus's story from Jenni Fletcher in
The Highlander's Tactical Marriage
On sale March 2022

And Elspeth's story from Madeline Martin in
The Highlander's Stolen Bride
On sale April 2022

Author Note

When asked to consider working on a connected project with Jenni Fletcher (with whom I just worked on the Sons of Sigurd series) and Madeline Martin (with whom I just collaborated on the multi-author self-published Tourney World project last summer), I jumped at the chance! We set up a couple of Zoom chats to brainstorm and, along with the inspiration of Neil Oliver's Scottish history videos and our love of Scotland, came up with the Highland Alliances series.

As usually happens with me, the universe sends me signs that I'm heading in the right direction— the castles I needed in my story showing up on Facebook and on TV, the period we chose pointing us to some wonderful conflicts and many other surprises as we moved along with writing the series.

So, we begin Highland Alliances in the southwestern part of Scotland, near the islands and where powerful men move as they wish.

I hope you enjoy the series and my story. It features:

1. Cinnamon-roll hero (crusty outside, gooey inside!)

2. Slow-burn love

3. Fast-burn sex

4. Marriage of (in)convenience

5. Enemies to lovers to LOVE

And Scotland, too.

Happy reading!

TERRI
BRISBIN

———

The Highlander's
Substitute Wife

HARLEQUIN®
HISTORICAL™

Recycling programs
for this product may
not exist in your area.

ISBN-13: 978-1-335-40761-0

The Highlander's Substitute Wife

Copyright © 2022 by Theresa S. Brisbin

This edition published by arrangement with Harlequin Books S.A.

For questions and comments about the quality of this book,
please contact us at CustomerService@Harlequin.com.

Harlequin Enterprises ULC
22 Adelaide St. West, 41st Floor
Toronto, Ontario M5H 4E3, Canada
www.Harlequin.com

Printed in U.S.A.

When *USA TODAY* bestselling author **Terri Brisbin** is not being a glamorous romance author or in a deadline-writing-binge-o-mania, she's a wife, mom, grandmom and dental hygienist in the southern New Jersey area. A three-time RWA RITA® Award finalist, Terri has had more than forty-five historical and paranormal romance novels, novellas and short stories published since 1998. You can visit her website, www.terribrisbin.com, to learn more about her.

Books by Terri Brisbin

Harlequin Historical

Highland Alliances

The Highlander's Substitute Wife

Sons of Sigurd

Tempted by Her Viking Enemy

A Highland Feuding

Stolen by the Highlander
The Highlander's Runaway Bride
Kidnapped by the Highland Rogue
Claiming His Highland Bride
A Healer for the Highlander
The Highlander's Inconvenient Bride

The MacLerie Clan

Taming the Highlander
Surrender to the Highlander
Possessed by the Highlander
The Highlander's Stolen Touch
At the Highlander's Mercy
The Highlander's Dangerous Temptation
Yield to the Highlander

Visit the Author Profile page
at Harlequin.com for more titles.

Prologue

Caistéal Suibhne (Castle Sween), Argyll, Scotland—
August in the Year of Our Lord 1360

Their ancient enemy had arrived with the late-summer-morning fog. It had formed in the estuary and spread up the river and over the shores, hiding their presence until it was too late. Half of his men were killed before a warning cry rang out into the eerie silence. When the fog cleared, many of the MacMillan warriors, some of their villagers and, worst of all, their chieftain lay slaughtered.

Ross MacMillan stared out from the battlements of Castle Sween and surveyed the loss of life and the damage to the outbuildings and village. With each breath he tried to control his rage and his grief as he sorted through the choices facing him and the clan.

The name of Alexander Campbell was known by all in this area for his villainous and deadly acts two decades ago. He'd not been heard from since his forced exile from Scotland as punishment for his heinous crimes. No one, not a clan around here, had ever expected him to return. And now they'd paid the price for their wilful ignorance.

'Ross.' His brother Fergus stood closer behind Ross than he realised. Turning to face him, Ross let out the breath he'd been holding.

'The elders are finished and await you in the hall,' Fergus said. Ross nodded, but his brother glanced away before meeting his eyes. 'Will you accept?'

'If they offer it, aye.'

'You are the eldest male of Cormac's relatives. You are already commander of his, our, warriors. The only others who would offer any resistance to you lie in their grave cloths awaiting blessings and burial,' Fergus argued. Though why his brother did so, he knew not. Fergus usually kept his thoughts and words to himself, so this was more than Ross had heard him speak in a long time.

'Aye, I will accept.'

They walked to the steps leading down into the yard and Fergus stopped at the bottom before moving on. Something yet unsaid bothered his brother. Considering all that had happened this day and the things yet left to come, Ross could not pick out just one vexing thing from the dozens that he'd thought on before Fergus's arrival.

'Everything will change,' Fergus said.

'Aye.' Ross waited for Fergus's true question. His brother's habit of taking a while to get to the real topic of concern was familiar.

'What will you do? What will we do?'

Although both of them had stood high in their uncle's regard, neither had expected Cormac to die before producing an heir of his body. Ross understood the enormity of what he faced—he must gather their allies, organise their people and resources, protect the clan and carry out his duties as their new chieftain.

'We will do our duty, Fergus.' He stared at his brother. 'I will need your help and co-operation.'

'You always have my help. I will swear my fealty to you as my chieftain.' Ross could not fault his younger brother if he was not looking at the wider situation as he so easily pledged his loyalty.

Ross followed his brother across the yard to the door of the keep. Their path was slowed by many who stopped him to ask questions and by others who sought his advice and orders. As they reached the hall and stood before the gathering of the elders and counsellors of the clan, Ross whispered his warning to Fergus.

'Doing our duty means marriage, Fergus.' Fergus nodded and smiled, believing Ross spoke only of his own betrothal.

'I will stand at your side, Brother,' Fergus replied.

'As I will at yours.'

Fergus turned, shaking his head and shrugging. When Ross began to walk past him, his brother grabbed his arm.

'What are you saying?'

'We have been struck hard, Fergus. Our only path to survival and to defeating the Campbells is with allies.'

'Aye. I ken.'

'Well, consider this then, Brother. You and our sister Elspeth are now of use in establishing connections with several other clans to benefit us in the coming battles.'

Ross understood immediately, as would the elders, that he and his marriageable siblings would draw offers from the neighbouring clans. Treaties, supplies, gold and warriors would be negotiated in marriage contracts, all necessary if he, if they, hoped to prepare to destroy their returned enemies. And none of them would have much choice when it came to the marriages to be made.

As the truth struck Fergus, his eyes widened at his own prospects. Then fear filled his gaze, but Ross believed that to be the sensible fear of any man facing marriage. Finally, Fergus shrugged.

'Marriage,' he whispered, in a voice flushed with trepidation.

'Marriage. For each of us and Elspeth as well,' Ross confirmed.

'I am glad you will be chieftain and be the one to tell Elspeth of her fate,' Fergus said. 'My chieftain,' he mocked with a bowing of his head.

When Ross's name was called, he turned his attention to the matter at hand and the oath he must swear to protect his clan.

Marriage would come later, but it would come.

He just wished he would not be the one to tell their sister about hers.

Over the next weeks, and as he'd expected, none of them was happy with the decisions made about their betrothals. One of the elders tried to assuage his concerns by explaining how arranged marriages were the most successful. Watching his sister's and especially his brother's reactions to the news of theirs did not portend much happiness for either one. Ross was the only one who'd not met or known his intended before and now he knew not if he should feel comfortable or if the tiny sliver of pure dread that inched down his back was the warning he should heed.

Only time, and the arrival of his bride, would tell.

Chapter One

Caistéal Dùn Naomhaig (Dunyvaig Castle), Islay,
Scotland—three weeks later

The noise of people and their work in the keep and around it woke her long before she was ready to wake. Separated by water from the mainland, Iona—her home for the last three years—was never this noisy. Contemplative brothers and sisters never yelled out commands or questions. No, she was definitely no longer on Iona.

Ilysa MacDonnell yet wore the clothing she had on her back when her father's men took her from the nunnery. She'd given up the garments of privilege soon after her arrival on the holy island and took to the simple habit of those who had taken their vows and among whom she worked.

Shifting on the unfamiliar soft mattress, she ached from the top of her head to the soles of her feet. Which, she now realised, were bare. Leaning up on her side, she stared down at them and tried to bring to mind the memory of removing her stockings and shoes. A shake of her head told her that her veil and wimple remained in place.

'You look like a nun, Ilysa.'

'And I live like one, Lilidh,' she replied with a shrug. She'd not heard her sister enter so she must have been in the room already, waiting for her to wake. Swinging her feet over the side of the raised bed, Ilysa slid off to stand.

'I took your stockings and shoes off,' Lilidh admitted. 'I remember that you like to sleep with them so.'

Tears filled Ilysa's eyes as good memories of her elder sister tending to her flooded her thoughts. That was all it took for Lilidh raced across the chamber and pulled Ilysa into a fierce hold. 'I have missed you, Sister.'

'And I, you, Lilidh.'

Remaining in a tight hug for several long moments, Ilysa savoured the warmth and emotions of such an embrace. Other than tending to injuries or illness, there was no such physical touching at the nunnery. And, in this moment, she realised how very much she'd missed such a thing.

Loud, boisterous, emotional and physical in every move they made, the MacDonnell kith and kin were the furthest thing from the community in which she'd lived for three years. How had she survived without all of this?

As Lilidh released her and stepped back, her glance moved down Ilysa and fixed on her arm. 'Did I hurt you?' she asked. 'Your arm?'

'Nay.' Ilysa's useless left arm hung at her side and had not been caught up in the hug. ''Tis fine. Truly.'

Years ago, mayhap five or so, Lilidh had not realised the extent of Ilysa's injury and the undependable control she had over the damaged arm and had sat on it by accident. Only the cracking sound of the bone breaking had alerted Ilysa to what had happened. At least, she'd felt no pain in it…then.

'Do you ken why I am here? Father's men would say nothing but for the call home by him.'

She leaned her head to one side and then the other, trying to ease the tightness and discomfort from sleeping on too soft a mattress. Reaching up, she took hold of the wimple's strap just as her sister did.

'Here. Sit,' she ordered. 'I will see to it.' Lilidh lifted the veil off and had the wimple loosened and the coif moved aside before Ilysa could warn her about the…

'They have cut your hair?' Lilidh dropped the headdress and gauzy fabric and touched Ilysa's now collar-length locks. Her hair had reached well below her hips, as Lilidh's blonde tresses did. 'They cut your hair!' The soft caress of her sister's fingers belied her anger. 'How dare they?' Lilidh moved from behind her to meet her gaze. Ilysa took her sister's hand and tugged her closer.

''Twas my decision, Lilidh.'

A deep silence surrounded them while her sister stared at her hair and thought on her words.

'Pray tell me you have not taken vows?' Lilidh shook her head wildly and squeezed her hand. 'I beg you, tell me you have not.'

Something in the tone of Lilidh's voice alerted her to more than sisterly concern. A desperation deep within her voice, in the pleading way she asked about vows made Ilysa uneasy. Very uneasy.

Although that had not been her plan, it should not be a surprise to anyone if Ilysa chose to enter the full life of the nunnery rather than continue to live as a lay sister. No one had ever asked her about it, but then her father had, until just two days ago, allowed her to fall from his memory or concern. She'd received no messages or letters from him, no orders or questions, nothing since the day she'd climbed on to the birlinn that had taken her to the island.

'I have—' Her words were interrupted when the door swung open, crashing against the wall, and both of them jumped in surprise.

And there he stood—Iain MacDonnell, chieftain of this branch of the mighty clan that controlled huge swathes of the islands and highlands here along the south-western coast of Scotland.

Her father.

Still tall. Still wide in his shoulders, chest and arms. Not looking any older than when she'd seen him last. Even his hair had not dared to thin or go grey and reveal his age. The cruel slant of his mouth was the same. The way he strode into a chamber as well. So was the manner in which he fisted his hands as he moved—always ready to strike out. Always ready. Nothing different in three years. Ilysa could not stop the shiver that raced through her at the sight of him.

'Vows?' he said in a whisper. Oh, it was much safer for anyone involved if he was shouting out his commands or insults. When his voice dropped low and he spoke slowly, someone would pay a price. 'You had better not have taken vows!' He closed the space between them and reached out. 'What the hell happened to your hair, girl?'

He grabbed hold of her hair, tugging her up on to her toes and closer to him, and studied her face in silence. The grimace of pain she could not help, but she clenched her jaws and lips together to make certain no cry left her mouth. When she did not speak, he pulled again and shook her. 'What happened to your hair?'

'Father?' Lilidh's soft voice broke the tension. 'I pray you, let her speak.'

He released his punishing hold on her so quickly Ilysa lost her balance and fell to her knees. Her scalp screamed from his abuse and she let out a breath before even trying to speak.

'I had my hair cut to make it easier to wear the habit like the others. For my, for our, work around the nunnery. Though the prioress harbours a wish for me to join their community permanently, I have made no such commitment.'

'Oh, does she? Well, I paid too much for her to accept you until I make a decision about your place.' He crossed his massive arms over his chest and snorted. He did not like to be challenged and especially not by a woman. Not a wife, a noblewoman or even a holy woman. The MacDonnell paid no heed unless he wished to.

Ilysa bowed her head not to let her anger show. He did not want her around, did not want to see her deformity and did not wish her shame to be his. But, he also wanted no one else to wish for her presence. Living at the nunnery had given her comfort. A place where her efforts were valued, not her appearance. A community where they lived in peace without the constant violence and furore of her father.

From her position, on her knees, on the floor before him, Ilysa understood she would never feel that peace again. He had jerked her chain and she was back in his control once more.

'Get up now. Get her out of that…that—' She glanced up to see him pointing at her clothing. 'Make her ready. The agreements are signed and the ceremony takes place this morn.'

Lilidh's trembling hand slipped into her own and Ilysa knew the explanation would be bad. Luckily for her, her sister wrapped Ilysa's arm under her good one and had a firm hold when her father explained.

'You are contracted for a marriage. The MacMillan needs a bride and I need the alliance.'

'Marriage?' Ilysa searched her memory for anything she knew about the chieftain of the MacMillan clan. 'But, Father, I cannot marry…' The expression in his eyes then warned her off finishing her words or voicing any objection.

Though Lilidh had a tight grip on her, her sister would not meet her gaze. One thing she'd learned about Lilidh while growing up together was that her sister was always the one who came away unscathed. So, somehow, Lilidh had something to do with Ilysa being considered or chosen when this marriage was being negotiated.

'Cover that disgraceful hair,' her father ordered. 'Be in the hall in an hour.'

She could not think of a thing to say to him, so she lowered her gaze and watched him walk to the door.

'Make certain you keep that useless flesh and your face covered. Wear your heaviest veil and do not take it off or raise it unless I give you permission.' When she did not answer, he took one stride back to her and grabbed her chin to force her gaze to his. 'Do not think to naysay me or offer anything but your word of consent when asked. Do you understand me, Daughter?' He squeezed her chin until she feared his fingers would bruise her skin.

'I do.' She managed to force the words out against his brutal grasp.

After another brief glance at her hair and then at her arm, he released her and left. The sound of the door slamming echoed through the chamber as his heavy footsteps moved down the corridor outside.

Ilysa stood unmoving for several moments, trying to sort through her physical pain and her emotional distress. Lilidh held on, not releasing her or speaking. Which meant one thing. Turning to face her sister and witnessing the guilt in her eyes before she controlled her expression, Ilysa shook her head.

This. This constant threat of lies and treachery she had not missed at all. It had taken three years for her to forget this part of her family's, and her sister's, habitual backstabbing and only hours to remember it clearly.

'Lilidh, what have you done?'

It took her less than an hour to go from a young woman who had found a measure of happiness and peace to a bride bartered for her father's purposes, who now faced a life of uncertainty amid his schemes and plans.

Lilidh explained little as she gathered her own gowns and veils and dressed Ilysa in finery she had not worn in years. Over it all, Ilysa would wrap a length of plaid around her shoulders as a shawl so that she could tuck her arm under it. Ilysa allowed the silence to continue until the maidservant was dismissed and she remained alone with her sister.

'Tell me,' Ilysa said. When Lilidh ignored her demand and fussed over securing her short curls under a simple coif, Ilysa asked again, 'Tell me.'

'A request came from the MacMillans for an alliance with Father,' she said. 'He did not seem happy to do it at first, but then more messengers arrived from here and there and, suddenly, he agreed to a marriage alliance with the new chieftain.'

'New chieftain? When did that happen?'

On Iona, she'd received little news of the world outside. The prioress would share bits with the community when she received missives or when visitors brought word, but without steady communications with kith or kin, she'd learned little. And since none of her family had written to her in the last three years…

'A few months ago? Mayhap more recently than that.' Lilidh shrugged. 'I pay little heed to Father's machinations.'

Such an atrocious lie should make her sister burst into flames. Somehow, though, she managed to speak the words without hesitation. Since their mother's death, Lilidh had not only paid heed to her father's actions, but turned herself into his apt pupil. Did Lilidh think her sister's memory had remained on Iona? She shook her head.

'Others may believe that about you, Lilidh, but I did not leave my wits at the nunnery. What did you do when you learned of Father's decision?' The answer became clear before her sister opened her mouth. 'You suggested me.'

Silence descended and filled the chamber. Lilidh's hands stilled and then she let out a breath.

'I am not ready to marry,' Lilidh said. 'And you of all people should remember that my mind is set on marrying The MacLean's son.'

Ilysa's throat tightened at the mention of Lilidh's choice. Graeme MacLean had been the man Ilysa was supposed to marry. Right after a visit to Dunyvaig and meeting her in person for the first time, he'd seen Lilidh. Within weeks, Ilysa had been banished to Iona and the match between her sister and Graeme became a topic of negotiations. Negotiations that were not yet settled, it would seem.

It was not that she cared about Graeme or even wanted to marry. It was her sister's complete disregard for anyone or anything that did not centre on her. Ilysa had learned that early in life even while wishing it was not the truth of her sister's nature.

'So, you are not betrothed and yet you offered my hand for this…this…alliance Father wants?'

Her sister turned away and put several paces between them and did not answer, making the truth clear without words. Ilysa grabbed the rest of the veils from her hand.

'Ilysa.'

'Nay,' she said, waving her sister away. 'I will finish here and see you at the ceremony below.'

Lilidh opened her mouth to say something and then

stopped herself. Ilysa watched her elder sister walk to the door of the chamber and lift the latch before Lilidh turned back.

'I am sorry, Ilysa. Truly sorry. I beg your forgiveness.'

Ilysa did not breathe again until the door closed. Lilidh's words and expression told her that she would not see her sister at the ceremony.

So, there was still more she was not being told. More intrigues and being manoeuvred by her father to get what he wanted. And he always got what he wanted, no matter the cost to anyone else. Part of her understood that her sister did what she must to survive, yet that did not help the pain in her heart over Lilidh's disregard for her.

Ilysa stood then and placed the veils over her coif, angling them so they overlapped in front of her face. Light barely passed through the layers as she went to the bed and searched for the special sleeve that lay tangled within her discarded habit. Tugging it free, she smoothed it flat and found the straps on each end.

The design of it by the seamstress at the nunnery was ingenious, for it supported her arm and kept it from harm. With the sleeve in place and its straps tied around her—one end down from her shoulder, across her back and tied at her waist—the sleeve kept her arm covered so people did not gawk as much as when she did not wear it. It supported her arm and kept it close to her body which meant there were fewer accidental injuries. And, it eased the pain in her shoulder and neck from the weight of an arm that could not support itself.

With her arm secured and the veils in place, Ilysa

walked to the door and reached out to lift the latch…
and could not do it. Her hand, her good hand, trembled
so badly she could not make her fingers touch the latch.

The urge to run, to escape, filled her until it was
nearly uncontrollable. For three years, she'd lived in
peace. She'd lived without fear. She'd lived with purpose.

Now, she must survive her father's plans simply to
live.

The burning in her gut and the tightness in her chest
reminded her that she did not believe she would. Finally,
the realisation that her delay would bring her father
spurred her to push past the fear and leave her chamber.

Only when she reached the great hall did she discover how truly strange this marriage indeed was. A
brief lift of the veils to see her way forward revealed
that, other than her father and his closest counsellors
and warriors, two men who were strangers to her and
the priest standing at the ready, the hall was empty of
any other family members or friends. Even the servants
were missing if she went by the lack of the usual sounds
they made when carrying out their duties.

Crossing the stone floor and heading towards the
place where they gathered in the front of the huge chamber, Ilysa listened for any words or indications of what
was going on. When she reached the steps that led up
to the dais, she stopped and waited.

'Stand here,' her father said, from her left. He took
hold of her arm from behind and pulled her to a spot a
few paces away. Unless she lifted the veils, she could
see nothing more than the feet of those standing before
her. 'We are ready.'

The priest, an unfamiliar one, began to pray then in Latin, offering up pleas to the Almighty for the bride and groom, pleas for bairns, and offering thanks for various blessings. She understood these more after learning much of the ancient language while at the nunnery. After droning on for a long time, the priest paused and called out their names.

'Ross, son of Donald MacMillan and Margaret Mac-Lean, do you consent to this marriage?'

Ilysa waited to hear the voice of her soon-to-be husband. Her fingers itched to tear off the veils and see him, but she stopped herself from doing that. What did he look and sound like? Was he ruthless and brutal like her father? How old was he, if he was the new chieftain? Had he been married before?

So many questions raced through her thoughts in that long moment before he answered. As the man moved to her other side and stood close enough that she could feel the movement of his legs against the skirt of her gown, she waited on his vow.

'I, Dougal MacMillan, cousin to The MacMillan and sent under his seal and at his orders, do give his full consent and acceptance of this marriage and the bride here given.'

After he'd announced his name, Ilysa missed most of the rest of it. The man she would marry was not here at all. Instead, he'd sent a man to marry her by proxy. A man named Dougal was here to claim her for someone else.

And where could the man she was marrying be?

'Lilidh Ilysa MacDonnell, your father has given his permission and now you must give your consent to enter this marriage.' She was so confused by the name she'd been called, for the priest had switched her name around in the wrong order, that she again missed much that he said after the name was pronounced. Her father's jesting demand that his daughters share their names, each in a different order, had come back to haunt...her. He now tightened his grip on her arm.

'Pay heed, girl!' His rough whispered words were low enough that the others did not hear.

'Aye, I consent.' It did not matter that she did not want this marriage. Or that she still harboured the dreams of a young woman for a marriage of her own choosing and with a man she loved. All that mattered was to survive and to do that, she must obey her father. And she would.

The next time she was prompted to speak, she did so quickly. Her father's grip eased as they moved through the ceremony and as her fate was sealed. Too soon, all the words had been said and she stood waiting for whatever came next.

In a usual wedding, the customary feasting would begin and continue for hours if not days, with the ceremonial bedding occurring very quickly. But, this one? She knew not what to expect. Without a word of warning, her father dragged her forward to a table nearby and released her. Pushing a quill into her hand, he held her arm over the parchment.

'Sign your true name on the document, not your sister's,' he instructed in a near whisper.

Once more, the shuffling of feet told her that her husband's man approached. The movement of quill over parchment could be heard as a low scratching sound in the surrounding silence.

With her father's harsh breathing urging her on, she held the veils away from her face and leaned over the parchment document lying on the table. The marriage declaration. Her father plucked the quill from her grasp as soon as she finished signing her own name and pulled her back away from the table.

'Father Donald, if you would finish it?' Dougal Mac-Millan asked of the priest.

More scratching and then it was done.

She was done. Her dreams of a life of service and contemplation were done.

'Are you satisfied, Sir Dougal?' her father asked the man.

'Aye, my lord, I am as The MacMillan will be, too, once the supplies and men you have agreed to provide arrive at Sween.' He cleared his throat and continued, 'And, of course, his bride.' The man must have a kind side to his nature for he tried to make it seem that she was of as much value as the supplies and men she brought to the marriage were.

Those few assembled began to disperse and she was left standing alone, with no idea of what to do or where to go. The nervousness spread through her as the silence continued until she called out to the man who had stood for her husband.

'Sir Dougal, are you there?'

'Aye, my lady, right here at your side,' he said as he walked back to her. 'How can I be of service to you?'

She heard it again—that kindness, this time in his voice, and she was tempted to take the veils off and see him. Her father's cough reminded her not to disobey his orders.

'I ken not what is expected of me now.'

'My lady, we will leave at daybreak on the morning tide and return to Castle Sween where you will meet your husband.'

'Why is he not here?' she asked.

'Lilidh—' The warning was clear and dark in her father's single word. He was continuing with the farce that it was her sister who was marrying this man's chieftain. She drew in a breath to correct him, but his growl made her think better of it. 'Mind you respect your husband and his duties. I ask your pardon for her disrespect, sir. She is headstrong and will benefit from a firm hand applied generously and often to bring her to heel.'

Her pride bristled as she realised that her father was giving the man she'd just married permission to beat and mistreat her. A scream built deep within her, pushing against her self-control and the need to let it out. But the fear she'd learned in her father's household strengthened her resolve to remain silent.

'My lady, The MacMillan is overseeing the repairs to the keep and to the needs of his people. He meant no insult to your honour with his absence.'

Mollified somewhat, she nodded.

'Go to your chambers and pack your belongings. I will have your supper sent to you so you may prepare for your departure on the morrow,' her father instructed.

'My lord?' Ready to flee, Ilysa remained as The MacMillan's man addressed her father. 'There is no need to deny your daughter a wedding supper. This arrangement is different than most and hasty, for good reasons, certainly. But a bride should be—'

His words cut off so quickly she thought him struck dumb by the Almighty. Her father must have given their guest the glare that warned anyone from questioning his orders. Her hand was reaching up to remove the veils when her father grabbed it and held it still.

'Go to your chambers now, Daughter.' He released her and gave her a little shove as he turned her towards the stairway. 'Sir, until your chieftain receives her, she is still under my domain. She will be at the dock at daybreak.'

She reached the stairway and turned back towards her father. Daring a quick peek, she lifted one side of the veils and watched as The MacMillan's man strode off in the opposite direction. Anger poured off him with every step he took. In spite of it, he did nothing but walk away. Most importantly, he did not challenge her father's words or declaration.

No one ever challenged her father…and succeeded.

She did not have to be banished for three years or be returned on only a word from him to have forgotten learning that particular lesson. Though she was angry with herself for not speaking up about her name or alerting The MacMillan's representative that he'd accepted the wrong woman as bride for his chieftain, Ilysa had no choice but to remain silent.

The MacMillan chieftain would discover very quickly that he'd been duped into marrying her. The true question was whether whatever bargain he'd struck with her father would outweigh the man's pride.

Since the journey from Dunyvaig Castle to Sween would take less than a day, she would discover the answer quickly.

Chapter Two

'Ross, I must have a word with ye.'

Ross turned from the discussion he was having with the steward and looked past his cousin Dougal to see his new bride. When he saw no one, he narrowed his gaze at the man he'd sent, the man he'd trusted, to carry out the proxy marriage to The MacDonnell's daughter.

'Where is she?' Everyone within hearing went quiet at his tone.

'As I said, I must have a word with ye in private.'

Ross nodded his head towards the small chamber off the hall that he knew was empty now. It stood waiting for some of the supplies that were to accompany his new bride on her arrival here. Once within, he closed the door and crossed his arms over his chest. He did not like the feeling that was growing now in his gut.

'Speak, Cousin.'

'The MacDonnell... He... He sent this to ye,' Dougal stammered as he held out a large sack of coins to him. A very large sack of coins.

'And what did The MacDonnell do that requires such

gold to appease me?' Ross might be new to his position, but no one in Argyll could claim ignorance of Iain Mac-Donnell's ways. Or his schemes that tended to benefit himself and few, if any, others.

''Twas my fault, Ross. I take responsibility for the mistake.'

This must be bad—very, very bad. Of course, Dougal had served their uncle, and that man, may his soul rest in peace, was not known for his calm temperament or tolerance of errors made. Ross put the heel of his hand against his forehead and pressed against the building pain and pressure.

'Dougal. Tell me.'

'He switched the bride. He switched his other daughter for the one you'd contracted with.'

The MacDonnell had three daughters—the eldest was the one he'd agreed to marry, the youngest was too nigh to childhood for Ross to consider and the middle one was known to be…

'The disfigured one,' Dougal whispered. Ross shook his head. They'd made haste in setting up the marriages needed to provide supplies and warriors, but Ross was not so lacking in sense that he would agree to… 'The one he'd banished to the nunnery on Iona.'

'I am married to a disfigured nun?' The pain in his head spiked and his vision grew blurry from it. Rubbing his eyes, Ross shook his head. 'Why would you go through with it, Dougal? What is her…damaged about her?'

'I ken not, Ross. She was, she is, veiled.'

'So, how did you find out?' His thoughts swirled at the possibilities and the problems this would bring.

'She admitted it just before we arrived.'

'She? What is her name?' Who the hell was he married to? A marriage that, though by proxy, would not be a thing easily undone.

'You agreed to marry Lilidh Ilysa MacDonnell, but you married Ilysa Lilidh instead.' Dougal's regret echoed in his words. 'I thought I glimpsed a different name on the register from the one the priest called out during the wedding, but in the tense moment, I did not ask about it. I just thought I was mistaken. Ross, I am sorry.'

'With her true signature and yours and the priest's, the marriage is legal, no matter what name or names were uttered.' Dougal nodded and turned his gaze away.

What was Iain MacDonnell up to? The man did nothing by mistake. He'd deliberately switched his daughters, knowing that their similar names would likely slide by a man not expecting such sly deceit. Like Dougal. A man of honour who expected that others would uphold their own word.

'Who else kens?' Ross looked at the wall, waiting to learn how truly bad this was.

'Only the elders who attended and whomever The MacDonnell enlisted in his scheme,' Dougal offered.

Ross shook his head. A desperate man made mistakes. Mistakes that neither he nor his clan could afford. And such an insult as this one needed to be answered or his position would be questioned. He wished he'd not sent Fergus off so quickly to his own marriage now. With his brother and sister already betrothed, he had little choice but to…

'Where is she?'

'I left her on the birlinn. With guards. I thought you should ken before I brought her in.'

Ross walked to the door and opened it. With a wave, he motioned for Dougal to leave.

'Bring her now. The MacMillan will greet his bride as he should.' Duty. Duty to his clan must come first. Too much depended on this agreement.

'You will accept her?' Dougal asked as he shuffled to the open doorway. 'But she is…'

'I heard you the first time. The wrong bride. A disfigured bride. A bride from the nunnery. An insult to me and our clan. Anything else you need to tell me, Dougal? Och, aye, she is already married to me by proxy with no way out of that.'

Ross rolled his shoulders to relieve the growing tension. Dougal eyed him with suspicion as he passed him at the door. He shook his head at his cousin's concern. It was too late now. But forewarned now, he would be ready for any further subterfuge by The MacDonnell.

'Go. I will speak to Gillean, Munro and Innis before you return with her.' His steward, the commander of his warriors and the elder needed to have the truth before any word about his bride spread through the kith and kin here. 'And send for Father Liam as well.'

Ross followed Dougal out into the hall and called for the three men he needed to speak to before he did anything else. The urge to respond to this insult with one of his own grew within him. The feeling of being someone's fool did not sit easily with him and he wanted to strike out. If he was still just the chieftain's nephew, he could have shouted out the bold words in anger.

As the chieftain, he did not have the luxury of letting

loose his fury. Too many depended on this arrangement. Too much danger surrounded them as they prepared for another attack, one that could be disastrous without the supplies, the support and, damn it, the gold that his bride brought to him.

A short while later, giving enough time for Dougal to reach the dock and retrieve his bride and for the summoned priest to confirm his suspicions about the legality of the marriage, Ross walked outside and waited at the top of the steps leading up to the keep. With Munro behind him and Innis at his side, for Gillean was off securing the gold already received and preparing for what accompanied the Lady, Ross took in and released a deep breath, trying to prepare himself for…anything. Even before the Lady had entered through the gate, the crowd began gathering to catch a glimpse of her.

Even he wanted a glimpse of her.

Although he'd heard talk about her disfigurement, he remembered no details at all. When his uncle had first raised the possibility of marriage again after his wife had died, the eldest daughter of The MacDonnell had been mentioned. His uncle had initiated discussions. However, he'd turned his sights elsewhere not long after that, looking for a bride he'd never found. So, a MacDonnell bride seemed an obvious choice for Ross when the clan needed the connections and the wealth she would bring with her. While discussing the eldest daughter—known for her wit and beauty—no one spoke openly of her sister's defects.

Well, after watching her approach through the gate, holding Dougal's hand, Ross could see…nothing of her.

She was covered from her head to her feet in a long cloak that nearly overwhelmed her from the look of it. A hood was in place on her head and veils flowed over her face. Even a glove covered the hand laid on Dougal's. The whispers began immediately and spread like a wave over the crowd.

She—Ilysa Lilidh MacDonnell—walked with a slow grace, never faltering or hesitating in her progress. He could see Dougal speaking to her as they moved forward towards him and a smile even lit his friend's face at something she must have said. Soon, they stood before him at the bottom of the steps. He walked down to her and she curtsied before him, remaining low until he called her name.

'Lady,' he said. 'Lady Ilysa, welcome to Castle Sween.' He stopped then because he really did not know what else to say to her, there in front of his people. She rose and nodded to him.

'My lord, I thank you for your welcome.' Her voice was melodic and had a pleasing lilt to it.

'Father Liam,' he called out. The spry young priest ran down the steps and stood at his side. 'If you would give us your blessing?' Ross moved down next to his bride and waited as the priest made their wedding publicly official.

Well, this was not the final action needed. He tried not to stare at her, for the hood and veils concealed her thoroughly from his sight. After a few prayers in Latin, the priest laid his hands on their heads and asked in their tongue for the blessings of health and fruitfulness before ending.

When everyone watched him expectantly, he understood what they wanted. He turned to face the Lady, his wife, and nodded at her. 'My lady?'

A simple kiss. That was all he must do in view of his people to seal this bargain. A kiss. Without knowing the full extent of her appearance, he could only wait for her to reveal herself.

As she reached up and lifted the hood from her head, it seemed as though everyone watching held their breaths waiting. For them, it was to see their chieftain's bride. For him, it was to see if the rumours were true. Ross stared, trying to control his own nervousness over this revelation. The hood slipped down as she pushed it back to her shoulders and she lifted the veils away from her face.

His indrawn breath was not the only one.

Ilysa MacDonnell was a beautiful young woman. Searching her face for some flaw, he found none. Eyes the colour of the morning sky were outlined by thick lashes. A bow-shaped mouth with lips of soft pink. Gentle brows the colour of early wheat in the fields. Freckles lay scattered over her face and on her nose. Her countenance was pleasing even as it shocked him.

In his surprise, and as the crowd cheered, he took hold of her shoulders and pulled her closer to him. Then, he kissed her.

Other than a shiver that coursed through her, his bride had no other reaction to his kiss. Her mouth remained unmoving under his and so, after a few more moments of contact, he lifted his head. A blush filled her cheeks and the way she would not meet his gaze revealed her innocence.

Well, innocent in matters of the flesh, mayhap, but it

did not speak to her complicity with her father's plan to dupe him. There must be something wrong with her that The MacDonnell thought would render her unwanted as a bride or he would not have played this game. The size of that sack of gold confirmed his worst suspicions. Without stripping her naked before them, he had no way of knowing the truth.

That part would come later.

He smiled at her and held out his arm.

A meal would be served and he would have hours of daylight left to work on the battlements. At least now, the thought of what came next—bedding her—would not be the challenge he'd thought it might be.

His randy flesh made itself known and he almost let out a laugh. Nay, bedding her would be no problem at all.

It was a wedding feast unlike anything he'd ever seen.

His bride had travelled alone, but for guards sent by her father and one man who identified himself as The MacDonnell's representative. Why he had not made himself known as that *before* the blessing and this meal, Ross knew not. He suspected the truth, but without further questioning, there was no way to be sure. Without a maid or companion at her side, Ilysa sat wordlessly through the simple meal.

'You brought no maidservant with you, Lady?' he asked. From the stares and glares of those gathered around the awkward table he knew he should be speaking to her. Ross held out his cup for more ale.

'I only just arrived at my father's home and have had none…recently.'

'Nuns need no servants, then?' The words had slipped out as his curiosity had built since her arrival. 'My lady, I—'

'If truth be told, and this is something my father does not ken,' she said, glancing over at her father's man and lowering her voice before she continued, 'I was the nuns' servant on Iona.'

His eating dagger dropped from his grasp and clattered on the table in front of him. Ross reached for it, trying to ignore the other curious gazes now. And the surprise of her admission. A lady working as a servant was not done. Her father would be furious if he learned it.

'I have shocked you, my lord?' She smiled as she lifted her cup to her mouth. He could not look away as her tongue slid out to taste the liquid left on the cup's rim from her last mouthful. She traced the edge and Ross swore he felt the touch of it on his flesh.

'Aye,' he admitted, taking another drink of his ale and hoping it would cool this unexpected lust.

'I ken it would displease my father, so I do not speak of it.' The lady was smart. How smart? he wondered.

'Did you ken of your father's plan to substitute you for your sister in this marriage?'

Ross kept his voice down, so that only she heard his words. No matter, for the result was as he'd expected— she inhaled quickly and began choking as the ale she'd swallowed just then became stuck in her throat. Now, every eye in the hall was on her, and him, as she struggled to draw in a breath. Taking hold of her shoulder nearest him, he steadied her body as he smacked her on her back several times to help clear the blockage.

The third whack worked and only as he was letting her go did he feel the strap around her shoulder. Glancing down, he did not see it over her gown and without demanding she drop her shawl, he would not see more.

'Are you well?' he asked, watching as she drew in and exhaled several breaths, each one smoother and quieter than the last.

'I am, my lord.'

She reached up and smoothed the veils back in place where they perfectly framed her heart-shaped face. Was the rest of her hair the same golden colour as her brows? Ross could not imagine where that thought came from. It was not unseemly to be curious about a woman you had only just met…and married. Except as she reached across her plate and picked up the linen cloth on the left side did he realise she only used her right hand. Something not usual.

'I think there are many things we need to discuss, my lady,' he said. After a glance at her untouched plate of food, he stood. 'Gillean.' When his steward drew near, he introduced them. 'If you would see to the Lady's needs and show her to her chamber? If the journey has not exhausted her, mayhap a look around the keep and castle?' Ross turned to walk away, for the battlements needed his attention. And he remembered one thing more. 'The Lady will need a maidservant, Gillean. See to that.'

His steward nodded once more and Ross made his way to the stairway in the far tower that led to the roof. He'd nearly reached it when The MacDonnell's man who'd also accompanied his wife here stepped into his path. And, barely a moment later, Munro stepped in between them.

'My lord,' the man said. 'I would speak to you.' With a glance at Munro's obvious position, he continued, 'Privately.'

'Your name?' Ross asked.

'I am called Eachann.' For once, the name matched for he was indeed a plain-faced, brown-haired man.

Ross nodded at Munro, who moved to stand at his side. 'Well, Eachann, you may speak freely to me and my commander.'

'My lord…' Eachann hesitated.

Ross shook his head. He was not going to like what this man had to say. Munro's glance over at him said the same.

'Get on with it, man! My work does not do itself.'

'The MacDonnell ordered me to remain until proof of the bedding is shown. And not to release the rest of the Lady's dowry until then.'

Ross could not help it—his face did not hide his shock. Munro might have growled. 'He what?' Ross demanded.

'I cannot leave until the marriage is consummated and I see the proof. Or you get none of the goods I brought. And the men will not arrive as planned.'

Munro did growl then, which was what Ross wanted to do but could not. His commander waited on his word. And yet Ross could not think of a single word to say. So, he nodded to Munro to follow him and walked past MacDonnell's man, leaving him standing where he was.

Another complication. Another insult?

Did the man wait for proof Ross's new wife was a virgin or not? Which outcome would be worse? God's truth, he did not know. Did her father worry that he would ultimately refuse his daughter and was trying in every way to bind him to her tightly?

If he'd wanted to deny the marriage or turn his bride away, he would have done so at first word of The Mac-Donnell's machinations. If he'd wanted to claim the insult done him, it was too late even now. Consummation would be but one more nail in this trap.

There would be a reckoning over this when it was safe to call for it. This night, he would seek one with his bride. And a consummation. Though which one would turn out better, he dared not predict. Then, the one with her father would happen when he had the facts in hand to make it most effective. If his reputation suffered briefly, it mattered not. What did matter was the end result—his castle restored, his lands and people protected, his allies strong once more and their enemies vanquished.

The next hours of hard labour did little to lessen the tension building within him. Seeing the ship sent by Ilysa's father, yet filled with the supplies that he, they, needed sitting at the dock raised his sense of impending danger and his fury over his hand being forced.

He'd never planned to consummate this union so quickly. If their marriage had been face to face, he could have simply given her time to adjust to it. But the proxy vows demanded that it be finalised and formal—and consummated—as quickly as possible so no accusations could be raised later.

Finally, when the moon rose high in the sky and the others had sought their rest, Ross could avoid the inevitable no longer.

The MacMillan entered the keep, ready to carry out his duties. But his first duty was to discover what secrets his wife hid that could imperil his efforts to protect his clan.

Chapter Three

No matter the condition of her nerves, Ilysa somehow fell asleep in the tall, wooden chair in her bedchamber. She woke on a gasp, staring into the darkness around her. Confusion controlled her thoughts for a few moments, for she could not remember her place or the day, or night. As she listened and searched for clues, it was the moon's light that entered through a crack in the shutters of the window across from her that told her hours had passed since she'd first sat there.

The steward, Gillean, had tried to make her welcome and she'd smiled as he'd found ways to pry bits from her about all manner of things. Oh, he'd couched his questions carefully and explained how he needed to know to carry out his duties, but Ilysa did not doubt that Gillean could outpry even Mother Euphemia on Iona. That older woman had interrogation skills that a royal torturer would appreciate and a glare that would loosen most tongues.

Ilysa smiled at the memories of that woman and her friendship these last years. Because the sister could not walk easily, one of Ilysa's duties was to help her. The woman might be sworn to the Lord's work, but she had the most irreverent sense of humour Ilysa had ever known and it had made some of her hardest times pass much more easily.

So, The MacMillan's steward now knew far too many details about her. And on the morrow, the gossip would begin. The Lady did not wish for a maid's help. The Lady could indeed read and write in several languages. Though she could not sew—the reasons she left to his imagination—she was accomplished in other household tasks.

She'd refused a bath, but had asked for hot water to wash up in preparation for…her husband's arrival. But the water remained in the bucket, nigh to frigid now. And the fire set in the hearth had long since gone out. All her plans to prepare for his arrival had fled when she'd sat down and closed her eyes.

A smile tugged her lips as she realised that it was one of her skills, if it could be called that. She could sleep anywhere, in any position, when she was tired and given the chance. In the nunnery, it had helped her catch rest as she could when the long days of work and prayers kept her busy.

Ilysa only wished she'd put a cushion under herself on this chair before she'd sat down. Its hard surface had punished her body and now the protesting muscles in her legs and back warned her of the coming pain. She shifted her body first and then pushed up out of the chair.

The low, unfeminine moan that echoed around her revealed only a part of the deep aching pain that filled her. Her body was familiar with hard work and these last few days of sitting or standing and doing little else was taking its toll. Mayhap once…once this night was over, she could find a way back to doing some sort of work. Though Gillean made it clear that servants would be at her call and do whatever she needed or wanted done, Ilysa could not survive being as useless as…her left arm. Making it halfway across the chamber before a spasm in her back forced her to bend over and another moan escaped, Ilysa never saw him standing at the door.

'A hot bath might have helped your discomfort, my lady.'

She gasped and turned to face him, but the spasm had not yet relented and she lost her balance. The only thing that kept her from landing on the floor was his speed. Well, and his strength. He wrapped his arms around her, twisted somehow and placed her back on her feet without any apparent effort. Ilysa was about to thank him when she realised he yet held on to her. He held on to her left arm. Unable to feel sensations in most of it, she did not know he'd not released it.

His gaze lay on her arm and then it moved to her shoulder as he was clearly trying to sort through what he felt under her wrap. When he took hold of the edge of the woollen shawl, she did not fight him. If they ended up…together this night, he would see it all. Letting out a sigh, she looked past him, unwilling to see the disgust that would fill his eyes when she was exposed.

'May I?' His voice, deep and masculine, broke into her reverie. He'd not done any more than grasp the edge of the cloth. 'May I?' he asked again.

Was he asking for her permission? He waited until

she gave it with a jumpy nod. He slid his fingers under the wool and took a firmer hold of it. He moved to her side and she held her other arm away so he could remove the shawl. Standing this close to him, she could see that his hair was damp from a recent washing. That hair hung to his shoulders—his very broad shoulders. She had to look up to see past those broad shoulders.

He'd recently washed with a soap that carried the scent of some earthy ingredient—given time, she would recognise which it was—and she found it appealing. As the weight of the shawl left her shoulders, Ilysa focused on that scent, inhaling slowly and trying to gain control over her fear. The heat from his body, so near to her, infused her with comfort even as she felt the chill of the chamber around her.

Her husband tossed the plaid on the bed and walked around her, examining the sleeve and the straps that held her arm in place. The sleeve hid the worst of the deformities and she prayed he would not demand its removal. He backed away, his gaze never pausing in his inspection. The furrow that formed between his brows revealed his puzzlement. She waited for him to do what he surely must want to do—tear off the sleeve and see the hidden shame it covered. Closing her eyes so she did not have to watch, she held her breath for his next touch.

'When you arrived, covered as you were, I expected that the rumoured defect you hid was under your veils,' he said. His calm, even tone took away some of the sting that words so personal usually gave. 'But, then,' he began as he reached out and touched her cheek with just one finger, ''tis clear to even a blind man that only beauty was hidden by the veils you wore.'

She twisted her good hand in her gown to keep it from trembling at his touch. The roughness of the tip of his finger teased her skin as he caressed her cheek and along her jaw. Then he slid it under her chin and on to her neck. Would he continue from there? Would he touch…? When she was about to move into his caress, he stopped her with his words.

'But then no one kenned that The MacDonnell simply hid the wrong daughter under those veils—'

'My lord, I pray you to—'

'Am I wrong, Lady?' he asked, dropping his hand to his side. 'With the clever rearranging of your names and a handful of veils, your father kept the true prize and instead fooled me with his…' The MacMillan paused and she steeled herself for the inevitable cruel words that always described her '…his middle daughter he'd banished to a nunnery.'

When she opened her eyes, his nearness startled her. She'd not heard him move. So close that she needed to lift her eyes to meet his. The hard angles of his face belied the softness of his voice. The growth of his beard shadowed the curves of his cheeks and the edges of his jaw. The beam of light from the moon made the reddish colour in it shine like burnished copper.

She'd not been this close to a man in…ever. Not even her father approached her so. None of his men would dare. And, of course, at the nunnery there were only the holy brothers and a few laymen who did the heaviest labour on their farm and in their buildings.

In spite of him being taller than her father, she did not feel threatened by his closeness. She should. She would never underestimate the danger of a man's insulted pride. And her presence here, rather than her older sister, was so much more than a simple insult— he'd been called out for a fool, whether he had been or knew what her father had planned.

'Aye. I am that one,' she admitted.

'The one who worked as their servant.'

'Aye.'

'The one who hides her beauty and her infirmity.'

There was a momentary pause before she could say anything. His eyes flashed and his nose flared as though he was scenting danger. Truly, she had only one answer she could give and it was something that must be shown.

Never breaking from his intense gaze, she reached up and tugged the lone veil she wore off. She stuffed it into her pocket and then went to work loosening the coif. When he lifted his hand, she shook her head and he stopped. It was never easy to do, but soon she pulled it free and watched his face as the condition of her hair was exposed to him.

The expression was not the one she expected to see. The corners of his lips rose and his eyes widened, but not in disgust. Lust glimmered there. And something else. Almost…approval?

Ilysa shook her head and ran her fingers through the curls that happened whenever her locks were released from the control of the coif. She'd hated it at first, but once the weight of its length was gone, the relief had been palpable. Though it had grown a few inches since the prioress had cut it, she liked it.

Now, on to the revelation she truly dreaded. The one that would not make him smile at all. When she reached for the strap to untie it, he shook his head and stopped her.

'Vows taken?' he asked. Ah, so he suspected that was her father's plan, then? It pleased her somehow that he would not be an easy victim of her father, even if he could not, had not, avoided that completely.

'Only with you,' she said. The sound that he made was something between an exhalation and a grunt. No matter how she described it, it was clear he approved of her reply.

'Had you intended to take holy vows on Iona?'

He did not wait on her words and instead walked to the hearth and stirred the embers seeking fire. Only when he paused and glanced over his shoulder did she speak.

'I had no plans to leave the nunnery, but I did not wish to swear the vows of a holy sister.' She'd hoped and even prayed many times that she could remain for ever. But she was not so daft to think she would not be used to further her father's ends when the need arose. As it had.

'When did you learn of this arrangement?' He stood and rubbed his hands together, shaking the ashes at the bottom of the hearth.

'An hour before I married you.'

She shivered then, suddenly realising that she was indeed married to the man, the warrior, the chieftain who stood before her. Ilysa studied him, much as he had her, gazing from his boots to his head. The fire's flames highlighted the auburn and red shades in his hair and set them alight.

'Come closer.' She blinked at his words. 'Come closer

to the fire, lass. Warm yourself here until the heat spreads into your chamber.'

She moved without hesitation then, for she was cold. And fearful. And sore from sitting. In this moment, she felt as old as Sister Margaret.

'What made you smile just then?' He'd moved aside to give her the best position before the growing flames.

'I was thinking of Sister Margaret.' At his raised brow, she smiled. 'She has difficulty moving quickly and I just gave you a fair sense of how she looks in taking those few steps.'

'So, your father brought you back and told you of his plan to deceive me an hour before Dougal pledged my word to you? Is that correct?'

'Nay!' she cried out. Taking a step back away from him, she tripped once more. And once more he saved her from injury since she stumbled towards the fire this time. When several paces away from it, she shook free of him. 'I was told I was to marry you. I did not wish to. But that did not matter to my father. I had thought he'd forgotten me. I thought I would never have to marry. I followed his order to cover my face. I thought it was about…about…'

'Your hair?' His gaze flicked over her shorn hair.

'Aye. Until the priest called out my name wrongly, I did not ken.'

'And when you heard it? When he said your sister's name, did you not think to tell my man?' His words were calm and measured and she could see he was assessing every word she offered. Yet the very question angered her.

Ilysa wanted to scream. Rage built within her at the

unfairness of this man's judgement against her. Many, so many, had tried to oppose The MacDonnell. Or to disobey his commands. Or to disregard his opinions. And, be they kith or kin, or enemies, they usually ended up ground beneath his boot or left much worse for their attempts.

'Damn you!' she said, fighting off the tears of fear and frustration. 'You think to hold me up and show me my own weakness?' She walked away. 'Well, I confess, my lord. I am but a weak woman who could not stand up to her father's wishes.' In that moment, what she truly wanted was something to throw at him. So, she flung her words instead. 'And when you discovered his ruse, my lord? Did you? Did you stand up and decry his dishonesty?'

What had she done? His face went blank at her accusation. She could see nothing in his eyes to warn her, but his body shifted slightly and he closed his hands into fists. He had no reason to believe anything she said or any excuse she gave him. She had deceived him. She had complied with her father's order without speaking up. All of that was true, but this loss of control? This outburst at him?

What had she done?

She did the only thing she could think of in that instant—she dropped to her knees before him and bowed her head, praying he would accept her obeisance. Pulling her useless arm in tight, she curled her body and waited for his acceptance or the first blow.

Ross could not comprehend how things had gone this badly with such haste. Staring down as his wife stumbled to the floor—for the third time, but only the first of her choice—he could not bring to mind words to say to her. Or what to do to sort through the mess between them.

She had astonished him in every encounter and in each conversation so far. Her intelligence, her wit, her practicality and even her hidden beauty. But, in spite of the fact that neither of them wanted this marriage nor, he suspected, the consummation of it this night, he did not want this to go as badly as it was. The sight of her crumpled at his feet, trying to make herself small and less of a target, sickened him. Oh, he recognised the position. He understood her intent.

Something told him that taking hold of her, even to help her stand, would be the wrong thing to do. So, he moved away until he felt the door at his back and he waited. When her body slowed in its quaking, he walked in careful, slow steps to the table where she'd been sitting and filled the cup from the jug left next to it. Then, he crouched before her.

'Ilysa, take my hand.' He repeated it several times before she lifted her head and looked at him. Her eyes were unfocused and moved quickly, darting to and away from him. 'Ilysa.'

Ross fought the urge to reach out and take her hand before she was ready. Like a skittish animal fearing capture, she stared at his hand without moving. When she finally held hers out, he watched it tremble as she reached across the inches between them. When her hand was closer to him, he slid his fingers in between hers and drew her slowly up as he stood. The moan was impossible to miss as she straightened to her full height.

'Sit.' He let her set the pace of her steps to the chair, guiding her with a steady hand. 'Drink.' Ross held the cup out in front of her. 'More.' He wished he had his flask to add a bit of liquid strength to the weak ale, but it would do for now. 'Where is your maid?' He had already talked to Gillean and knew about the Lady's refusal, but it would give her something to think about.

'I did not want a maid,' she said in a whisper. An honest answer, according to Gillean.

'Do you want a bath?' He almost smiled at the surprise in her gaze now. He watched as she warred with herself over what to say. Without waiting, he left the chamber, found the waiting servant and ordered a bath for her—and *uisge beatha* for himself.

He feared it was going to be a very long night.

Ross studied her as the servants arrived and they carried in the wooden tub and bucket after bucket of steaming water. Inappropriately, he wanted to touch her hair. The servants noticed when they passed her by, for he saw the way they exchanged glances. The golden curls framed her face and gave her the look of a magical fae creature.

When it was half filled with the hot water, they tempered it with some cool water and left extra of both sitting by the hearth, along with drying cloths and soaps. When the last of them left and the door closed, he turned back to Ilysa.

'My lady, your bath awaits.'

He'd thought on how this might proceed tonight, how to consummate their vows with a woman who'd lived in a convent for the last three years, and he'd not truly come up with a plan. How would she react to the intimate meeting of their bodies? Would she resist his efforts to bed her?

Oh, the consummation part was the least of it—*that* he knew how to do. But how was he supposed to undress and coax an almost-nun into bed so that he could get to that part? Especially one who had just a short time ago fallen to her knees in fear of him and his reaction to her honesty? No matter how he'd contemplated this night proceeding, bathing her was surely not part of it. As he watched her consider her choices, Ross realised he wanted to believe that her anger was about being played as a pawn in her father's game.

'I do not understand, my lord,' she whispered. She shook her head as though clearing her thoughts. 'Do you not wish to punish me for my boldness? For my insults?' She clutched the arm of the chair as if preparing herself. 'If you do, I pray you to proceed, for the waiting is the worst part for me.'

'I do not usually punish people for what they say, Lady. If I did, half my kin and most of my enemies would be dead.' He waited for her to smile. 'And I cannot fault you for doing what you had to do to survive with your father. I, too, am doing what I can to ensure my clan's survival.' Her eyes widened at his words, but her grip did not lessen on the chair. 'But now you are my wife and we are in this endeavour together. Now I will hold you responsible for your actions.' He crouched down in front of her and waited for her to meet his eyes. 'Do you understand, Ilysa?'

A slight nod was her answer.

'And do you agree?'

'I gave my consent.'

'I wish to hear you agree to be my wife. And to obey me. Do you, Ilysa?'

'I have said so in my vows,' she said. He noticed her lower lip quivered as she spoke.

'But you spoke those to my man and not to me. Say it to me.' He stood and put some distance between them. He did not want the words if his nearness threatened or forced her to say them.

'I am your wife, my lord.'

'Ross.' She blinked and shook her head. 'Ross is my name. A wife should use it.'

'I am your wife, Ross.' She let out a breath and nodded.

'Then take your bath and seek your bed.'

Chapter Four

The MacMillan had arrived with one purpose in mind—consummation—and left her alone with a bath for her comfort and a bed that beckoned her exhausted body and soul to its plush mattress. Oh, and a fire that filled the chamber with warmth she'd not experienced since moving to the nunnery.

Ilysa slid down into the steaming water and felt the constant cold in her limbs ease. Aye, it was the end of summer and the seasonably warm days and pleasant nights should have banished that cold. But, living in the stone nunnery building that was set on the edge of Iona and surrounded by the constant winds coming off the water could not provide comforts such as the heat pouring off the fire or the thick blankets lying over a plush feather-filled mattress on a rope-strung bed did.

Reaching over the side of the tub, Ilysa scooped out some of the soft soap and spread it between her fingers before rubbing it over her shoulders and arms as best she could. Her left arm lay at her side, tucked against the linen that covered the bottom and sides of the tub.

Ilysa leaned her head back and enjoyed the heat as her thoughts filled with questions about her husband.

Ross MacMillan was as complicated as her father. Not as powerful as The MacDonnell, but he was smart. Certainly not as violent in his temper or treatment of others. Considerate in unexpected ways. Unexpected.

For a man, a powerful chieftain in his own right now, a man insulted and fooled and expecting a bride he did not get and getting a wife he did not want, he was completely unexpected.

That she sat in this bath, still a virgin in spite of his intent when arriving in her chamber, was a testament to his self-control. And his intelligence.

She knew he was biding his time with her. Though her father's man had said nothing to her, she'd witnessed the angry exchange as Ross left the hall after their meal. Her father was committed to making this marriage unbreakable, so she suspected what that conversation was about.

Consummation.

Ilysa sank down, wet her hair and then slid back up. This would be the difficult part—washing her hair and then manoeuvring her way out of the tub. He'd offered a maid to help her, yet something had held her back. As she scrubbed the soap into her curls and the soothing lavender scent surrounded her, Ilysa realised why she'd declined.

Ross had not demanded to see her arm in spite of knowing it was the centre of her shame. And she could not dishonour his consideration by allowing others to see it, and gossip, before he did.

When some of the soap got in her eyes, she reached

over the side to find a cloth. She tugged one closer, wiped the lather away and found him standing in the shadows near the wall watching her. No words were spoken and yet Ilysa understood he would not move or touch her or do…anything if she said nay.

Should she naysay this? Would she submit to his touch?

He moved slowly from his place, approaching and moving behind her. Initially, fear held her still while anticipation and curiosity began to bubble up inside her.

After the debacle with Graeme MacLean, his reaction to her disability, the transfer of his affections quickly to her sister, she had put aside all thoughts of marriage. And love. And the possibilities of those. So, never had she thought that a wedding or wedding night would happen for her. Yet now she had a husband who stood next to her as she sat completely naked and open to his sight.

Ilysa did not move, though she trembled and wanted to try to cover her bareness. No one had ever seen her thus. Not servants or her sisters or anyone. His touch earlier was also the first time for such intimate caresses. She heard him move closer behind her and could see him from the corner of her eyes as he sank to his knees.

Then his heated breath on her neck sent shivers down her body and a wave of fire race through her blood. Her breasts felt swollen somehow and the place between her legs throbbed as she waited for his next movement. Her body understood what to do even if she did not.

'Lean your head back, Ilysa.' She did and found his hand waiting to support it. 'Close your eyes.' Warm water poured over her head, rinsing the soap from her hair and face. He guided her forward and she took hold of the side of the tub. 'Lean up now.'

Her body followed his instructions and she let out an unexpected sigh when his strong fingers spread soap across her back and over her shoulders. He did not dwell or hesitate in one spot or another, instead he used very thorough motions to spread and then rinse the soap. Her body did not relax under his ministrations, for the core of her ached for something more with each soft caress of his fingers.

When he moved to her side, Ilysa knew that he would see the worst of her. She held her breath and closed her eyes then, waiting moment by moment. Somehow the shame she bore felt heavier as she waited for his reaction. If he, a warrior who had seen death, mayhem and carnage, could not bear the look of it, what would he do?

Ross lifted her right arm from where it rested and stroked from her fingers to her shoulder, spreading the soap before rinsing it with handfuls of water. Now...

Now...

She had to see. Her eyes opened and met his gaze. He stared at her face even as his hand moved lower. She felt his touch on her hip as he slid his fingers around her senseless left arm and lifted it from the water. Never once did he look at it as he washed it from shoulder to fingertips. Never once did he glance away from her eyes. Again, she only knew he'd returned it to the water when his hand grazed her skin.

Then, only then, did his gaze move, but not to her damaged arm. He gazed at her breasts. A quick look of her own revealed that the water did not cover them. Indeed, it held them up as though inviting his inspection and touch. The tips of them tightened at the warm caress of the water as she looked up at his face and saw the way his eyes widened. Then, an intense, heated expression of hunger entered his eyes and she shivered at the desire she saw.

Though she expected him to touch her, she did not expect him to dip his hand into the soap and spread it across her breasts. Her mouth opened in silent shock, but he did not hesitate.

His hand moved in circles, over and around one and then the other. She did gasp then, once and then again when he shifted his hand and let his fingers slide over the taut nipples. Though her inexperience made her want to pull away, her traitorous body urged otherwise. As he flicked his thumb over one tip, ragged breaths escaped her mouth at the stimulating touch. When her back arched, pressing the fullness of them into his grasp, she knew she'd lost any semblance of control in this situation.

He eased up on to his knees and faced her next to the tub, using both hands now to cup and caress her. When his thumbs slid once, twice and thrice, over the sensitive tips, a moan forced its way out and her body arched again into his hands. Her own hand covered one of his, but whether to stop him or encourage him, she knew not.

'Should I stop?' he asked in a hoarse, masculine whisper. His hands did just that as he waited for her answer.

'Would you?'

He smiled in reply, a wicked, tempting curve of his lips that made her want to...want to do...something.

'Nay,' she whispered, not waiting for his answer and giving in to what would happen between them this night. 'Do not stop.'

He laughed then, a low, slow, sound that made her ache deep inside. He did lift his hands then, rinsing them before removing the soap he'd spread on her skin with several handfuls of water. Soon, the bubbles surrounded her in the water and her skin tingled in a way she'd not felt before. And he just stared at her, studying what he could see as if he could not settle on the next step. If she thought that was the end of it, he quickly proved her wrong.

If her eyes opened any wider, he swore they would stick open and never shut. Ross wondered if she would allow what he wanted to do next as he watched her skin pebble with gooseflesh that had nothing to do with cold. His little inexperienced nun of a wife surprised him with the way she'd accepted his caresses so far, but if he washed the rest of her would she stop him?

Things between them would certainly be easier if she was not fearful and if she lay on their marriage bed prepared for him to complete the act. A quick glance at her face tempted him to be bold. So he was.

Ross reached into the water and slid his hand down along her leg, encircling her ankle when he reached it. Then, sliding it under her leg, he lifted it out of the water and leaned it on the edge of the tub. She trembled at his actions, but once she'd adjusted her position and grasped the edge with her one hand to stabilise herself, she did nothing to resist.

The soap he'd spread on her skin eased his touch

and his hand glided over her leg. Each time, he moved closer and closer to his target—the curls at the junction of her legs. Ilysa's body tensed less with each swirl, until he spread his hand over her thigh and massaged his way under the water. He was not a brute given to harsh ways with the women he'd bedded so he went slowly. His aim was to tease and entice her body and when his fingers touched the very edge of the curls, she arched up under his touch.

But he was under control no matter the size of his cockstand and he did not dip inside the folds of feminine flesh that waited just there. Ross eased her leg back into the water and moved to the other one. This time, she aided him in lifting it on to the rim and he smiled. His bride might not have been the one he'd planned to marry, but he was not displeased with her response in these intimacies. As he applied the soap and spread it over her leg, repeating his caresses of the other one, something yet bothered him.

Ross took one last bit of soap and closed his fingers around it, keeping most of it in his palm until he reached those curls. He rubbed the back of his hand over them and then down into the folds of flesh. Her gasps turned into moans as he pressed a knuckle deeper within and massaged there. Stroking her with it, he added another. When her body opened to his touch, he moved his hand and stroked with his soapy hand. As she pressed into his grasp, he asked his question, while not even knowing if he should trust her answer.

'Are you a virgin, Ilysa?' She was caught up in her passion and did not hear his words. He stopped his

movements and held his fingers against the soft flesh.
'Will I be the first inside you, Lady?'

He'd had to ask—the question of what he would discover had plagued him since her father's man had told
him of this last demand. Would he find proof of her
virginity when he consummated their union? Once he
entered her, it would be too late. But no matter what he
found, he would have to provide a bloodied sheet to her
father and whether hers or his would matter not. The
MacDonnell would be the only person who would know
the truth, while Ross would know he'd been played for
a fool once more.

Her body tensed under his touch and she lifted her
head to meet his gaze. Though her face was the one of
a woman being pleasured and filled with arousal, he
knew she saw him and considered his question.

'Aye, my lord,' she whispered as she rocked against
his hand and then blushed as she realised she'd been
helping his efforts. 'You will be the first.'

She shifted her hips, pushing his fingers into her
flesh. As she slid away slightly and repeated that movement on his fingers, her breathing changed, becoming
more frenzied. The lass was mimicking his actions and
his own blood surged through him, sending heat and
need into every part of him.

Without removing his hand from between her legs,
Ross leaned over, slid his other hand behind her head
to hold her steady and kissed her, plunging his tongue
into her mouth as his fingers thrust into her woman's
core. He tasted and felt her excitement and the tenta-
tive touch of her tongue on his. When he moved his
thumb against the small, hardened bud hidden within

her flesh, she screamed into his mouth. The way she thrust her hips into his hand told him she was accepting of his caresses. She clutched his hand and pressed it against her body, not allowing him to stop.

Ross lifted his mouth from hers and watched as she reached her peak. Her body tightened and trembled against him, inhaling quickly over and over as pleasure filled her. He held her until her body went still. His own body craved release and his flesh throbbed against his breeches. All in good time.

Once she'd calmed, he eased away, letting her head rest back, and stood. She did not speak as he stoked the fire back to a roaring blaze and then he found the large drying cloth next to the tub. Shaking it open, he tossed it on the bed and then leaned down and lifted Ilysa from the water. He noticed that she took hold of her damaged left arm and pulled it across her body as he did so.

Ross carried her to the bed and placed her on the cloth he'd spread. Climbing up next to her, he took the sheet-sized cloth and rubbed it over her hair, removing most of the wetness, before turning his attention to the rest of her. From the sounds of soft panting she uttered as he'd stroked the cloth over her body—those lovely breasts, the curve of her hips, the place between her legs—he knew his wife was ready for the rest of it. She watched him silently as he moved closer and kissed her again. But when he lifted her deformed arm, she pulled away.

'My lord,' she said as she tried to sit up. 'What are you doing?' She shifted and tried to tuck her arm out of his sight.

'Tell me how to...' He glanced at her arm. 'If we are

to do this, where will your arm be most comfortable? I do not wish to hurt you.'

Any other woman would have burst into tears by now. But an innocent woman, who'd lived in a nunnery for years, with a deformity that was whispered about and that had prevented at least one marriage contract, should be running screaming down the corridor to escape him. Though The MacDonnell thought him completely witless, Ross had sources of knowledge about the great chieftain and his family. No one had been able to give an explanation about her disfigurement and he'd thought as his kith and kin did—that it was under her veils.

But now seeing it, Ross thought it was not as bad as rumours made it out to be. Aye, he'd seen worse, much worse. From its appearance, the worst of the damage with lasting results centred just below her shoulder. The upper and lower bones were canted—signs of previous fractures and imperfect healing.

'I cannot move my arm without help,' she said. Her eyes filled with tears. As she reached across her body, he did it for her. Sliding his hand under her elbow and taking hold of the damaged wrist and hand, he followed her instructions and moved her arm until it lay away from her side, as comfortably as possible. Able now to move over her, Ross wiped the tears that trickled from the corner of her eyes.

'Hush now,' he whispered. 'If the thought of me bedding you did not make you cry, this, my seeing this…' he nodded at her arm '…should not make you greet.'

Her quiet dignity, especially when considering her parentage, impressed him. After they did this and the marriage was unbreakable, she could settle in here while he turned his attention and efforts to repairing the damage already done and preventing their total destruction at the hands of Alexander Campbell.

His body urged him to hurry now, for her body's scent and the way she moved against him roused his blood and his own needs. Sitting back, he tugged the laces on his now-wet shirt and pulled it over his head. Her eyes widened. Had she never seen a man naked? That question made his other decision for him—he left his trews in place.

Ross eased himself between her legs, pushing them wider as he settled there. His flesh surged against his breeches as their chests and bellies touched unimpeded by clothing. Only after he had kissed his way from her mouth to her neck and shoulders and on to the tops of her breasts did he reach down to free his hardness. He tested her readiness and then placed the blunt head of his manhood against her flesh. She clutched at his back as he pressed forward, entering her body a scant inch before retreating and beginning again.

Tight. So very tight. He fought to keep control over the sheer pleasure of such a grip on his flesh.

Wet. The slickness of her arousal coated him and allowed him to move deeper and deeper within her without causing her pain.

Then, his flesh felt the resistance of hers and he lifted his mouth from her skin and paused, waiting for her gaze to meet his.

'This may hurt a bit, Wife,' he whispered.

Taking the taut tip of her breast in his mouth, he teased it with teeth and tongue to distract her until Ilysa's hips rose and pressed against him. Without hesitation, he thrust all the way into her heat. Then, he allowed a momentary pause between withdrawing and sliding back inside her. Ross moved slowly at first, waiting for her body to adjust to his invasion.

He felt the exact moment that her body accepted his. He relinquished his control as his body took over, pushing her towards another peak of pleasure. Lifting his head, he watched his wife as she reached it and, with a few deeper, harder strokes, his seed spilled within her heat.

It took some time for their breathing to calm. He would like to think that this was simply an act to complete their vows—and for her, it most likely was—but he could not help but notice his wife's unabashed reaction to him and to accepting the pleasure he offered. Yet, even as he moved off her body, her warm and welcoming body, he understood that this had been something he'd simply had to do and had done.

Now, after he showed the bloodied cloth to her father's man and got the supplies and other prizes he'd negotiated for, he could return his attention—all his attention—to carrying out his duties as chieftain here. Ross slid off the bed to stand and crossed to the tub. Using the water to wash himself and tugging his trews back in place, he dipped a washing cloth into the one remaining bucket of hot water and walked it back to her.

'This will help,' he said. 'A hot bath in the morn will, too, I suspect.' She reached for the cloth and used it, without otherwise moving. 'I will tell your maid.'

'You already know I want no maid.'

He did not reply for the glare in her eyes as she said

it showed that she understood it was not open to discussion now. Regardless, she would need the comfort of the bath and the help to have it.

'I can call her to help you ready for bed, if you'd like?' He could not resist teasing her with this. 'Or you can see to it this night and accept her help on the morrow?'

He held out his hand to her. Only then did she take notice of her own lack of garments. She looked away as he helped her from the bed. Ross did not—he took the opportunity to study her as she made her way to the chest near the door and found her shift and what looked like another sleeve.

'Who made those for you?'

Curiosity got the better of him and he followed her across the chamber. What he did not expect was the speed with which she donned the shift and then pulled the sleeve over her arm and began to tie the straps to hold it in place. Practice had made her efficient in dressing by herself.

'One of the women at the nunnery came up with the design of it.' She ran her hand through her hair and he watched the still-damp curls spring loosely around her face. 'I have two made of heavier fabrics and this lighter one for sleep.'

'Ah, different strengths for different purposes.' She nodded. 'But they each secure your arm to the rest of you?' He pointed to her waist and body.

'Aye,' she said, touching the one she wore. 'I was grateful when the prioress gave unprecedented permission for such a luxury.'

She faced him then and he was hit with the realisation of her innate beauty once again. His flesh rose, reminding him that he had just been inside her body and he could be again, if he would bend to his body's desires. Nay, better to keep this under control and keep her in her place rather than be distracted from his duties.

Remembering the most crucial one, Ross walked back and gathered up the now-marked drying cloth to take it to the man waiting on the birlinn at his dock. Ilysa lost the colour in her face as he neared.

'That is what he told you?' she asked. She moved away from the doorway and watched him with horror in her eyes. 'I saw his man stop you in the hall. My father demanded proof?'

Ross nodded as he lifted the latch and tugged the door open. 'Aye.'

'That is why you asked me if I was…untouched?'

'Aye,' he admitted. 'But I also wanted to ken how to proceed—if I should be slow and careful because you were inexperienced or…' he shrugged '…or more enthusiastic if you were not.'

Ah, the colour raced back into her cheeks at his words, proving in another way that he was married to a woman who'd lived with nuns. No matter her body's frank response to his touch and his body, she was practically a nun.

'Seek your bed, Ilysa.'

He left then without looking back, certain that she had fared well and had not suffered from their joining. Now, he would finish the last task connected to this hasty marriage and then seek his own bed, knowing his clan would finally have what they needed to prevail against their enemies.

Chapter Five

A soft knock on her door made her tense.

It had not disturbed her sleep, for she'd been awake since the moment the sun's light crossed the horizon. As she had every morn since she'd moved to Iona. When no one had called on her at that time, Ilysa had allowed herself to remain there abed.

Part of it was that her body ached. From head to toe and especially in the middle places. Especially the place her husband had claimed as his right. Part was uncertainty, plain and simple.

The steward had made it clear she had no official duties here. And he did not have to say aloud that neither her husband nor his people needed her help, other than what she'd brought to the marriage. Though she had no delusions about her position here, she also had no idea what her place would be.

Just as she'd decided that lying abed too long was not something she could tolerate, the knock came at the door, spurring her to rise. From her husband's words last evening, she knew this would be her maid. Expecting the customary young serving girl, Ilysa instead found someone completely different standing there.

A woman, stout of form, with kind eyes and the face and body of one past their childbearing years, walked closer. She wore the practical garb of one in service—a plain, sturdy gown with an apron tied around her waist and a kerchief covering most of her hair.

'Good morn, my lady. I am called Gavina and my lord asked me to see to ye.' The pleasant greeting was followed by other sounds as the woman glanced around the chamber, shaking her head and mumbling under her breath. 'Have ye a robe, my lady? Ye will take a chill if ye walk aboot in only yer shift.' The woman walked to the trunk and lifted its lid. But then she stopped before doing what any other maid would do—begin searching the contents for what she sought. 'May I, my lady?'

'I do not have such a thing, Gavina,' Ilysa said as she walked to where the maid stood. There had been no opportunity in her life the last three years to linger about in a stage between rising and working or working and sleeping. A robe was simply not a necessity.

'There is another trunk in the corridor, my lady. Mayhap 'tis in that one?' The woman waited on her permission.

'I only brought this one, Gavina. I have no other.' Sad, yet the truth of it.

The woman opened the door and pointed to another trunk that did, indeed, sit there. One she'd not seen. One that could not be hers. When she nodded her permission to the servant and Gavina tugged it into the chamber and lifted the lid, she recognised some of the garments within it.

Lilidh's gowns and other clothing filled the trunk. Not her newest ones from the look of them, but some of her cast-offs that would have been adjusted for their youngest sister to wear. Since she'd not packed this one, Lilidh must have. Ilysa shrugged at Gavina and motioned for her to move as she grabbed hold of the trunk and pulled it further into the chamber.

'Weel, 'twill take some time to sort through these, but sit ye down here and stay warm until I get the fire going and this bath replaced.'

The next two or so hours were spent doing whatever the maid told her to do—from sitting wrapped in several blankets waiting for the tub to be emptied and refilled by a constant stream of servants to choosing which garments she wished to wear. Some time during the blur of activity, a tray appeared before her filled with a bowl of steaming porridge that made her mouth water, a thick slice of buttered bread, a chunk of cheese and some beverage that filled a large mug and drew her attention as the appealing aroma spread from it.

As unaccustomed to so many people and so much talking and noise as she was, having so much food presented to her, for her, surprised her. At the nunnery, everyone shared their very plain, very sparse meals together. If someone stayed abed or otherwise missed it, they waited until the next gathering to eat. So, having food brought to her for her comfort was shocking.

It did not take long for Ilysa to realise that this woman had been chosen by her husband for her manner of speaking directly and her bold manner of ordering her betters around. He must have surmised that his wife was more familiar with following orders than being on her own. And, he'd guessed correctly in this.

Half the morning had passed before she descended the tower stairway to the main hall. If Gavina had been shocked by Ilysa's unusual hair or her damaged arm, the woman never showed it. Her constant stream of gossip and questions made it difficult to dwell on one topic for too long. Yet she had an uplifting sense of humour and a practical approach to everything that faced this morn and Ilysa found herself liking the woman. Was that the true reason behind Ross's choice of her?

Since she'd eaten more this morn than she usually ate on most days, she accepted Gavina's offer to walk around the yard and to see the lands closest to the castle. Ilysa needed to move about, to breathe the air and regain her balance. Eschewing a cloak, she followed the servant out into the yard where everyone looked very busy, carrying out all sorts of tasks. Though most paused to look at her as she passed and many offered some gesture of respect, no one spoke to her.

Ilysa took the measure of her new home, watching those at work and taking note of the general condition of the keep, the yards and the people. The MacMillans were not the wealthiest or most powerful of the clans in this area, but their attitudes and loyalty to their new chieftain and their clear willingness to work hard were apparent in their behaviour.

Even if they all but ignored her. And that was not new to her.

Gavina followed along, mentioning names and pointing out different places as they crossed the yard towards the gate. When the guards watching from both above and there on the ground questioned her, Gavina boldly demanded their apologies for delaying their Lady in her duties. It took all of her control not to laugh as the jovial servant became a serious guardian of Ilysa's honour and position.

A small collection of cottages lay spread out just beyond the gates. The burnt doors and knocked-down walls and other breakage revealed they had been attacked and yet most of the repairs being done were within the keep instead. As they walked towards the dock, she noticed that nary a cottage had escaped destruction of some kind. Only when she realised she was counting the number of damaged houses and the people near or in them did Ilysa wonder who saw to the villagers' needs and when that might be accomplished.

Her thoughts were filled with questions and she did not see anyone in front of her until it was too late. Strong hands grabbed her shoulders to avoid her running into…him. Glancing up, she saw that she'd nearly slammed into her husband.

'Forgive me, my lord,' she said, stepping back and waiting for him to release her. Instead, he motioned Gavina off with a nod of his head and held her firmly in his grasp. 'I am well, my lord. You can let me go now.'

'Are you, Wife? Are you well?'

Now that she'd left her chamber and had the opportunity to walk and stretch her legs, unused to sloth, she did feel well. It was only the intense scrutiny in his gaze and the way his eyes darkened to a deep brown from their usual mix of brown, golden and green that made her think there was more to his question. Startled that she'd actually noticed his eye colour, she nodded wordlessly, staring at him.

Only then did the true meaning of his question strike her and the heat of a blush rose in her cheeks. He was asking about…the marital act. When she remembered her reaction to it, to him, the heat coursed through her body and the place, the one he and only he had touched, began to throb.

Though she'd known the basic process of joining with a man, no one had revealed the unbelievable pleasure that could be part of it. Oh, men bragged about it. They revelled in seeking it out and they glorified attaining it. But, as the sheltered, ignored daughter of a powerful man, no one would have told her about such a thing. And no one had. Nor about the touching before the act. She'd heard the stories about a woman's skirts being tossed over her head and the deed done, but nothing about *before* the deed.

The man standing there, holding her securely, had touched her in ways she'd never conceived of. As her husband, he had the right to take, but last night was not about that. He'd shown patience and a care that had shocked her. He did not shame her when her father's actions towards him would have been reason enough to do so. Even the sight of her malformed arm uncovered before him had not elicited anything but a question.

His pride had been insulted, his honour questioned, yet he'd still treated her to pleasures she did not know existed between a man and a woman. She had readied herself, expecting a completely different experience, one of pain and shame, and instead this man rose above what most powerful men would have done.

And now? Now he asked after her comfort and condition.

'I…am well, my lord. And…' She paused, searching for the right words to say that would bring this conversation on to safer ground. 'I hope that everything arrived as promised?'

He released her and stepped aside, allowing her to see the crates and barrels and other supplies that had both accompanied her and followed her arrival here. She had no knowledge of what he'd agreed to or whether her father had fulfilled his part of the arrangement. So, she asked.

'Is all as you expected it to be?' She was proud that her question came out in an even tone of voice. It was not that she wanted to know, it was more that she needed to know what to expect here. Was he satisfied with the payment he'd received for his marriage to her? Was he angry that he'd received her rather than her sister?

He tilted his head, studying her, before answering her question.

'Do you wish for honesty between us, Wife?'

'I would rather hear the truth than live in fear of the rumours or gossip, my lord.' And she would. She had learned over the past three years that she could indeed deal with the knowledge of the situation being clear and truthful than to ignore what everyone knew and she wished to ignore. His gaze narrowed and he shrugged.

'Everything arrived as promised, except for the wife I was promised. However, there was a large amount of gold included for the purpose of soothing my insulted honour.'

His words were not unexpected—his cousin had told

her about the additional large sack of gold coins when she'd revealed her identity to him on the journey here. But she could not gather any sense of anger or disappointment in his words or tone about her replacing her sister.

'Before you ask,' he said, just before she could do just that, 'I accepted the gold and the bride and will not protest either one.'

He sounded so serious and yet she saw a flash of mirth in his eyes as he met hers. He confounded her with his even temper and lack of reprisal against her. Mayhap this marriage would not be as onerous as it could be for her?

'And now, my lord?' She turned and, with a hand above her eyes to block the brightness of the sun, she looked back at the cottages and then over at the keep. 'What do we do now?'

'I use the benefits of our arranged marriage to strengthen our fortifications, repair the damage wrought during the attack and prepare for the next one.'

'And…me?' In a usual marriage, the wife of the chieftain held a position of honour and influence. Her sister would be perfect in that role, having been groomed by their father for such a marriage. But Ilysa had no such training since there were no such expectations for her. Any glimmer of hope for her match with Graeme had been crushed and had revealed to her the truth of her life. 'What would you have me do?'

'I do not require anything of you, Ilysa.' He looked past her then as someone approached quickly. 'You are safe here from your father's further machinations.' The steward walked to his side and leaned in, whispering something she was not meant to hear and did not. 'I must see to my duties.' He nodded and then followed Gillean back towards the gates.

Little would she have guessed that she would not speak to him for the rest of the week. Actually, with the exception of an occasional glimpse here and there, Ilysa did not even see her husband over that time. Her days passed in peace with no call for her help or advice or labours of any kind.

Day by day, her chamber filled with comforts. Later that first day, a thick, plush robe was on her trunk. One day after that, cushions for the chair and the bench along the window appeared, making it a much nicer place to sit. A lantern capable of burning for a long while and a pile of books were placed on the small table next to the chair. Thick stockings and sturdy low boots that kept her feet warm and dry as she walked through the keep and village awaited her one morning. Having lived these last few years with few possessions and little comfort lately, these were truly gifts.

Tempting as it was to remain within her chamber, Ilysa was determined to do more than sit reading. *'Idle hands do the devil's work,'* the prioress had warned, and being lazy filled her with a restlessness she'd not felt before. Given the extraordinary gift of time on her own with nothing to do simply clarified for her that a life at leisure was not what she wanted.

The first morning after that week of silence from her husband, Ilysa put on one of her working gowns, tied on her handkerchief and sought out a place to be of help.

* * *

"Tis not a shameful thing, you ken?'

Ross faced his cousin and raised a brow at his statement before looking away once more. He did not take his cousin's bait. So, as he expected, Dougal tweaked him again. His closest friend always seemed to find the unguarded places to pick at.

'She is your wife after all. A man should have a care about his wife.'

Ross put down the hammer he held and had been using on the modifications to the dock and faced Dougal. Ignoring his friend's taunts had not worked.

'And how many wives have you had that you can give me advice on mine?' he asked as he crossed his arms over his chest and glared at Dougal.

As he suspected, sarcasm did not work to slow down Dougal when he wanted to discuss something. Especially the something, or someone, he felt responsible for.

Ilysa MacDonnell.

'I do not think the lass, er, the Lady played a part in her father's deception, Ross.'

'The Lady and I sorted out her part in the deception, so let it go.'

'You did? Then why are you acting as if she does not exist?' Pick. Pick. Pick.

Ross let out a growl then, not worried about doing something a chieftain should not.

'Have a care, my friend. You stray very close to a line you should not cross with me.' Dougal's gaze narrowed and Ross knew his cousin would not let this go. Nay, he would chew on it like a tasty bone tossed to the hounds would be. 'You ken how much work we have yet to do here, Dougal. I have made things clear to *my wife* on the matter of our marriage and she understands.'

Dougal began to speak and Ross held up his hand— the one he wished still held the hammer—to stop him.

'Gavina apprises me of the Lady's welfare and needs. Gillean does as well.' Hell, even Munro added his bits. And so did the cook, the blacksmith, the baker and even the fletcher. Everyone seemed very at ease in making their opinions known to him about his wife. Except for the woman herself. 'So, I ken well what *my wife* is doing and how she fares and that she wants for nothing,' Ross explained.

As if the very fates he taunted heard his words, the breezes carried a laugh he did not recognise. Feminine and cheerful, it sent a shiver through him. Glancing in the direction where it had originated, Ross saw nothing amiss. Then, a woman he did not know walked from between two of the cottages.

Lithe and graceful, she wore the plain garb of a servant and the hair covering of a married woman. The basket on her arm was filled with all sorts of things and must be heavy from the way she shifted it on her arm. Her one arm. When Gavina stepped over to her side and said something to her, they turned away and headed to a different cottage.

His right hand formed a fist before he faced Dougal, knowing his friend would be smirking with self-satisfaction. And Ross could not argue with it either, for he'd ignored what his wife had been doing these past days since their wedding night. Oh, aye, he'd heard about her discoveries in her chamber. If Gavina was taken aback by his requests or suggestions, she never said so. The woman, the widow of another of his cousins, was the perfect maid for his reluctant wife.

Ross understood what he was doing. He wanted her content and out of his way. He did not need the distraction he knew she was. From the first touch that she'd permitted him to the sighs and moans of her pleasure, Ross knew the danger she presented to his well-ordered plans.

He wanted his wife.

He wanted her with a fierce need that surprised him.

He wanted to take his nunnery-trained wife to bed and pursue every kind of fleshly pleasure he could think of—and more.

And now? Now that his body urged him to slake his desire on her body? What was he to do with an arranged wife who was growing more inconvenient by the moment?

Chapter Six

After giving in to his curiosity—damn Dougal for spurring it on—he sought out several of the villagers he knew well. He learned of Ilysa's most recent efforts and was baffled to hear of her instructions to the women and weeuns who lived outside the wall of the castle. She gave no such directions to the men, but then they had theirs from him or from Munro. His people knew their duties and carried them out.

Only after speaking to his commander and steward did it make sense. His wife was taking the women and children under her protection. While he had seen to the defences, she'd seen to the welfare of those not able to defend themselves. In spite of his instructions to do nothing, Ilysa MacDonnell could not remain idle.

Regrettably, he now stood in the shadows of an alcove where she could not see him, watching her speaking with the cook and the baker and the other servants who worked here in the kitchen. If Dougal saw him, he would mock him relentlessly and Ross would be unable to argue it. But, Ross wanted to see if what he'd been hearing was true.

Although their first reactions to his new bride had been tempered by his own behaviour and the immediate suspicion he'd expected they'd feel towards any newcomer, they had changed their minds rather quickly considering...

Well, considering her.

All of her. The man who was her father. Her appearance. Her deformity. The knowledge of her past three years as almost a nun. Yet, from the way they attended to her every word, it seemed that none of that mattered now. In the time it had taken him and his men to rebuild the damage to the keep and the dock and then the village, she had won her own kind of war within the walls.

He only noticed the silence gradually and then realised that those he watched were now staring at him. Since his wife stood with her back towards him, she turned now to see what the others were looking at in the corner. The lively expression in her eyes and on her face muted in the first moments as she comprehended he'd been watching her. Even her body altered as she saw him—her shoulders lifted back and her chin raised in a moment, changing from a relaxed stance to something resembling a battle-ready one. All she needed was a sword in her hand and she was prepared for anything.

'My lord?' she asked, giving leave to the others with a nod before walking closer. 'Is there something you need?'

Although he was very certain of his decision to keep his new wife at a safe distance, a part of his body did not accept his decision and readied itself for something more. Ross shifted on his feet, hoping his rising erection was not visible to one and all and especially not to her. Now though, he must give some explanation of why he was following his unwanted wife. Ross searched for something to say. Something that would explain away his skulking in the shadows observation of her.

'I...' The spot between her brows tightened then and he could not help noticing the lone curl that had escaped from under her kerchief. No one knew about the riotous curls hidden beneath that drab scrap of fabric she contained them under but for him and her maid. Ah! That was it. 'Did you find the book I sent to your chamber?'

'My lord?' She approached him as he stepped from the shadows. 'A book?' Curiosity now brightened her blue eyes.

'A book of hours that was my mother's. I thought you might enjoy it.' He could not explain this unwelcome habit of late of sending a variety of comforts and even luxuries like this to his wife. And, at this moment, he did not wish to examine it more closely. He concentrated on the fact that if she was reading that or any book, she was not meandering her way through the keep or yard or village.

'Truly?' she asked.

The fingers on her visible hand began moving as though she was touching or stroking something...or as though she wanted to. His misguided male flesh reacted to that small gesture.

'My thanks, my lord.' Her words came out as a breathy whisper, urging him to drag her to her chamber and touch her until all her words sounded like that.

Ross needed to regain control of himself, his wayward desire and his hardness. He needed distance to do that. This distraction was dangerous and he could not allow it to be so. His duties demanded his attention. Now. Staring at his wife and following her during the day were outrageous and placed his clan in peril. Until the Campbells were destroyed, Ilysa MacDonnell could have no place in his life other than the means to the necessary end she was.

'I will be very careful of such a valued possession of yours,' she added, misunderstanding that it was now hers and hers alone.

Tempted to explain that to her, he realised it would draw him into deeper conversation with her, so he stood up to his full height and nodded at her. When it appeared she would say more, he turned and left her standing there. The echo of her gasp at his rudeness almost weakened his intent.

Almost.

He did not look at anyone as he strode out through the kitchens and into the yard. He did not stop or speak to another soul as he made his way to the stone steps that led to the battlements.

The guards must have read his expression, for they moved away from the place he claimed at the corner where he could see for miles in all directions. Tearing his thoughts away from the woman in the kitchens, he stared out over the water of Loch Sween towards the south and west.

The walls and docks were repaired. Their dead were blessed and buried. The harvest was underway with a large contingent of guards—mostly those sent by The MacDonnell—and their stores would be refilled soon.

When his sp—trusted men returned from their assignment, he expected to have more insight into the location and numbers of their enemy.

For though Ross MacMillan might be a new chieftain, he was not new to the dangers facing them. He'd served his uncle for years, since his father's death, and he understood more was at play than a random attack. The Campbells who had followed Alexander and been exiled with him did not simply decide to sail back to their former lands one day and attack.

The attack had been more than that—it was meant to take out their defences and it had. But it was incomplete. Oh, they had killed their chieftain and many of their warriors, but it was not the last attack the Campbells would launch against them. Ross understood that a bigger strike would be coming soon. And Ross would not fail again in the preparations needed to keep his kith and kin safe.

He could not fail.

His indifferent behaviour towards her confused and angered Ilysa.

He dismissed her without hesitation whenever they met up even while his gifts were some of the kindest acts she'd witnessed. Oh, it wasn't the expense of most of them, for many of them were simply making something available to her that she might need or want.

As Ilysa considered this latest one, she realised that her maid was at the centre of those. Though her husband rarely conversed with her, Gavina questioned her with the deft skills of a diabolical interrogator each evening as she readied for bed. Having no experience in others being interested in her opinions or even her needs or comforts, Ilysa found herself ill equipped to protect her privacy from her maid. Worse, or sadder still, she had no desire to turn her maid from those conversations.

Ilysa turned to find the servants who had scampered away at Ross's appearance now gathered back around her, awaiting her instructions. For the next while, she applied her experience and what she'd learned and observed in the nunnery and even the nearby abbey to help prepare those dependent on the chieftain's protection for the next attack.

Oh, no one had said to her of such a thing directly, but Ilysa had learned to listen in silence and she'd heard many details that would surprise her husband. When she first noticed that his attention was taken by the defences of the castles and the warriors, she'd begun seeing to the villagers and servants. With an eye to supplies, she'd taught them how to seek cover when the attack occurred, how to protect their bairns and more. Though she doubted the chieftain knew or cared, she was careful to never contradict her husband or his men's orders or directions.

Though she had not been in an attack or invasion before, she paid heed to the stories of the villagers and simply tried to sort out better ways to do things to ensure that none, or fewer at least, came to harm. She busied herself from morn to night and found that she slept well now that the bed and the chamber grew familiar to her.

Then, something extraordinary had happened. After that first evening, when Gavina would ask about supper, Ilysa had asked for a tray in her chamber. The difficulty and embarrassment of partaking in a meal in front of others, especially if it included foods that needed cutting, usually overrode any desire of hers to be at table. In the quiet of her chamber, it mattered not.

A few days ago, Gavina invited Ilysa to join her in the evening meal down in the kitchens. It was something as the chieftain's wife or the daughter of a powerful man she should never even have considered for a passing moment. Yet…she had to admit she'd thought on it. The refusal at the first invitation was easily done, but something within her could not stand firm in her resolve. At the nunnery, they ate a communal meal and, though silence was preferred by the rules of the house, the prioress used that meal to share news and interesting bits that she'd learned of or thought might be of use. Any sense of being ill at ease at the large table faded as her need for company grew.

Strange that, and stranger still that her desire to sit with a large group did not involve the chieftain and those who sat in honour at the high table, but the lowly servants. Mindful of that, she made her way down to the lower level of the keep later that day, passing the busy great hall and making her way to the place Gavina had pointed out to her. Stilted silence surrounded her as she made her presence known to those gathered at a long table until Gavina rose and greeted her.

'My lady! Ye came to join us!' Gavina had a space cleared for her with a few whispers and nods and Ilysa sat in the proffered chair. A cup appeared and was filled with ale. 'Ronald, bring something for the Lady.'

With her maid's guidance, the conversation began once more and Ilysa sat listening to the story of the cook's boy who, even though not a child, had fallen off the dock and the chaos that had followed it. Alarm filled her at the thought, for she herself could not swim, but the cook explained that it was a prank on the young man's part to draw his friends into the water. Without knowing all those involved, Ilysa smiled and listened.

A bowl was placed before her and the savoury aroma made her belly growl. Covering her stomach, she nodded at the man in thanks and found a spoon next to it. Glancing around at the others, Ilysa discovered that their meal was different from hers. Their food required cutting or tearing and hers was a stew made up of bite-sized chunks of…mutton in a thick gravy with root vegetables of the same size.

Someone had taken pains to give her food she could manage with one hand.

Before she could shame herself with tears, Gavina held out a platter of torn pieces of bread and Ilysa swallowed several times before meeting her maid's eyes. 'My thanks.'

Concentrating her efforts on eating without spilling, Ilysa did not participate in the lively chatter, but she enjoyed hearing it. They spoke of the common things in their shared lives—bairns and kin and duties and the coming danger. Through it all, one thing was clear to her: Ross MacMillan had their support and loyalty. Whether her presence caused the comments about him or not, none could find fault in their new chieftain or his efforts. She emptied the bowl before raising her eyes to those seated at the table.

'My lady?' Ronald asked in a soft voice that belied his size and strength. 'There is more if ye havena eaten yer fill.'

Ilysa glanced at the bowl and saw that she'd eaten every bit and wiped the delicious gravy up with her bread. What surprised her was that she could have eaten more of it. Her appetite, barely present for a very long time, had reared back with great force since her arrival here. Thinking on it now, she realised that she'd eaten more in the last week than mayhap the month before!

'Nay, Ronald,' she said. ''Twas delicious and my thanks for making something in addition to all your other dishes.'

The cook smiled and nodded.

''Twere no trouble, my lady.'

As she rose, they all did. Ronald eased out the chair from beneath her and she nodded to the others. 'Gavina, I will not seek my rest for some time. No need to rush.'

'Aye, my lady,' her maid said.

As she made her way to her chambers and, for the hours that followed before she slept, Ilysa found herself smiling over the small moments at the table with the servants. For a time, she felt as though she belonged— or, at the least, did not stick out as an obvious outsider. No one stared or remarked on her inability to eat as they did.

So, when she did seek her bed, a sense of comfort filled her. And the sweets that Gavina brought from the cook added to a feeling of satisfaction.

She'd fallen so quickly and deeply into sleep that she did not know what woke her until he stepped forward from the shadows. She shifted in her bed and lifted her head to see.

'My lord? Is all well?'

Only the light from that small lantern, an extravagant luxury he'd provided, lit the chamber and revealed his presence. The chieftain stepped closer, frowning as he glanced across, his gaze moving from her to the hearth and then to the lantern and back to her.

His frown deepened as he took another step and then another. When his hands fisted and rested on his hips, a tension stirred in her stomach and bile rose as she waited on his next step. It would take only two more paces for him to reach her bedside and be within...striking distance of her. He'd not threatened her before, nay, he'd actually withheld punishment when she'd insulted him the night of her arrival.

Yet, too many years of recognising the signs of an impending beating forced fear through her body and readied her to do what she must to survive. And then, when she thought he would move towards her, he turned and walked to the hearth.

'This chamber is always cold,' he muttered as he knelt before it. 'Tell Gavina the fire should be larger each night,' he said over his shoulder. 'I can see my breath in the chill air here.'

Ilysa slid to the edge of the bed and let her legs drop over the side as she sat up. The cold he'd mentioned tempted her to tuck her legs back under once it reached her. She'd fallen asleep without putting on the sleeve that held her arm stable as she slept. So, she adjusted her arm so that her hand rested in her lap and she tried to explain.

'My lord, 'twas not Gavina's fault,' she said. 'I have been abed for some time and it simply—' The flames stirred and heat rushed across the chamber as he stood and faced her, ending any excuse or reasoning she planned to offer.

'Do you have something against being comfortable, Lady?' he asked. His voice softened as he walked towards her then. His hands dropped and he held them open at his sides.

'Nay. I am comfortable.' Her gaze flitted over the lantern she had boldly left burning. Unfortunately, the wick sputtered out in that moment. Sliding her hand over the thick pile of blankets covering the bed, she held them back to show how many were layered there. 'You see, my lord? I have claimed several blankets to keep me warm through the night.'

A strange and indecipherable expression passed over his face. He cleared his throat and for a moment she thought he looked guilty. Guilty of…something. And the urge to ease his guilt filled her. Yet she knew not how or why she should.

'Was there something you wanted, my lord?' She tugged the blankets over her legs. Now, his expression was filled with an emotion she did recognise—desire. Wanting. When he did not speak, she drew up her courage and asked him directly, 'Have you come to claim your conjugal rights?'

'You were frightened a few moments ago. Now, you are bold.'

The light and shadow thrown by the flames in the hearth made his face look grave and then pleasant as though the lines and angles of his face changed as she watched.

'I would rather ken what I face, my lord.'

She made the mistake of letting her gaze roam over his body. That male part of him made itself apparent as she did so. The chamber suddenly grew warmer and the place between her legs where he would enter her began to throb.

'Aye, Wife. I would claim…my…conjugal rights.'

Her body seemed to understand his intent before she did. Their joining had been filled with the most wondrous pleasure in spite of the short time when she'd first felt the thrust of his flesh into hers. He'd had a care for her as he'd claimed her.

Then, he'd left and not returned to her bed.

She'd heard that men liked bed play. That they sought it out as frequently as they could. That a man could have more than just one woman to satisfy his needs. Though she'd seen no sign of that behaviour in her husband, how would she know? But, if he'd not sought satisfaction in her bed, where did he seek it?

'You are thinking many thoughts at once, Wife. I can almost hear them swirling inside your head.' He smiled then. 'Does that mean you do not wish for me to do so?'

'Why do you wish to?' She gasped as soon as the words left her mouth.

He laughed first, leaning his head back as he did. It eased her concerns and she felt the corners of her mouth lifting at the sound of it. How did he manage to do that? He went out of his way to soothe her fears and lessen any she might feel for him. Her father used his punishments to increase her terror and the anticipation of it to leverage his control over her.

But this man did exactly the opposite with her. And she had no idea of his motivations or what he hoped to accomplish. Would he answer her?

'I wish I kenned, Ilysa. I wish I kenned.' Uncertainty filled his eyes as he watched her. He lifted up his hands and ran them through his hair, shrugging as he did it. 'You can say nay.'

His offer to allow her permission befuddled and touched her at once. Whatever the urge was that brought him to her chamber, it was clear he regretted it. Or battled it in some way. Yet, it had brought him here and not taken him to another woman's bed.

'Aye, my lord.'

Her consent increased the perplexed expression in his eyes, as though he could not believe she'd said aye. So, she eased over a bit in the wide bed and lifted the piles of bedcoverings to allow him in. At first, he narrowed his gaze, studying her face, and then he moved closer, tugging his belt free and allowing the wrapped length of tartan to drop to the floor.

Her breasts swelled as he tugged off his boots before grabbing the edge of his shirt. As his body was revealed in the golden glow of the flames, she lost her breath. Without the fear of their first joining, anticipation heated her blood and made her mouth go dry. By the time he stood before her, naked and even bigger than she remembered, she was hot enough to push back the covers.

When he approached and climbed on to the bed next to her, she lost all thought and could not find a way to breathe. Every part of her was tense as she waited on his first move. Would this be the time he would toss up her bedgown and take her? Would he…? Would he…?

The touch of his mouth on hers startled her from her reverie. His hands slid into her hair and his fingers moved up to cup and hold her head.

'I have wanted to touch your hair from the first moment I saw it uncovered,' he whispered against her lips. 'It has taunted me every time I have seen you with that damned kerchief over it.' His finger massaged her scalp and the pleasure of the simple movement surprised her.

'I am a married woman now. It should be covered, except in my bedchamber, my lord.' His hands spread out in her hair and then his fingers clutched it tightly, giving him control over her movement. He tugged and she leaned into his hold.

'And if your lord and husband told you to uncover it outside your chamber?' His mouth was hot against the sensitive skin of her throat as he kissed it. 'So that he might enjoy it whenever he looks at you?'

'I w—' she said before his mouth returned to her skin just above the edge of her shift. Then, she could not speak.

His lips tightened on the spot and he suckled it, causing inexplicable ripples of pleasure to flow out to all sorts of places within her. The tips of her breasts grew tight. Her body arched closer to him of its own accord. The place between her legs throbbed and grew wet. She lost control of her breaths and the sounds slipping from her own mouth. The touch of his mouth became something more urgent and then his teeth bit the skin as he suckled and she moaned aloud.

One of his hands continued to hold her head and he slid the other down to cover the aching tip of one of her breasts. The caress satisfied for a moment and then the craving began to grow anew. His fingers encircled her breast and he rubbed his thumb over the tip—in spite of the thin fabric between them every pass of his calloused skin forced her hips to arch. The tip grew more sensitive with each stroke and every caress built up the tension within her.

She wanted more. She wanted his mouth on her flesh. She wanted him to ease the ache between her legs. Even if it hurt at first, she knew now it would release the built-up tension centred there.

Ilysa managed to reach up and loosen the laces of her bedgown. He lifted his gaze to hers as he tugged the edges of the shift until she was exposed to his sight. His eyes and his nostrils flared as he took what she offered.

'Lie back now and let me pleasure you, Wife.'

And so she did.

And he did.

Chapter Seven

The fire had burned down, leaving only some smouldering ashes giving off their last vestiges of heat. It mattered not to her now for her husband warmed her more efficiently than any hearth could.

Ilysa should be embarrassed or ill at ease and yet she was so comfortable and so satiated that she had not the strength or the will to move out of his intimate embrace. Her limp body was not her own to command, as he'd shown her.

Actually, he'd demonstrated his control over her body and her pleasure thrice before she collapsed into a deep sleep. Each time was different from the others, whether in pace or vigour. And each time he seemed intent on pushing her further into pleasure than the last.

Oh, the things he had done!

She reached up and touched her face where her cheeks heated with a deep blush from the memories of the way he'd used his mouth and his tongue and his hands and body to arouse her until she begged. Though whether it was begging for cessation or for more, she could not tell now.

He shifted a bit and she waited to see if he awakened or settled back into sleep. His arm, placed over her bad arm in a way that sheltered it, enfolded her in his embrace. He'd done that each time—protected her arm from being caught under and between them and he'd even put her sleeve on her before taking her in an unexpected and scandalous way. Her hips arched at the thought of being on top of him while he watched her sitting on his…

That part of him hardened behind her, pressing its length against her back. The deep, low chuckle that rumbled through him revealed his wakefulness. Her body recognised the meaning of his masculine flesh rising so, for she'd seen it and felt it three times this night.

'I did not mean to disturb your rest, Wife.' He leaned closer and rubbed his cheek against her hair. She did not understand his fascination with the wild curls that most everyone thought unattractive and for which her father would have beaten her if he'd had more time.

Ross eased his arm from under hers and rolled away, allowing the chill air to rush in as he got out of her bed. As she turned on her back and pulled the bedcovers up, she wondered at his departure. Without a word, he circled the chamber and collected the garments he'd strewn in his haste to join with her. Now, he pulled his shirt on and gathered the length of the plaid he wore and tossed it over his shoulder. He made no attempt to put his boots on.

And not once in the time it took him did he look or speak to her. Had her unrestrained passion displeased him in some way? Should she have resisted? Lay silently beneath him? Not touched his body as he'd touched, caressed and tasted hers?

'I do not understand, my lord,' she said, adjusting her sleeve and struggling up straight. 'Did I do something wrong?'

How could he explain that she'd done everything perfectly? That he could not have expected anything more from her? Worse, that she'd given him such pleasure in her acceptance of his touch and his possession of her body? Ross sat on the stool near the cooling hearth and dropped his boots once more.

How did he explain something he did not understand himself?

His brilliant plan to keep her out of his daily life and to concentrate only on his duties as chieftain had made sense when he'd come up with it. She was not the wife he'd sought or wanted. Truth be told, he was not ready to marry until the elders forced his hand. Well, until the Campbells forced it.

And in spite of her being everything a man would not want in a bride, she was everything he wanted. Watching her, from near or afar, these last days had not assuaged his desire for her. Indeed, it had…

'My lord?' Her voice was soft and guarded—as it always was—yet, he could hear the sense of vulnerability in it. 'Have I displeased you?' Ilysa now sat up on the bed, watching him and waiting on his words.

'You have not,' he said, letting out a breath as he spoke. 'I did not mean for this…' He paused and motioned at her bed. 'I did not mean it to happen.'

She startled at his admission. A deep frown marred her usually pleasant face. But only for one long moment. Then, she nodded and looked away. She shifted on the bed and tried to cover herself with the prodigious pile of blankets. Blankets that kept her warm when her husband did not.

Something told him that her comments about the bedcovers had not been meant as a rebuke of his absence. Her next words, in their even tone, confirmed it somehow.

'Ah, I understand. Your leman was not available to you this night.'

'Leman?' He choked on the word and rose as he said it. 'My leman?'

'I understand why you would seek to take your pleasure on a woman experienced in the bed play you prefer over…' Stunned at her assumption, he waited, unable to predict what she would say. 'Well, as your people call me, your nunnery wife.'

'What the hell—?'

'I am not insulted by that description, my lord, since it is true.'

She opened her mouth to add something, but his growl, his loud growl, stopped her. He strode to the bed, standing so close she had to look up at him.

'Who has said that?' When she shivered, he asked again, 'Who has called you that, Ilysa?'

'Those who do not call me that usually just whisper my father's name as I pass.' She shrugged then as she rearranged her shift. 'It matters not. I am what I am.'

'You are the wife of The MacMillan,' he said.

Unease crept through him as he uttered the words.

The simple rise of her eyebrow said more than any conversation could. Gavina's whispered warnings and Dougal's taunts came to mind.

'A wife you do not want.'

He glanced at the bed and raised his own brow. 'I think you ken that is not true.'

'Ah,' she said with a slow nodding of her head. 'Even an unwanted wife has her benefits. At least when the one you truly desire is not available to you.'

Her words echoed with the faint tones of righteous indignation and—could it be?—jealousy or resentment? Should he disabuse her of the mistake in her assumption or let it lie between them? Nay, he would not treat her as her father did, nor as his uncle might have.

'I have no leman.'

Disbelief shone in her gaze. Which surprised him.

'Then I do not understand,' she whispered on a sigh.

'Ilysa, I mean no insult to you.' And he did not. He wished things to be clear and distant between them. 'I need all my attention on defending my people. I need to concentrate so that I am not outwitted or undermined again.'

'Well, at least you will not be fooled into taking the wrong bride again.'

That would always be his biggest failing—so he could not argue with her. Yet, he wanted her to know the true reasons behind accepting her without rising to a fight with her father.

'I would do anything to protect my clan. After losing my uncle, I was chosen to lead.' He sat on the side of her bed and stared across the now-chilling chamber. 'I would do anything to protect my brother and sister.'

'I did not ken you had siblings,' she said.

'Did your father tell you nothing of me before he presented you to Dougal?'

'Nothing, my lord.' A soft sigh escaped her. 'My sister mentioned that you were a new laird. I confess feeling some relief when I saw Dougal there.'

'Relief?'

'Aye. I feared the only man who would have me would be some elderly one in need of a helpmate or such.'

No matter that she had been part of the scheme, unwilling or ignorant at best, Ross felt angry for her. An honourable man did not need soft feelings about a woman to be outraged at the callous use of her. The need to beat her father to the ground rose in him, for this and so much more. Shaking his head, he closed his eyes and imagined the pleasure in doing just that. He heard and felt her shift behind him.

'Where are they?'

'My brother Fergus has married one of our allies and my sister Elspeth will await her marriage at an abbey near her betrothed's lands.' He chose his words carefully, not yet willing to share all his secrets with The MacDonnell's daughter until he had determined her true role in his machinations.

He smiled then, remembering his sister's, and brother's, reaction at his decision. Fergus understood, as Ross did, their responsibilities and the duty expected of them. When Elspeth calmed down, he had no doubt she would as well. The abbey seemed the best place for her safety and to give her some time to understand that he had not made that particular alliance to punish her. Fergus, though…well, he was more difficult to convince considering his past with the widow of Nevin Barron.

'What amuses you so?' she asked, laying her hand on his back for a moment. She'd not approached him before and the weight and warmth of her slender hand burned his skin with an awareness that should not happen.

Yet it did. Ross felt every inch of his shoulder under her touch. A simple touch. He ignored it to answer her.

'Elspeth could be a hellion when she wanted her way in things,' he said.

'And she did not want this marriage?' Her hand slipped away. He noticed.

'Expectations for them were always different,' he said. 'We all kenned that our uncle would control our marriages, but Fergus and Elspeth thought they would have more control over their choices.' After their father's death at the hands of Alexander Campbell, their uncle had become their guardian. 'Even as his heir, I never expected—'

'Me?' Though trying to jest, he could hear the vulnerability in her voice. Ross turned and slid back to face her.

'I never expected to inherit.' She nodded at his words, but he could see she did not believe them. 'My uncle planned to remarry soon. He had even looked to your sister as a possibility, though he made no attempt to discuss it with your father yet.'

'Was your uncle very old?'

'Not so young, but not as old as you feared me to be,' he said. 'Still young enough to have sons. So, I never anticipated being in control of…all this.' He spread his hands out to mean the whole of the MacMillan holdings.

They sat in silence for a short time, Ross caught up in the concerns that faced him in the coming fight for the survival of their clan. And for a reason he could not explain, it was a comfortable situation. He did not have to justify or detail a plan or outline his duties.

Sliding the rest of the distance across the bed to lean against the wall, he decided he was not quite as ready to leave Ilysa's chamber as he'd thought he was.

'You'd best climb back under your pile of blankets,' he said to her. 'The chill is returning.'

From the expression in her eyes and the tilt of her chin that exposed the graceful lines of her throat, it seemed his wife wished to say something. The slightest shake of her head, one that would have been unnoticed but for the way it made those curls shift, and she lifted the bedcovers and slid under them.

The silence gained hold, but then she whispered a question about his family, about his parents.

Another followed and another until her voice grew softer with each word. When her slow, even breathing told him she was asleep, Ross eased off the bed and collected his boots. The cooled hearth drew his attention and he stirred up the ashes, added more fuel to it and waited for it to catch.

There would be no need for it if he warmed his wife through the night.

Shaking off any regrets or the temptation to climb in with her, Ross gathered and tossed the length of plaid over his shoulder as he walked in silence from the chamber and closed the door behind him. As he made his way to the other end of the corridor towards his own chamber, his fortune ran out and he turned the corner into Gavina.

She began to smile even as he shook his head in warning at her. The woman had taken her Lady under her protection and would see this as...more than it was. More than it could be.

'Not a word,' he whispered, stepping to his chamber door. 'Not a word.'

'I would never, my lord.' Her words acquiesced, but her tone mocked.

Ross entered his room and dropped his boots by the door. Though Gavina would torment him, he did not doubt her loyalty or that she would keep her silence.

Glancing at the shuttered window, he knew the sun would rise soon. With little time left in the night, he lay on his bed and his satisfied body sought rest.

At least it would not happen again. He could not regret this small respite amid the strain of carrying out his duties, but it could not happen again.

It would not. He would not allow it.

But the next night, as he approached her door in the dark of night, Ross assured himself that giving in to the growing need to seek comfort in her embrace and body was not a distraction.

As his men returned warnings of boats gathering in the south, he was learning about the woman he should not have married.

He discovered that her feet were sensitive to his touch.

He learned that she allowed him to have his way in intimate matters. She refused him nothing.

* * *

On the morning after the fourth night spent in her bed, he realised that there was so much more to the daughter who Iain MacDonnell had banished and shamed than Ross could have known…or hoped.

Chapter Eight

This time, the enemy arrived at the gloaming, when the setting sun's light created strange reflections on the surface of the loch and made their approach harder to see. But unlike the first attack, the MacMillans were prepared for the attack.

Ross was out of the keep within moments of the alarm being raised. Following Munro, he took his place next to his commander on the wall and watched as their warriors gathered just outside the gate. As Munro called out orders, Ross was pleased to see that the Campbells seemed unprepared for the resistance they met this time.

The speed with which villagers reacted to the call to arms startled him. As he watched, they fled their cottages at the first warning and ran towards the gate. When he would have called out to the guards, the men separated and spaced themselves out along the approach, allowing the villagers to flee into the yard and protecting them until they were inside. The lines gathered again before the gates, ready for any attackers who made it that far.

'Who ordered that?' Ross asked, disappointed that he'd not been the one to think of it.

'A suggestion was made about the villagers after the first attack.' He glanced out of the corner of his eyes at his commander. Something was wrong but this was not the time to sort it out.

Munro strode along the parapets and called out to the archers waiting. Ross watched as his men aimed the barrage of arrows for the boats nearing the docks. Not waiting for their enemies to reach land, Munro ordered the burning arrows loosed. Dozens flew into the air, over the walls towards their targets—the boats and the men in them. The few who jumped into the water attempting to make it to shore on their own were taken down. Not without effort—the Campbells manoeuvred their birlinns away, far enough to be out of the range of the archers with their burning or simply deadly arrows. A warning cry drew Ross and Munro to the southern part of the keep's battlements where a smaller force approached on land.

Ross smiled grimly, knowing which men awaited them once they broke from behind the rocky protection of the bedrock of the castle itself. It took little time for the attackers to accept the futility of their attempt and to flee. His men chased them, catching a few as they did. Munro let out a yell and Ross nodded.

'We will speak later,' Ross said. 'See to any wounded and work with Gillean to repair any damage.'

'I will send men to follow them as before,' Munro added before he called out to several men to follow him and rushed down the stairs.

Preparation had won the day. Ross made his way

down to the yard as his men waited for the guards to allow the gates to be opened. The yard was crowded with those who'd fled the village when the warning had been called. They gathered in groups and as he paid heed to them, he realised that the men stood listening to one of his guards. Glancing across the yard, he found the larger group of the women, elderly and children in the area between the wall and the stone storage shed.

Expecting to hear whimpers of fear from those most unable to defend themselves, the soft singing shocked him. The weeuns sat on the ground, surrounded by the women and the eldest of his relatives, and all of them faced someone in the centre. The clear, rhythmic words and melody of a waulking song used by the women in their work echoed in rounds from the leader. Ross knew who it was before he got any closer.

Ilysa MacDonnell sat in the centre, singing the familiar song and encouraging the others to join in.

Ilysa MacDonnell, smiling at the little lasses who pushed closer and touched her skirts. And the wee laddies, too.

His wife.

He knew every curve of her body now, every secret sensitive place on her skin and every sound she made in passion. But he had never heard her sing.

As she glanced around those singing, her gaze moved to him and her voice faltered in her song. The blush that seemed to happen every time she looked at him outside her bedchamber crept up into her pale cheeks. She wore her innocence like the shawl around her shoulders. No matter what sort of private pleasures they found together, she yet blushed every time he met her gaze.

'My lord?' she asked as she climbed to her feet. She waved for the children to remain as she nodded to one of the women—Suisan, he thought her name was—to continue leading them. She stepped through the group and approached him, concern in her expression. She tilted her head for a moment. 'Is the battle finished?' she whispered so only he would hear.

'The men are finishing it now,' he said, nodding to Munro who passed him by just then. From his commander's expression, Ross could tell that the fighting had been too short and not enough vengeance wrought on those who'd caused so much damage in the first attack. ''Twill be safe to allow the villagers back to their homes shortly.'

'I will let them know to wait on your signal, my lord.' With a glance over her shoulder, she leaned in closer to him. 'Have you any other need of me before I return to them?'

If the blush had not burned brighter in that moment, Ross would have been convinced that, of the two of them, only he heard the double meaning in her words. But, her cheeks pinked and she blinked as she moved her gaze from his and he could not rid himself of the damned smile.

She'd turned from him and approached those nearest, whispering to them and waiting as they passed along the news and instructions to those closest to them. And not once did the singing slow or pause as the word spread. Then, she moved into the centre and sat down to sing with them.

He stood and watched as she gathered the children close again and began another song, involving them in the singing to keep their attention on her. Though they'd just been attacked and it could have ended differently, Ilysa had created a separate place within the terrifying and loud fight, while flaming arrows flew over her head and men fought just over the wall from her. But not just for her. For those who could not defend themselves. For the young and very old. For the women unable to fight. For those too ill.

For his people.

'Ross?'

He turned from his thoughts to find Dougal waiting there. At his cousin's nod, Ross followed him out of the gate and towards the loch.

'This was not their full force,' Dougal said quietly as Munro joined them.

'They played with us,' Munro added, as he joined them. 'A few boats, a few dozen warriors and another score or so approached on foot from the south.'

'So, they toy with us after their first attack did not wipe us out?' he said. 'Why?' Ross crossed his arms over his chest and turned back to face the keep. 'The well within, the stores, the preparations all mean we could withstand even a siege.' He shrugged. 'It makes no sense.'

'They must be dividing their men,' Dougal offered. 'But where else would they target?'

'Send word to Fergus at Castle Barron and to the MacLachlans about this attack.' His brother held a smaller keep that was also part of the old Campbell lands and would be in danger and their allies from that area, the MacLachlans, should know as well. Ross looked back across the loch and to the south. 'This was small enough to get past Islay without attention, especially if they separated and met down there—' He pointed to the place where the land jutted out just enough to block the view to the south. 'If the boats then stayed close to shore, they could hide themselves until the last moment.'

''Twas a good thing then that we had men watching the approaches,' Dougal offered.

'It still makes little sense to me,' Ross admitted. 'The Campbells are gone for a score of years, attack in surprise, but leave the deed undone. Now, they trickle back into their old lands expecting to succeed?'

'I think The Campbell has help, Ross,' Munro said. His commander spit in the dirt. 'Our men returned with stories about his eldest son, Calum. The old Campbell is not strong enough any longer without his help.'

'So, we have two Campbells, each able to bring war to our doors? The older and the younger?'

The implications and possibilities filled Ross's head and none of them was good for the MacMillans or their allies who now held lands the Campbells wanted back. Lands now connected to himself, his younger brother and, soon, his sister.

Places that he'd sent them to oversee.

Places that would now be attacked and possibly lost.

More of his kin dead.

'What do we ken of the son, Munro? Do we ken which of the Campbells is behind these attacks?'

'Alexander was seen nearby and several of our elders reported seeing him during the first attack. But the son was a wee lad when last here, so I fear no one would recognise him now.' Munro glanced at some men approaching them from the gates. 'I will find out from those who fought in the thick of the first attack if anyone heard of him being there.'

'Nay,' Dougal said as he nodded to their guards. 'I do not think this...' he waved his hand over the area '...was planned to be more than it was.'

'Another attempt to tease us out into the open and waste our advantage?' Ross asked. 'Or to discern our preparedness? If that, what did he discover? What did this give him except burned boats and a score dead or wounded?'

'They killed our laird in the first attack.' Dougal's voice lost any hint of its usual wit. 'And, they learned this time that we are indeed prepared for them.'

'Aye.' Ross nodded. 'But did we expose any weaknesses to them?'

No one spoke as all three turned their gazes to the collection of cottages that sat there outside the castle. Though only a short time had passed while the villagers rushed inside, that small delay had left the gates open and the entire castle vulnerable. And now, their enemy had witnessed it.

'Who gave the orders to protect the villagers?' he asked.

'I did,' Munro said. Something in his tone told Ross his commander answered truthfully, as he expected him to do, but that there was more he was not saying.

'And who brought that tactic to you, Munro? Though it worked successfully, 'twas not something we'd discussed before.' Strange that the man would keep anything from him. It was known that any man could bring his suggestions or questions to the chieftain or his man and be heard. Especially the older men experienced in battle or strategy. So, if Munro had not given the name…

'My lord?' Ross turned to the one who'd spoken. A guard from within the keep.

'Aye?'

'The Lady wishes to ken if 'tis safe for those within to return to their homes outside the walls.'

'Munro?'

'Aye, 'tis safe, Robbie,' Munro replied. 'Let them leave.'

The guard went off to relay the news that would allow the women and children to leave the castle. When Ross turned back to his commander, he almost missed the hasty, yet guilty glance shared between his two closest advisers. Almost.

In that moment, he knew where the suggestion had originated from. Or suspected he did. When Ilysa appeared on the path from the gates to the village, holding the hand of a young lass, he knew it to be true.

His wife giving his commander advice.

His MacDonnell wife.

A sudden burst behind his eyes had him blinking and shaking his head. Not pain. Surprise. And more.

'Ross, I—' Munro said. Ross cut off his words.

'My wife gave you advice about defensive strategies and you did not think to tell me?'

He forced the words through clenched teeth. He was angry. Nay, not angry so much as…aye, he was angry. At his men. At himself. At Ilysa.

'You did not wish to speak of her,' his commander said. 'Regardless of the one who suggested it, I thought the plan a worthy one, Ross.' Munro closed his mouth and stood waiting. Dougal's face took on a slight green-ish hue.

'But you purposely did not bring it to me for my approval.' Ross closed his eyes for a moment, trying to hold his temper under control.

His uncle had always struck out first, when angered or insulted. Be they man, woman or beast, none was safe when Cormac MacMillan was on a tirade—whether righteous or not. He was not generally a cruel man, just one with little patience for fools…or those smarter than himself.

He was not his uncle, nor would he be. His anger felt too raw now and, as he felt it surge, Ross suspected that some of it was aimed at his own ignorance. His wilful ignorance that paid no heed to the woman he'd married.

'See to what needs doing now,' he said. Nodding at both men, he stepped away. 'We will speak, all of us, after supper this night.'

The two said nothing else as he walked down the shoreline towards the south. Let them think it was for whatever purpose they would, but Ross understood he needed to sort out his thoughts before broaching them with anyone else.

An image of Ilysa shrinking back in fear from him filled his vision then. Every time when he first approached her, the colour would leave her face and her body would shift as though preparing to take a beating. Only these last several nights had seemed to ease her initial terror of him, of him hitting her as her own father had, and he'd be damned before he let that return. Or to allow her to believe he would ever raise his hand to her in anger.

If he saw her now, she would not understand his reaction. Hell, he did not. So, until he'd sorted it out—the
anger, the lingering suspicion of her and her connections
to her scheming father and his plans—he'd walk the cir-
cumference of the castle and search for any Campbells
left behind and hopefully pummel them to release this
tension within him.

Then, he would have the discussion with his wife
and his advisers that he needed to have.

She could not help it—a sense of accomplishment
unlike anything she'd ever felt filled her as she made her
way back to the keep. Ilysa walked with a bit of light-
ness in her pace she usually did not feel. And, when
people called out greetings to her as she passed, for
once, she did not walk in shame or fear.

Her confidence weakened just a bit when she saw her
husband speaking to his closest kin. Pausing to watch
the exchange for a moment, Ilysa could see the anger
sparking between them. Ross was furious. Dougal and
Munro looked like they'd rather be washing laundry
with the women than standing there with their chieftain.

She walked on and returned to the keep, seeking out
any who had need of help and remained busy.

After some time when things calmed, Ilysa went to
her chambers and cleaned up a bit. She'd just finished
washing her face and replacing her head covering when
she heard Gavina enter.

'My lady?' Ilysa turned at the call. Her maid approached, huffing as she rushed towards her. 'Gillean
seeks yer advice.'

A slight wind would have knocked her off her feet at those words. The steward had been the last in the household to accept her. He brushed off her questions with polite retorts. He disappeared, conveniently busy, when they were supposed to speak. Only in the last several days had he begun to thaw in his icy disregard.

Since his chieftain began seeking her bed at night.

A shiver shook its way through her at such a realisation. Was the change in her husband's attention the cause of the shift in Gillean's attitude, then?

Ilysa stared for a moment, counting in her thoughts those in the keep who had also had such a turnabout in their behaviour towards her. Not only the steward, but also several of the MacMillan elders and a few cousins. She brought her attention back to Gavina and motioned for her to lead her to him.

Gavina knew the truth—that her husband had started visiting her bedchamber at night—but Ilysa could not imagine the woman sharing that knowledge with others. The efficient servant had learned other personal details about her and yet there was not a whisper about those from anyone in the household. Since her husband had not made any change to the way he treated her in the light of day or around others, she doubted now that was the reason behind this shift.

She followed Gavina down the stairs to the lower level usually inhabited by the warriors. Along the length of the large, open chamber ran one corridor and she knew that Munro used a private chamber off this hallway as his own. They did not pause there. Instead, Gavina continued on to the end where a small, locked door faced them. As did Gillean.

'My lady, I appreciate your haste,' he said. Without an explanation, he turned and lifted a large ring of keys from his belt and found the one he wanted. Before inserting it into the lock, he rapped twice on the door and called out a name, warning of their entrance.

'Gavina?' she asked in a whisper. When the servant did not speak, she looked at the steward. 'Gillean, what is this about?' He glanced past and over her, before pushing on the door.

'My lady, we can speak within. I pray you enter.'

She tugged the shawl around her shoulders a bit where she clutched it and took one step, then another into the chamber, praying she could face whatever or whomever was within it. Gavina followed her, giving her a bit of comfort. When Gillean stopped and stepped aside, Ilysa looked across the small room and saw only a pallet in the corner.

And an unconscious man on it.

Only when she stepped closer and a lamp was lit, did she see who the man was. A moment of utter panic flooded her and she shuddered as it did.

For there on the pallet, unconscious and unmoving, lay her husband, Ross MacMillan, the chieftain of his clan.

Chapter Nine

'Can you tell me what happened?' she asked as she dropped to her knees next to him. Touching his face, she found his skin cool to the touch and the heat of his breaths barely warming hers.

'He was——' Munro stepped from the shadows, but paused in his reply. Glancing at Gillean and Dougal, who she'd not seen until then, he continued. 'Ross went to…check the southern edge of the castle after the attack. When he did not return for some time, we found him like this.'

She saw no blood on the places she could see. 'Where is he injured? And where is the healer?' Ilysa did not wait on the answers this time. Instead, she began to lift him as much as she could to search for signs of injury. Which they would have noticed already. 'His head?'

As she leaned over closer to him, he made no sounds. She did something she'd seen the healer at the nunnery do once when one of the servants had been struck by a bucket when it fell from a height. Sliding her fingers into his hair, she felt along his scalp for any bumps or signs of injuries. And there it was! Just along the back edge, a large, raised lump hidden by his hair.

'Roll him to his side, I pray you,' she said, unable to manage it. 'Have a care for his head as you do so.' It took little effort on their part and she then could feel the outline of it. 'Here.' She pointed it out to those watching.

''Tis why he does not wake?' Dougal asked.

'What does your healer say?' Silence met her question. She sat back on her heels and looked at each one standing in the crowded, small chamber. 'Why have you not called for him?' She knew there was one. She knew his name even—Kevin—though she'd yet to meet him. 'Were there so many wounded that he cannot see to his chieftain?'

'Lady,' Munro said. He stopped. And then started once more, but barely made a sound before shaking his head. A few grumbles echoed around her.

This was bizarre. Their chieftain's condition should be utmost in their concerns. After just losing the previous one, they should be...

They were fearful. Now, she saw it clearly in their gazes and in their hesitations. The clan had just lost a strong, powerful chieftain in the prime of his life but weeks before. Their new one, younger with less experience, lay unconscious and unmoving, a dangerous head wound which meant an uncertain future. If those above stairs knew of Ross's condition or the uncertainty of it, panic would spread quickly. As would word that the MacMillans were without a chieftain once more. And before his brother could return to take control, if he could, it would be too late. She could almost hear her father's gleeful chortle at such news.

'We do not wish the news of this to spread,' Gillean explained. 'Not until we ken he will wake.'

'Too much danger in allowing our enemies to learn our chieftain is not well and in control,' Munro added. Exactly what she'd thought.

But they'd told her.

They'd told her.

The momentary feeling of being included and not considered an enemy was quickly replaced by a different fear at the sight of her vigorous, strong, brave husband lying before her. That he might not wake. That thought sickened her in ways she did not understand and did not want to right at this moment.

'What can I do? I have no training as a healer,' she explained.

'I have seen this before,' Munro said, crouching down at her side. 'The first thing he needs is time.'

'The one thing he does not have if the Campbells return.' She stood, accepting Munro's arm as he held it out to steady her. 'What is your plan?'

'Well, Lady, while we complete our work on our defences, we will put it out that he has ridden to meet his brother about the threat, so he will not be expected to be here for at least a day or two,' Dougal said.

'Would he do that? In times like these?'

'Aye. He did it once before you arrived here,' Dougal explained, glancing at Munro as he explained it.

'Why am I here?'

'We need to keep him from sight until he is awake and well, Lady,' Gillean said.

'Here?' Ilysa looked around the small, cramped, inhospitable chamber and knew that Ross should not be here. An odour she could not identify teased her nose. Dampness oozed through the rock wall and an uncomfortable chill was strong here even now in summer.

'You cannot leave him here.' Ilysa gathered her woollen shawl tighter. 'Bring him to my chamber,' she offered. 'I will see to his care.'

'Are you certain?' Munro asked. ''Twill mean you will have to keep his presence a secret. And see to his... more intimate...care.'

Munro had barely uttered the words when Dougal grabbed him and pulled him away, whispering fiercely at him the whole time. Gillean leaned in and added his words in their little discussion, throwing glances at her as they argued. She'd thought they all knew about Ross's dark-of-the-night visits to her and that no one could mistake his purpose—to...seek his conjugal rights. She'd blamed Gillean's change towards her on those visits. Looking over at her unexpectedly silent servant, Ilysa noticed that Gavina had offered neither words of wisdom nor suggestions to them.

'With apologies, Lady,' Munro said as the little cluster of men broke apart. 'Will you help us?'

'Gavina, come, we will prepare the chamber as best we can without inviting attention.' Ilysa walked towards the door and turned back. 'Gillean, announce that he will not be at table so that none expects him there. Then, whisper about his visit to his brother. Your people understand that protecting him protects themselves.'

And she knew that they would do what must be done to protect Ross. She'd heard them speak of him while working in the kitchens and in the village.

'We will see to bringing him there once the keep is settled for the night, Lady.' Dougal nodded his head respectfully.

'I will work with Gavina to make sure the chamber is supplied during his stay there.' Gillean reached out for the door.

No one had spoken of the other thing that could happen—that Ross might never wake from this injury. And she did not wish to either. However, there was one matter that no one had mentioned of yet. As she waited for Gillean to open the door, she waited for their attention and then asked the question that had truly plagued her.

'Why are you not summoning your healer to see to your laird?'

Gillean paused after unlocking the door and looked at Munro. As did Dougal. Some look passed among them before Munro stepped closer and leaned in to speak.

'We think the healer is a spy for your father.'

Of all the explanations she had reasonably expected, that certainly was not one of them.

Ilysa opened the shutter and looked out at the rainy night. Truly, she could see little past the heavy rain, but she stared none the less. She should be asleep. She should have been exhausted by the excitement and worry of this day, from its beginning to its end.

She should be worn out by her husband's attentions of the marital kind. These last nights spent in his arms exploring every sort of pleasure between a husband and wife had been enlightening and more than she'd ever expected. After those nights, simply meeting his gaze in the light of day made her blush at the intimacies they'd shared—and the things she'd done.

Securing the shutters against the growing winds, she turned and looked over at him there on her bed. He'd not moved at all once Munro and Dougal had placed him on it. Not a twitch of his hand or arm. Not a leg shifted. He'd not even reacted when she'd lifted his head and placed cold cloths beneath it, against the wound.

She'd thought he surely would have moved when she'd leaned closer while replacing the cloths and her breast had accidentally brushed his face. But, he had not. Nor when she'd spoken to him. Or when she'd threaded her fingers through his hair as he liked to do to hers.

Nothing seemed to make a difference.

Ilysa sat in the big wooden chair next to the bed, on the cushions Ross had arranged for her to have. Munro and Dougal had dragged it from nearer the hearth for her. Was the chamber warm enough for him? Standing once more, she stoked the fire with the iron poker and added a bit more peat to it. Either she or Gavina would see to it through the night and day, taking turns so that someone was in the chamber at all times.

Until he woke.

The rest of the night moved slowly for her. Unable to sleep. Unable to stop the worrying thoughts that filled her as each quiet moment passed. When Gavina arrived, Ilysa used a small pallet arranged in the far corner to get some rest. Once she'd gained a few hours of sleep, she left the room and went to speak to a few of the villagers who waited for her in the hall and then summoned her husband's closest advisers to meet with her after supper. As she went about the few tasks she needed to accomplish, she was pleased when whispers of Ross's visit to his brother followed her steps. So far, their ruse was accepted.

After arranging with Ronald for some strong broth to be made and sent to her chambers, she walked out through the kitchens to enjoy a moment or two in the break in the heavy rains. It was not her way to stay inside for such a long time—she preferred working outside and breathing in the freshness of the breezes off the sea and loch. At a rumble of thunder, Ilysa turned to escape the rain's return when she heard some men talking. Looking for where the voices were, she followed them until she found them.

Leaning back against the wall so she was not seen obviously listening, Ilysa waited as they did. Nothing seemed untoward until the taller man called the shorter one by name—Kevin. As she peeked around the wall, she saw the tonsure on his head and the wooden case he carried and knew this was the healer. When they began to walk away, Kevin turned and she could see the whole of his face.

She'd not seen him for years, a long time before she'd left for the nunnery, but she could recognise him now. Her uncle's younger son, Kevin had been sent off to study with the brothers at the Cambuskenneth Abbey near Stirling to learn his craft. Now, here he stood, in her husband's keep, serving as healer.

But, did he also serve as her father's spy? Something told her that his presence here was no coincidence.

Taking care as she stepped away from them, Ilysa made her way inside just as the clouds opened and the torrential rains began once more. Now, the darkening skies matched her mood.

What was she to do? Did she admit that she did know their healer? Worse, that there was a good chance Brother Kevin was indeed working against the MacMillans, or, at the very least, reporting knowledge gained back to her father.

Would he do that? Would he risk his vows to serve The MacDonnell while he served the Almighty?

That question plagued her for the rest of the day and even as she watched the commander, the steward and the chieftain's friend enter her chamber. After each of them approached their laird to see for themselves that he yet lay unresponsive on her bed, they gathered before the hearth and waited for her to sit in the chair closest to the bed.

It was interesting to her to see the differing expressions on their faces as they realised that things might go from bad to even worse. Munro, the man in charge of strategy and defence, was stoic with no sign of any emotion. His ability to give nothing away was needed certainly in negotiations. Gillean looked as if he was calculating in his thoughts. His eyes darted here and there and his fingers moved as though he was writing or counting something. And then there was Dougal.

The first MacMillan she'd met and the man whose trust of her father had actually brought her to this place and this clan, the man showed his concerns and worries on his handsome face. As Ross's confidant and cousin, there was true affection in his gaze as he watched Ross lying motionless on the bed.

And there was nothing any of them, or she, could do to make a difference in Ross's condition. But what was certain was that Ross needed the attention of someone practised in the skills of healing.

'I think a healer must see to him,' she said, breaking the silence in a voice that was hoarse from hours of praying. Glancing from one to the next, she added, 'His condition is beyond my meagre if any skills.'

'But, Lady—' Munro said. He stepped forward and crouched before her, meeting her gaze at the level of his. 'I told you what I believe about the man.' Munro glanced over his shoulder at the others and then faced her. 'We cannot—'

'He cannot go without care any longer, Munro.' She stood and he did as well, backing away a pace or two before pausing. ''Tis not an easy decision, but one we, *we*, must make.' How could she tell them the truth about their suspicions about their healer?

The truth. It must be the truth. After everything that had happened in her life between her father and her, Ilysa knew she owed him no allegiance. Despite the honesty of knowing that, it was difficult to break the bond of kin. A glance across the chamber at her husband and understanding how he'd changed things for her and offered her a safe place for the first time in her life, she knew it must be the truth.

'I finally saw your healer,' she said. As she did when nervous or fearful, she tucked her arm closer and pulled on her shawl. 'He is my uncle's son.'

'Your uncle?'

'Kin?'

'A spy!'

All three began arguing among themselves and their voices rose. Such loudness would draw attention from any servant on this floor, so she shushed them.

'Quietly, I pray,' she whispered. 'Quietly.'

'Lady, does he ken you recognised him?' Dougal asked.

'Nay.' She shook her head and sat back down. 'I heard some men speaking and sought them out. I have not seen him in many years, but 'tis him. He left for the Cambuskenneth Abbey in Stirling years before I was sent aw—' She paused. 'Before I went to Iona.'

'You are certain?' Ross's friend asked.

'I am.' Something struck her. 'I think that's why he has avoided me in the weeks since I arrived. He could not take the chance that I would reveal him to you. To Ross,' she said.

The widening of their eyes made her realise she'd called their chieftain by his first name, something she'd not done before. Well, the times she had were not ones that they had witnessed. Only in the privacy of this chamber. Only when he had demanded it of her to continue or to cease the relentless pleasure between them. The heat built in her cheeks and she fought the urge to touch them, for fear it would bring attention to her blush.

'So, he is your father's man?' Munro broke the tension with his question.

'I do not ken if he is or is not.' She lifted her shoulders in a shrug. 'I have not seen him in years. I have never heard my father speak of him other than when arranging his education with the Abbey.'

'And he did not return to Dunyvaig or another holding when he finished? Assigned by the abbot?' Gillean asked.

'I was…away by then.' She hated how her voice always quivered with the shame of her exile. Only when her hand lifted of its own volition did she realise what she was doing and stopped. 'I have not heard him spoken of or seen him until this morn.'

'I do not think we can trust him any longer,' Munro said.

'I do not understand,' she said, interrupting the commander. 'How did he come to be here? Did the abbot send him to you?'

''Twas the old chieftain who requested the abbot to send a holy brother to us,' Gillean said.

'Holy brother, my arse,' Dougal said under his breath.

'When did that happen?' she asked. 'When did he arrive?'

'Lady, he has been here for several months and given no sign—' Gillean offered at first.

'That's not true,' Munro said, waving Gillean to silence. 'You found him searching in your chamber. Looking in the chest where you keep the parchments recording the clan's business.'

That was how the argument started, though from the sound of it this was not a new disagreement, but an ongoing and persistent one. From one to another and back around, the words meant nothing. What she saw and heard was their anger and fear for Ross's future.

'None of this helps your chieftain,' she said softly. When they did not stop, she repeated it just a little louder. 'None of this helps your friend. Cease, I pray you. Cease.'

They stopped and met her gaze then. Sheepish expressions on grown men. She'd seen it before when the prioress would catch one of the lay brothers in some minor transgression. Now, they looked at her.

'Spy or not, has he given any sign that he is less than what he claims—a healing brother?' She walked to the bed and leaned down to touch Ross's hand. 'He needs help. He needs it now.' Entwining their fingers together, she looked at them. 'Make a decision, for I cannot order you to any action.'

If they'd been married differently, if she'd been accepted as a true wife from the beginning, the wife of a chieftain, she might have had a say in the matter. But these men knew the truth behind her marriage and the insult given by her father in fooling their chieftain into it. Though they might trust her on some matters, even disclosing their belief that her cousin was a spy, it was not endless. Never would she be able to give an order that they could not countermand. Never could she control the household of her husband, no matter her abilities or experience in dealing with such matters.

Now when it was critical that she do something, she could not. And the man who'd given her some measure of hope as he'd treated her with respect and kindness would be the one to pay the cost of it.

If only they'd had more time together. If only he could know her heart and that her loyalty lay not with her father, but already with him.

She closed her eyes and felt his skin against hers, warm and strong. And waited on the word to be given.

Chapter Ten

They were too late. By the time the others had agreed with her reasons to summon the healer and sought him out the next day, Brother Kevin had disappeared. Without creating more gossip or raising an alarm, they could do little but check his chambers and the other usual places where he would be. And he was in none of those.

Mayhap he had seen her when she had thought herself well out of view? Whatever the reason, it mattered not now, for he'd fled Castle Sween and could not be found. That was the only thing certain to her.

Finally, after more discussion and arguing, Munro agreed to allow Gavina to bring the old woman from the village who saw to many minor ailments. Since women's complaints were beneath the brother's notice or skills, she—Morag—usually answered any call concerning the megrims associated with the women. So, after banishing the men, Ilysa waited on her arrival.

Morag followed Gavina into the chamber and nodded her head in greeting. Then, catching sight of her laird on the bed behind Ilysa, she nodded once more.

'Not the Lady with a womanly condition then, eh?'

'That is what you will say if asked about the summons here, Morag,' Ilysa said. She tried for a stern tone, one that would make it clear that the woman must comply, but she knew she'd failed when Morag let out a cackling laugh. The woman leaned to see past Ilya and look at Ross.

'What has happened?' Morag asked as she ambled over to the bed. She had such an uneven gait, Ilysa was tempted to hold the woman up as she made her way across the chamber.

'He was found in this condition.'

'Has he wakened at all?' Morag reached out and touched his face, lifted his arm and dropped it again and opened his eyelids to peer at his eyes. All that Ilysa could do was watch and answer.

'Nay. Not awake. No movements on his own. No word or sound,' she offered. 'The only injury we could find was the lump on his head.'

Ilysa stepped aside and allowed Gavina to assist Morag in moving Ross. The men had placed him closer to the edge so the woman could reach him more easily. Over the next short while, Morag poked and prodded as she asked questions about him. When she reached out and pinched Ross's forearm roughly, Ilysa gasped.

'Hmm…' she whispered after getting no reaction. Then she moved to his head and slapped him while calling out to him. 'My lord,' she said. 'My lord, you must come!' When Ilysa would have stopped her, Gavina grabbed her and tugged her back a step.

'Nay, my lady,' she whispered. 'Let her do as she must.'

'My lord!' Morag called again. 'Fergus needs you!' Another slap echoed in the chamber. Gavina tightened her hold as it happened and Ilysa turned her attention to seeing if there was any reaction at all.

Nothing.

A third blow, but this time Morag's attempt to wake him surprised Ilysa for the woman called out her name instead of kith or kin.

'My lord! Ilysa is in danger!'

If she'd not been staring at him, she would have missed the very subtle change in his breathing. Morag placed her hand on his chest, so she must have noticed it as well. Ilysa held her breath, watching and waiting for some sign of Ross waking up. Moments passed with no change and the woman stepped back from the bed.

'The blow to his head pulls him down into this unhealthy sleep.' Her gaze narrowed as she looked at Ilysa. 'He did hear your name.' Morag smiled at her. It was a knowing smile that told of being proven right in some way. 'He heard her name,' she repeated, looking over at Gavina. Her maid nodded and shared that same smile.

'Will he wake?' The terrifying question hung out between them in a silence broken only by the crackling bursts of fire as the peat burned in its uneven way. Ilysa understood in that moment how much she cared if he would.

How much she cared.

'Aye, my lady. I think he will,' Morag said. Ilysa gasped and then her breathing hitched, a sob threatening to make her lose control. 'There, there now, lass,' she whispered as she patted Ilysa's hand. ''Twill be well.'

'What…?' She paused to take a breath. 'What must be done?'

'Lady, nothing more than ye already are,' Morag advised. 'Keep him warm. Let him be.'

'How long will it take?' Ilysa asked.

'That is for the Almighty above to decide. And he hasna told this old woman!' Morag walked to the basket she'd brought and reached in it. 'Put some of this on a cool cloth and hold it to his head. 'Twill help the swelling.'

'My thanks.' Ilysa watched as Morag whispered in a hushed tone with Gavina before making her way to the door. 'Morag, I must ask you again to keep your chieftain's presence here secret.'

'Aye, my lady. 'Twas a womanly complaint that brought me to ye.' That smile lifted the corner of the old woman's lips again as though she knew something or knew more and did not say it.

'Gavina? I will remain here,' she said, dismissing her maid with a nod. She watched as Gavina escorted Morag out of the chamber. Without hesitation, she found a clean cloth, dipped it in the cool water in the bucket and twisted out the excess. Folding it in a square, she added the ointment Morag had given her and placed it under Ross's head.

Soon, the chamber was silent but for the sound of his breathing, so she sat in the chair and leaned her head back. Then night fell and desperation filled her. Ilysa leaned over, pressed her forehead on the edge of the bed and let out her fears, her worries and her tears. Exhausted from too little sleep and too much worry, Ilysa closed her eyes and lost track of time.

* * *

The first thing she noticed as she woke was the tickling sensation against her nose. A sneeze threatened and she brushed her hand against the growing itch. A rub eased the itch until the tickle happened again. Ilysa realised it was her hair, which was gathered under her kerchief.

But when she reached up to straighten it, it was gone. She opened her eyes then.

'I asked you not to wear this,' Ross said. Now his fingers slid along her scalp, tugging the cloth from her head.

Stunned that he was awake and speaking, Ilysa remained still beneath his touch, as he entangled his fingers and drew them through her curls, over and over. Finally, she could wait no longer and lifted her head up and away, leaving his hand to fall to the bed.

'You are awake!'

'You were crying.'

'Let me get Munro and the others,' she said. 'They will want to hear of your condition.' Her muscles, stiff from sitting in such a bent position for too long, protested as she stood. Or as she tried to. Ross clutched her arm, holding her there, with a strength unexpected in someone who'd been bedridden and unconscious for more than two days.

'Nay, wait,' he whispered. 'Tell me what happened.' He eased his hold on her, watching with an intense gaze. 'Sit by me.' He shifted away to allow her more space and a groan escaped him. 'My head feels like someone hit me with an axe.'

'They may have done exactly that, my lord.' She

watched as he reached up and explored the back of his head in the same way he'd touched hers. Tugging out the cloth she'd placed there, he scowled at the odour and tossed it on the floor before she could get it. 'Do you remember anything? Did you fall or were you struck?'

'My lord?' he asked. He took her hand in his and stroked her palm with his thumb. 'Another thing I have asked of you, Wife, is to call me by my name.'

'How can you speak of such unimportant things when you have lain unconscious for nearly three days?'

'Three days?' He ran his free hand through his hair and shook his head, stopping when it pained him.

Actually, every move, even breathing, hurt him. Searching his thoughts, he remembered nothing of those three days. Blackness swirled when he tried. And dizziness threatened to pull him back down. He held on to the only thing he could to keep from sinking again.

The only one.

Squeezing Ilysa's hand, he waited for the light-headedness to pass.

'If not your men, I pray you let me call for Morag,' she whispered to him. 'She might have a tonic that could ease your pain.'

'Morag?' He shook his head. 'The village woman?' She turned to face him and he noticed a furrow forming between her brows and her lips tighten. 'What has happened?' The pain in his head pounded now as he tried to discern the reason for her hesitation. 'Ilysa—'

'If you lie back, I will tell you what has happened since you were found.' His practical wife.

'And I will lie back if you lie with me,' he said.

Two could play this strategy and he was losing strength quickly.

Only when she stood to take off her shoes did he realise she was fully dressed. Well, other than that damned cloth she insisted on wearing to cover up her short hair. She tugged the woollen shawl off her shoulders and held it out to him. Then, she walked to the end of the bed, gathered up the length of her gown and climbed up on to it. He closed his eyes, anticipating more pain as she positioned herself next to him, but it was momentary and slight compared to the feeling of warmth and comfort that spread through him as she settled there.

No sooner had she slid up against him, easing her bad arm between them, than she began to speak without him needing to prod her.

'You were found nearly three days ago, outside the castle, on the southern approach,' she said. He took note that she slid her hand across his chest and let it rest there.

'When?'

'After you'd given word it was safe for the villagers to leave the walls. I saw you argu—talking with Munro and Dougal and then you left them.' He slid his arm around her, cradling her against him. Her head rested on his shoulder and she gazed up at him. 'Do you remember any of that?'

From the hopeful tone in her voice, he suspected she did not want him to remember the topic that had made him angry after the battle. But he did and would take it up with Munro and Dougal, and her, later. And there were other matters to discuss as well with his practical wife. For now, though...

'I remember leaving them by the dock and walking the perimeter of the wall towards the south.' Towards Islay and her father's lands. 'Then, nothing.'

'Did you see something?' she asked. 'Someone?'

He rubbed his forehead, trying to remember what had happened, but the pain worsened, sending shards of it into his eyes and down his neck.

'Hush now,' she whispered as she stroked gently over his chest. 'Worry not about it for now. You were badly injured and it will take time to completely heal.'

Her hand moved slowly, down his chest and up. Then down his arm and up. Leisurely. Not stopping as she continued to whisper meaningless words to him. Ross thought she might have asked him another question, but the warmth of her in his arms tempted him back to sleep and he could no longer fight it.

Ross knew not how long he slept. From the faint signs of light entering through the shuttered windows when he opened his eyes next, he suspected dawn was not far off. If it was possible, Ilysa lay even closer to him now than before. Though he'd not moved, her leg was thrown over both of his and her hand was tucked around him in a tight hold.

He eased from under her and slid from the bed, somehow without causing her to stir, even when he placed three more blankets over her to keep her warm in his absence. After allowing the dizziness to ease, he made his way across her chamber to the door. Listening for the soft snoring she refused to believe she did in her sleep, Ross smiled and lifted the latch. He'd almost reached his own chamber when a young maid came around the corner and gasped when she saw him.

'My lord!' she said, lowering herself into a curtsy. 'I did not ken you were back.'

'Send word to my commander and the steward to come to my chamber,' he said as he continued to walk on.

'Aye, my lord.' The lass kept peeking at him as though she thought he was an apparition.

'And send to the kitchen for food,' he added. He did not remember his last meal. Ah, he was planning on talking to them, and Ilysa, at supper when he'd stalked off in anger. Glancing over his shoulder as he reached his chamber, the maid yet stood and stared. 'Now, girl.'

Only when she ran off did he realise he wore nothing but a tunic. As he opened his door, her words struck him—she did not know he was *back*? He'd fallen asleep as Ilysa was about to explain what had happened and he'd never actually heard the details. Just after he'd relieved himself and tugged a clean shirt into place, his door burst open and slammed against the wall.

So much for being discreet.

'Ross!' Munro rushed into his chamber. A moment later, his commander regained control of himself and took a breath. 'When did you wake?' The huge man crossed his arms over his chest and glared at Ross as though he was to blame for his behaviour.

'A few hours ago,' he said, gathering a length of tartan and preparing to put it on.

'Where is…your wife?' Munro glanced back at the doorway. Did he expect her to walk in? Ross only then realised that Ilysa had never been in his chamber.

'Sleeping. From the look of her, she has not been sleeping or eating recently. Close the door.'

As the image of Ilysa's strained features and gaunt expression filled his thoughts, Ross knew she had not been doing either of those. It had taken the few weeks since her arrival, of good and filling foods and hours of sleep each night, for her to begin to look less like a half-starved nun and more like the young, vibrant woman she was.

'Before anyone else comes, tell me what happened?' he asked. Then he held up his hand and shook his head. 'Nay, I do not remember what happened. The last thing I do retain any memory of is walking away so that I did not raise my fists to the commander of my warriors.'

Munro's expression turned sheepish as a knock came on the door. Without waiting to be acknowledged, Dougal pushed his way past Gillean to enter first.

'Are you well, Ross?' he asked. Again, Ross saw the strain of exhaustion on his friend's face as it was on Munro's and Ilysa's.

'I will be, Dougal. Once I discover what happened and what has transpired since—' He pointed to his head. 'Well, since I got this lump.'

'Ross—'

'Munro was just telling me as you arrived.' He nodded over at Gillean. 'Munro?'

Over the next short while as Munro did explain what Ross had missed while in his unnatural sleep, Gillean accepted the tray of food that arrived and Ross ate while listening. He'd swallowed the last mouthful of ale when his door crashed open a third time. He stood as he beheld Ilysa there—her eyes wide, her lovely curls uncovered and her hand on the door frame as if it would support her if she found something disturbing within.

She looked like a warrior goddess ready to fight her enemies and protect those in her care. Did she know what effect she was having? Glancing at the others, he saw that they were also enthralled.

'You were gone!' she said in a breathy whisper.

'I needed to get up and you needed rest,' he said, holding out his hand to her. Did she realise that her uncovered tousled curls and wrinkled gown gave away that they'd been together? 'Dougal, a chair for my wife.'

Silence and stares were the first reactions from his men. Even Ilysa gasped in surprise, for—daft man that he was—this was the first time he'd acknowledged her position to those here while she was present. She took his hand and walked with him over to the large chair near the hearth. When he would have released her to sit, she tightened her grasp on his hand.

'Are you well? Does your head yet pain you?' Her gaze moved over him.

'I am well enough, thanks to you, Ilysa.' He lifted her hand to his lips and kissed it. 'And to you, as well,' he said, nodding at the others there. 'You protected our kith and kin while I could not. And you protected me.'

''Twas but doing our duty, my lord,' Gillean said.

'Aye. Duty first, Gillean.' Ross sat in the other chair. 'I have not been doing mine.'

No matter that he had no memory of most of what

happened after he left Munro and Dougal three days
before, he did remember one thing—his wife deserved
praise for her part in preparing the keep and people for
the attack. While he was trying to ignore her, except for
the comfort she offered, she was working to protect his
clan. While he spent hours wrapped in her arms seeking the pleasure of her body, she'd spent her time or-
ganising protection for the villagers if an attack came.
While he thought he was carrying out his duties to his
clan, she was actually doing that.

Now, it was time for her to receive her due and, if
she agreed, to take on the fuller role of the wife of the
chieftain.

'Ilysa, I have been told that the suggestion about
how the warriors should form up to protect the villagers as they seek the safety inside the walls was yours.'

No one breathed. No one met his gaze. No one dared
to speak at his statement. Because he'd made it clear
that she had no place here.

'Ilysa,' he said in a softer tone. 'I was not angry
that it came from you. Well, I was angry...' he laughed
'...but I discovered that I was angry at myself.'

He held out his hand to Gillean and nodded at the
keys on his belt. The steward untied them and handed
them to Ross. He thought her eyes wide and bright when
she'd entered, but they grew brighter now as he stood
and walked to where she sat.

'As my wife, you should hold these.'

'But, my lord,' she said as she shook her head, 'I was
not the wife you bargained for. I am not the...'

'You are the wife I married. Will you accept these?'

Ilysa met his gaze then and, for that moment, Ross

wondered if getting hit on the head had been the best thing that could have happened to him. Now he waited for her to take the keys from him.

Chapter Eleven

'Nay, Ronald, we must check our stores of ale be-fore—'

'Before the next attack, my lady,' the cook answered. 'Aye. And the flour as well.'

Four others, servants and household workers, all approached her after that. She walked with Gillean at her side, the steward accepting her invitation, or plea, to work with her this morning—her first carrying the keys her husband gave her yesterday that revealed her new position.

If he had concerns about her ability to carry out the tasks expected of her, he never said. When Ross had held out his hand for the keys, Gillean had not hesitated to place them in her hand. And there had been a moment when he could have spoken up and yet he did not.

From the time this change in her life happened, from the arrival of her father's men to bring her home until the time she realised the extent of his plan to substitute her for her sister, she'd never dared hope that it would work out at all. The truth was that she'd thought Ross

MacMillan, as any other chieftain, as her father, would surely kill or imprison her or at the least put her aside in response to her father's betrayal.

Here she stood, married, alive, in her husband's keep, guiding his people in this dangerous time. Holding the keys signifying her role in her hand as they approached a storage chamber, Ilysa fought back both a wave of euphoria and the threat of tears. Her years in exile at the nunnery, her duties there and the skills she'd learned with the holy sisters, all prepared her for this. But it was not the life she'd expected to lead. In the more than three years since her disastrous involvement with Graeme MacLean proved her unfit to be married, not once had this possibility entered her thoughts or her prayers.

She laughed aloud at the twist of fate and caught the notice of servants and others in the corridor. Nodding to them, she followed Gillean to their destination, but could not remove the silly smile from her face. Nothing could dim her enthusiasm as she and Gillean checked to make certain they had enough supplies to survive a siege, if, as Ross thought, the Campbells' next and final attack forced them and all the villagers within the walls.

As if his name in her thoughts conjured him up, her husband stood in the doorway, watching her. His gaze moved to her head and he shook his own at the sight of her kerchief. From the glimmer in his eyes, it was difficult to say if he was serious or just jesting with his demand that she go about with her head uncovered. He mentioned it every time he encountered her, never embarrassing her, but never missing an opportunity to remind her of his demand.

'Gillean,' he said. He stepped inside, but leaned against

the archway that held the door. 'I would speak to Lady Ilysa.'

His steward nodded to her and was gone before she could raise a question. Her hand was halfway to tugging on her shawl when he shook his head at her. He straightened away from the stone wall and walked to where she stood, each stride eating up the space between them with the languid grace of a man in control. When he reached her, she could not catch her breath.

'Are you yet afraid of me, Wife?' he whispered, lifting her chin with the tip of his finger. 'Do you worry over my reaction to your continued disobedience?' He took hold of her hand and held it. 'This is the clue that tells me the truth of your worry even while you are preparing to utter a denial of it.'

She could not help it—she did fear his response to her denying his wish. Mayhap it was that she did not know if he was serious or not about it? That was never something to consider about her father's orders—if he spoke it, he meant it and God help the pitiful person who did not take it seriously. She had not and learned quickly to do so.

'I am,' she confessed. Two words exposed that underlying fear that lived within her. No matter that Ross had not raised a hand, or even his voice, to her. Years of knowing to heed that fear had kept her alive. 'I am afraid. For I cannot tell if you jest, if your disapproval is feigned or if you are angry that I have not obeyed you.'

He took that final step before she could move back and wrapped her in his strong arms. Their bodies touched and she sank against him, into his heat and strength. Even in this intimate quiet, he had a care not to crush her bad arm between them.

'I will stop teasing you,' he said. 'Ilysa, I would never raise my hand to you. I took a vow to protect you and I will.' He lifted her chin and placed a gentle kiss on her mouth. That simple touch ignited a need deep within her for more. 'Something to think about, Wife. Your father can no longer harm you now. He thought he was giving me less than I had bargained for when, in truth, he gave me more. He was stupid enough not to recognise your value and now I have you.'

His flesh rose hard against her belly and, as they breathed against each other's mouths, her body reacted. The tips of her breasts tightened and a throbbing began between her legs. She felt his questing fingers in her hair before she realised she'd lost her kerchief. He tilted her head then and possessed her open mouth, filling it with his tongue as he pressed his rod against her. She used her tongue on his, tasting that part of him and wanting the other inside her. Only when he lifted away did she draw in a breath.

'I would have you now, Wife,' he said, even as his fingers grasped the length of her skirts and dragged them up. Her head fell back and she laughed aloud.

'You have turned your nunnery wife into a wanton, my lord,' she said. Holding the layers out of his way with one hand, he slid his fingers between her legs and she moaned at the sheer pleasure—the stroking of his fingers and now knowing what would follow.

'I am a lucky man then,' he said, his breaths growing rougher as he plunged two fingers into her body. She could only grab his shoulder and pray she could remain on her feet. 'Was that aye you cried out?' But when he slid his hand free and dropped her gown, she protested.

'Nay! My lord, nay. Do not stop, I beg you.'

He moved quickly, dropping the latch on the door and pushing a crate in front of it. Then, he slipped his arm around her waist and lifted her to sit on a tall barrel near the wall. Easing her back on to the lid, he lifted her knees and placed her feet on his chest.

'I do like you to beg, Ilysa,' he said in a deep, wild and wicked tone that sent shivers through her. Tossing her skirts up and leaving her legs and even hips naked to him, he stroked her thighs, moving closer and closer to her intimate flesh. Having experience now at being aroused by his touch, she leaned back against the wall and waited. He flicked the tip of his thumb along the folds of heated flesh until she moaned.

'I pray you...' She lost the words as he guided her legs over his shoulders, pulled her hips forward and placed his mouth where his fingers had caressed. She reached out and could only grasp his head, unsure if she wanted to press him closer or pull him away. But when he suckled there, it mattered not so long as he continued.

Her skin burned. Her body ached. Sensations built from deep inside at each stroke of his tongue and pull of his mouth. And all in one moment, one moment that spun out around them, her entire being exploded and released.

Barely had she come back to her senses when he pulled her to sit and eased her hips to the edge of the barrel. A pleasing throbbing continued which only increased when he entered her. And filled her. The sigh that escaped her was one of both satisfaction and anticipation.

She opened eyes she did not know she'd shut and met his gaze as he slid deep within her. He thrust further and she gasped, holding on to his shoulder as he wrapped his arm around her. Then he moved slowly, easing almost free of her before filling her once more. When she could not hold her head up, he eased his hand up and held her as he kissed whatever breath she yet had from her.

Pleasure, exquisite pleasure raced through her body, and soul, as he reached his own peak and spilled his seed within her. She leaned her head against his chest and waited for their storm of passion to ease.

'Are you well?' he asked, kissing her gently.

The tears filled her eyes before she could speak. He asked after her comfort every time they'd joined. Whether slow and tender or rushed and enthusiastic, it mattered not. He saw to her needs first and to her well-being after. She blinked them away and nodded, swallowing against the tightness in her throat. After he lifted her to her feet, she shook out her gown and pulled her shawl—now hanging from one shoulder—back in place.

'Are *you* well? Your head? I thought that when you did not visit my chamber last night—' She stopped, not knowing how to explain what she'd thought when she'd slept alone.

'Not visit your chamber?' he asked. His expression then spoke of confusion. Mayhap his head injury did plague him still.

Stepping back, he walked to the door and pulled the crate away from it. When he glanced back, she felt the blush rise in her cheeks. Even now, even after having had him inside her, she could not openly speak of such matters with him.

'That you can yet blush after allowing me to have my way with you, here in a storage chamber, surprises me. You wear the look of a well-tousled woman with your lips swollen from my kisses, your gown awry from my handling of it and your hair—' He smiled and reached out for her curls. 'Your hair looks like…well, it looks like you've just left our bed after making love for hours.' He laughed then. 'My innocent-while-wanton wife, you please me.'

A quick kiss and then he was gone as quickly as he'd appeared. Finally spying her tossed-aside kerchief, Ilysa grabbed it and turned her back to the now-open door to replace it. She was leaning over, shoving her curls under it when hands grasped her waist and pulled her to him. She knew his touch and the feel of his body now and did not fight him.

'What are you doing, my lord?'

She stood at ease in his hold. Ilysa thought she should, at some point, resist his approaches. To set up some boundaries and relegate these kinds of encounters to the bedchamber. It was not as though they were besotted newlyweds who were enjoying their first days of wedded bliss. Nay, theirs was a treaty. An alliance. And she an unexpected bride for the chieftain.

In truth, she did not wish to. She did not wish to rebuff him, to resist his touch or to refuse their…marital duty. She felt more alive than ever before and, in his arms—whether in the privacy of her chamber or an unplanned encounter—she felt cared for. The real truth was that she enjoyed their pleasurable pursuits more than she should or thought she ever would.

She enjoyed him. His touch. His kisses. His body. Him.

'I returned to order you to the table for supper this evening, but was so overwhelmed by the sight of your ar—attributes I could not help myself.' After a brisk but thorough caressing of her body, he turned her to face him.

'A poor example of leadership, my lord. A man led by his bal—' She could not. No matter that he would laugh. No matter. A godly woman who'd spent three years living as a nun would never speak those words or even in such a manner.

He laughed anyway. The sound of it surrounded her and warmed her heart towards him even more.

'You will join me at table,' he said. This time authority and command filled his voice. He waited until she nodded before he released her. 'You may wear that damned thing if you must.'

Ross left her staring after him. The two biggest purveyors of idle chatter stood outside the storage chamber with the most self-satisfied expressions on their faces. Gavina and Gillean perfected the spreading of gossip when they wished to, using bits of knowledge or rumours to build up their own positions. But they'd both protected Ilysa since she'd arrived from prying eyes and malicious tongues. That did not mean they would not babble about this between themselves though.

From those faces, they could not wait to do just that.

'The Lady will join me at table,' he said to them. 'Make certain all is prepared as she needs it to be.'

He knew she'd been eating her supper in the kitchen with the servants. Gavina and Gillean were not his only sources about his wife's activities, even if they thought so. And, until now, until he'd been made to see how big a part she'd played in preparing for the dangers they faced and would face again, he'd been content to keep her as a separate part of his life. To allow her to hide herself and her actions from him and the rest who lived here and depended on the chieftain for their livelihoods and protection. To accept the comforts she offered as she carried out her part of their vows without having to give much in return.

He'd thought he could succeed in spite of marrying The MacDonnell's daughter, in spite of being fooled into marrying the one foisted on him in his ignorance. But, with each detail he learned from Dougal, Munro and Gillean about her—her skills, her talents and her willingness to work hard before the attack and before his injury—he understood he could not and would not ignore her value.

As an ally. As a fighter. As a cunning strategist. And now he wanted more than all those things from her.

This night he would begin his campaign to win her trust so that she did not fear him.

'See to your Lady.'

He nodded and left, seeking Munro and a good fight. As the benevolent chieftain he was, he ignored the laughter behind him.

A strange sense of anticipation filled him for the rest of the day. Even as he trained with Munro or searched the site of his accident, his thoughts kept returning to what had happened between him and Ilysa in the storage chamber. And how it had happened. How she'd accepted him without hesitation. How she'd welcomed his every caress.

Although he'd witnessed some happy marriages, they tended not to be among those who held titles or wealth. Indeed, his uncle's first marriage had been a miserable one from beginning to end. His wife had been much younger than him and was not content being only a brood mare to his relentless pursuit of an heir of his loins.

She, Sorcha, had not resisted or had learned not to resist Cormac's bedding of her, but with each month's failure she'd faded away. So worn down by his uncle's steely control and constant belittling, she was too weak to give birth when his seed finally took and she'd died, with the child, in the bloody attempt.

Consumed with defeating their enemies, Ross had given no thought to having heirs. His only concern was survival and that his clan would prosper. He'd meant only to satisfy the requirement to bed Ilysa and put her aside until the MacMillans were safe. Then he could decide their future.

When he'd first realised who she was, he'd thought to send her back to Iona. If she truly had no part in her father's machinations, in his bold attempt to undermine their agreement, then mayhap she would remain when this was done. If innocent, he would not suffer her to remain in a marriage she did not want. After their long talks in the dark of night, he doubted she was involved in any way.

Aye, he would seek to end this sham of a marriage and free her. It was the right thing to do.

Unless she carried his bairn.

He stumbled then, at the thought of her carrying, saved from falling off the rocks by his quick reaction and Dougal's grasp. He'd not considered that complication before.

'Your head?' Dougal asked, as Ross regained his balance. They were searching for any clue along the beach or rocks there to explain what had happened to him after the battle.

'Aye,' he lied. 'The dizziness sometimes returns unexpectedly.'

'And you remember nothing? A sound? Someone?'

'A shadow. Voices.'

'So more than one?'

Ross walked towards the tree line and looked back at the castle from that position. Closing his eyes, he tried to remember something, some detail small or large, that could explain what had happened. The rustling of the wind through the trees at his back was all he heard. Then...

'You must stay here.'

''Tis not safe for me any longer.'

'The chieftain!'

'Three, I think, and one sounded familiar,' he said, rubbing the incessant ache on the back of his head. 'Behind me there in the bushes.' He turned and stared into the brush, hoping those brief bits of conversation would spur more to become clear. He spoke what he remembered to his friend.

'And then?' Dougal walked closer now, crouching

down to examine the ground for signs of the villains. 'Did you see them?' Ross shook his head.

'Nay.' *The chieftain!* 'Nay, nothing else. A blow from behind, then nothing.'

'The healer must have been meeting up with some of his kinsmen,' Dougal said. He spat on the ground. 'But what would MacDonnells be doing here so close to a Campbell attack?'

His cousin did not need a reply because they were both thinking the same thing. The very question was as damning as any answer would be. They—he, Dougal and Munro—had been right in their suspicions that there was more to this arranged marriage than was seen or known at first. Oh, the deviousness was no surprise, for with Iain MacDonnell it was not so much a question of would he betray anyone for his own gain but when would he.

'So, we have at least two wolves preparing to attack?'

'Brother Kevin's disappearance just after your injury is too much to be a coincidence. Especially after the Lady said she saw him and recognised him as kin.' Dougal stood and dropped the broken branch he was twisting in his grasp.

'You think he saw her?' Ross asked.

'I do, Ross. After playing my part in The MacDonnell's deception of you, I do not think anything related to the man is a coincidence or by chance.' Dougal nodded his head and walked off towards the castle gate.

'And? What about his daughter?' He let out the question that troubled him the most.

Dougal stopped and stared at him, quickly discerning the rest of the question and Ross's suspicions. Would his cousin be honest with him if he suspected that Ilysa was somehow involved?

'I saw her reactions when she saw you lying there unconscious and do not believe the affection and concern were false,' he said slowly. 'And I watched her do what was needed when you could not. Because *you* needed her to. I do not think she is a willing player in his game.'

Ross nodded at Dougal, wanting to believe that Ilysa wasn't part of her father's plans. Something unsettling rolled deep in his gut and he pushed the feeling away. Ilysa had proved herself—to those closest to him and to him. He was coming to realise that he wanted more of her, more of their marriage, in spite of all the factors that weighed on him about its origin, its true purpose and her father.

'Come,' he said. 'She is joining us at supper.'

Dougal blinked several times quickly, for he knew that she had not set foot in the hall for a meal since her arrival.

'How did you manage that?'

Ross did not answer until they approached the keep.

'I ordered her to eat with us. As a dutiful wife, she will obey.' He was jesting, but he did not think it so humorous as to cause Dougal to laugh until he choked.

'I would not eat anything she offers you, my chieftain,' he wheezed out between coughs. 'Have a care for your own arse now.'

Chapter Twelve

With her belly churning with nervousness, Ilysa doubted she could eat a bite. That would solve the biggest problem she faced—embarrassing herself by trying to consume a meal while others stared. That the people here had seemed to accept her made no difference for it was something that had not protected her in the past.

'Come, my lady,' Gavina said. Her maid had been quiet as she prepared for supper, dressing Ilysa in one of her better gowns. Though the trunk that had accompanied her here was filled with attire far better than her own, she had never worn one of them. She preferred the feel and comfort of a good, strong working gown over those sent that would tear in a brisk walk. As she glanced at the one she wore now, she realised it was the one she'd worn on her arrival here.

'Is this some sort of special occasion, Gavina? My brown gown is clean.'

'As is yer other brown one and the other one. Oh, so is yer grey one and the dark green as well.' Her maid's sarcasm made her wince.

'I told you I preferred the darker hues for they hide the dirt when I work,' she explained.

'Aye, my lady,' Gavina said. The sigh the woman let out was filled with her frustration over Ilysa's appearance.

'Worry not,' she said. 'I prefer function over a colour or the cut of a gown. I appreciate your patience with me.' Ilysa picked up the comb and used it on her curls. 'The kerchief.'

'My lady, yer husband likes yer hair uncovered.'

''Tis not proper. A lady should cover her hair at all times.'

'A nun mayhap, but—' Gavina stopped. 'I pray yer pardon for my insult, my lady.' The woman bowed her head.

'The kerchief will make this gown look shoddy,' Ilysa said, trying to give consideration to the beautiful garment and the work that went into making it. Gavina looked up expectantly. 'I will wear the coif and the blue veil with this.'

The older woman let out a sound that could only be described as a growl then, while never saying a word. She strode to the trunk in loud steps, making her feelings clear. And she mumbled under her breath the entire time that she placed and tweaked the linen straps around Ilysa's face and head to cover her hair and then secured the veil she had requested.

'You look lovely, my lady,' Gavina said as she made one last adjustment to the strap that held Ilysa's arm in place. 'There now, ye are ready for supper and for yer husband's gaze.'

The same two things that made Ilysa's stomach nervous.

Standing, she walked to the door that Gavina held open and then followed her maid down the steps to the hall. The noise rose as they drew closer and Ilysa prepared herself as they entered through the archway. She faltered at the silence that fell over the whole chamber.

'He has seen you, my lady.'

Ilysa glanced at the dais and saw Ross stand and walk to the edge of it. Though whispered greetings echoed around her, she did not look away from him as she made her way through the hall. By the time she'd reached the steps leading up to the main table, he was there waiting, his hand held out for hers.

'My lady.' He took her hand and guided her up to the table and then around it to her seat. A different seat from the one she'd occupied the first time. 'I did not ken if you would join me or not.'

'I did not think I had a choice,' she said softly. His command had been clear to her when he'd uttered it.

'And if you did?' He waited for her to sit and she discovered a large cushion in place on her chair. For her comfort.

She did not reply immediately. This kind of chatter made her nervous and she did not understand what he expected of her. In other circumstances and with other people, she would suffer no fools their jests at her expense, but this was her husband asking her before his kin. So instead, she closed her mouth and did not speak at all.

And he laughed.

He released her hand, leaned his head back and laughed.

Everyone at or near the table was staring, trying to sort out what words had been exchanged to make him react so. All the while, his laughter—joyous, explosive, refreshing, without guile or sarcasm—did something to her she could not explain. But the sound of it eased the tension that had filled her with every step she'd taken from her chamber.

'You are here and that is all that matters.'

Her husband sat down and nodded to the watchful servants. At his signal, they began filling cups and placing platters of food along the table. The appealing aromas spread as each new one arrived, but her choices were few. Most needed to be cut or handled before they could be eaten. This was what she had tried to avoid by eating in her chamber or even below in the kitchen, enjoying the bowls of soups or savoury stews that Ronald made for her.

'My lady.' So caught up in her worrying, Ilysa had not seen Ronald approaching. She turned to find him waiting next to her chair as a serving woman held out a tray. 'I hope you enjoy this one. I changed the seasonings more to your liking.'

Struggling to control her reaction, she watched as he placed a bowl of thick soup before her—the steaming scent made her stomach rumble in hunger—and smaller ones holding chunks of bread and some root vegetables. He bowed and walked off without another word and all that was left to do was eat without crying.

'That colour is very attractive on you,' her husband said. It felt strange to have him on her left and she only realised it as she turned to face him. His gaze moved to her coif for a single moment before returning to meet hers. 'You should wear brighter colours more often.'

Should she acknowledge the compliment? Should

she explain about her usual dull or dark shades of her gowns? She'd almost decided when he spoke once more.

'Gavina explained your reasons for the colours you choose. But you should be garbed in gowns more like this one when you are not working in the keep or village. If you need more cloth—'

'Nay, my lord,' she said, placing her hand on his arm. 'My trunks contain many gowns and garments my sister placed in them. A wedding present from my…family.'

''Twas in the marriage agreement. My bride was to have new clothing as befits the wife of a chieftain.' She could not help the surprise that showed then.

'My father fulfilled part of the agreement even while defrauding you of the most critical part.'

'Ilysa,' he said. Now it was his turn to reach over and take her hand in his. 'Let us put this to rest between us. I have accepted you as my wife. From the moment you stepped off the boat that brought you here, from the moment you stood before me, I accepted you.' He lifted her hand to his lips and kissed the back of it. 'Even if sometimes I ken not what to do with you.' She frowned at the admission and he smiled back. 'No matter your father's actions. No matter who should have been delivered to me. You were and you are my wife. Worry not yourself over it any longer.'

'Very well, my lord.' She slid her hand from his and lifted her spoon. 'If you can do that, then I must.'

He leaned in closer, whispering words softly so no others could hear. His warm breath tickled her neck.

'If I must not speak of your attachment to your head coverings, then you must give up your fight.'

When he said it in that manner, he gave her an honourable way out. She turned to agree and found his mouth within an inch of hers. She ached to kiss him. Her mouth opened and their breaths mingled. Closer now, he tilted his head to ease their mouths together. She closed her eyes, awaiting the touch of his lips on hers.

The crash of a metal pitcher of ale on the floor startled them apart. Only then did she comprehend that they had nearly kissed in front of everyone. If she thought that his polite kiss on her hand had been too much, what would his lips on hers have been?

The interruption brought back her wits. As she sat back in her chair and put as much distance as she could between herself and her increasingly appealing husband, she thought about why he could be so considerate of her with all that had happened. Did he truly not judge her for her father's deeds and misdeeds?

She filled her spoon and ate some of Ronald's potage. She might also have moaned at the taste of it. Ilysa felt her husband's gaze on her and fought not to look at him. Swallowing the delicious soup, she sipped another spoonful and fought the urge to make that unseemly sound once more, all while trying to ignore him. When she slid the tip of her tongue along her bottom lip to catch an errant drop, he took hold of her chin, gently, and guided her mouth to his.

His tongue boldly swept into her mouth as though seeking the taste of her meal. As he caught and suckled her tongue, her body readied itself for more. Aching and a hunger for pleasure at his hands filled her, erasing the need for food with a stronger one for him. How had she come so fully under his sensual spell? She'd told herself she was just doing what a wife must. She'd told herself she owed him obedience because of what he'd provided for her and especially for the safety that surrounded her now. As she opened to him, she suspected more was happening. Something she'd never dreamt was a possibility for her.

This time, loud cheering, banging of cups on tables and clapping brought her out of the pleasurable euphoria she felt. No force on this earth or in heaven above could make her raise her eyes and see all those before her who shouted out and cheered as they witnessed their lord kissing, nay possessing, his lady wife's mouth. She would never again be able to look at another of his kith and kin directly.

'Ross, she will never finish her meal and you'll have Gavina to answer to for that!' Dougal called out from his seat on the other side of her husband. The clapping continued to fill the hall.

Her husband lifted his mouth from hers and now laughed as he leaned back in his chair. She chanced to look at him to see if only she, the inexperienced one in their marriage, was affected by those kisses and caresses. His eyes had darkened with desire and he seemed to be struggling to breathe evenly.

She continued to take furtive peeks at him as they ate supper. Each time, his gaze would meet hers as though daring her to do…something. She distracted herself by eating her soup and listening to those who did speak to him as he ate. But that did not end the arousal within her. Or the need to know if he was affected by the same needs.

Did she dare glance down for a sign of whether that desire still flowed within him? He wore breeches now, fitted from his waist down to his knees and not the looser-fitting plaid that would hide such things.

She struggled against the need to see, but, oh, the sins she must reveal when next the priest held confession! In just several weeks, she'd gone from living a life of prayer and good works to one full of life and hard work and passion. Surely it was not a sin for a married woman to enjoy her husband's attentions? Even if he wanted her only for those desires and she thoroughly enjoyed it, was that then a sin? For they had little else connecting them but those minutes and hours wrapped in each other's arms.

Until this day.

When he'd handed her the keys to every storage chamber and important place in the keep, it changed so much.

At least on Iona she could seek out the counsel of Mother Euphemia or even Sister Margaret on matters that worried or perplexed her. Speaking to either of those good women about what she faced now would have sent them into apoplexy for certain! Mayhap she would talk to Morag about this? Gavina was good-hearted, and a widow of some experience, she thought, and would have practical advice as would the wise woman. But would they speak candidly about their chieftain with her?

'Do you wish more?' he asked, breaking into her contemplation.

'More?' Ilysa blinked several times, trying to clear her thoughts of desire and pleasure...and him! But his question stirred them up again.

'Ronald has more, if you are yet hungry. He told

me it was one of your favourites.' She looked down to discover her bowl empty and her hand with a piece of bread already scooping up the last of it.

'Would you like some instead, my lord? 'Tis delicious and as chieftain you should have the best of the food at table.'

'Ronald offered me some,' he said, shaking his head. 'I have eaten my fill.'

'My lord?' Munro had approached behind them. 'We are ready.'

'I will be there in a moment,' her husband answered.

'You must see to your duties?' Ilysa watched as he rose from his seat.

'Aye,' he said, drinking down the rest of his ale. 'Reports are expected from my men who have been following The Campbell's warriors.'

'Do you expect another attack soon?' she asked. She lowered her voice to keep this business private.

'Come.' He held out his hand to her.

'My lord?'

'We are about to discuss that and other matters about our preparations.'

No words formed in her thoughts. He slid her chair away from the table and helped her to stand. She walked at his side out of the hall and down the corridor to the steward's chamber which offered privacy. Just before they reached it, Gavina appeared from the shadows and greeted them.

'Worry not, Gavina,' Ross said. 'I will see the Lady to her chamber when we finish here.'

He did not give her time to react to the stunned expression on her maid's face, but Ilysa enjoyed it as they entered the chamber. When she finally gathered her thoughts, she laughed.

'I did not believe that was possible, my lord.' He guided her to a chair and watched as she settled into it.

'Oh, I have some tricks to use in dealing with the good wife. I have been around her all my life and ken her soft spots.'

'You must teach me.'

He'd taken a step towards her before he seemed to realise that Munro, Gillean, Dougal, Innis and another warrior she did not recognise were present and watching. This gathering was serious. Matters of life and death would be discussed and yet, in this moment, all she could think of was the excitement that lived inside her now at his words, glances, touches and kisses.

But...

But it was time to consider serious matters and so she concentrated her attention on that and let the feeling of wonderment at being included go. There would be time enough to savour this moment when their clan was safe from its enemies.

Was he losing his wits? Had the elders chosen the wrong man to lead the MacMillans and avenge the death and mayhem brought to their lands? For in this moment, Ross could only think of the taste of her mouth and the scent of her arousal as she sat at his side.

She still had no idea of the power of her beauty or her wisdom or kindness. Over and over, his people explained in great detail the contributions she had made to keep them alive and well.

Or of the strength of his attraction and need for her.

He was no innocent. Like every healthy, hardy, hot-blooded warrior, he'd sought the attention of the welcoming, lovely women around them. Visitors to his uncle often brought along relatives to be considered for future matches, but those were not where he found the women who welcomed him into their beds. Nay, it was usually the servants who travelled with their ladies, or those who worked in the kitchens, or on the outlying crofts. With no serious interest in marrying, he had not pursued a particular woman, but enjoyed any and all.

Until the day of the attack when the Campbells arrived and took the luxury of choice out of his hands and resulted in a wife he did not expect.

'What think you, Ross?' Munro asked. The gleam in his commander's gaze told of his intention of catching him lusting after his wife. As he had been. The only thing that kept him from complete disgrace was that he'd heard one of Munro's questions about the man who oversaw their spies.

'I do not believe we saw the entire Campbell force, possibly not even in the initial attack,' he said, glaring at Munro. Turning to Innis, he asked, 'You mentioned something after that, did you not? That the force did not seem large enough?'

'Aye, not to lay siege to a castle like this one,' the older man replied. Ross gifted his commander with a smug smile. 'They have more men than what we've seen. Have ye warned Fergus? And our allies?'

'Word has been sent. After this last attempt, we are certain he's split his men. The question is whether he has enough.'

'To defeat you?' Ilysa asked.

'Aye, my lady,' Innis said. 'Alexander Campbell was forced from these lands and exiled, never to return, by the order of the King. He didna go peaceably and swore to return to reclaim what was his.' The older man had lived through those turbulent and dangerous times.

'The question we need to consider is—does he fight alone?' Ross glanced at each person there and waited for their reaction. 'Other than his son, who would ally themselves with such a villainous creature as The Campbell?'

The question hung out in the silence between them for long moments. Then Innis spoke.

'I can speak to the elders and some of the villagers who might remember who aligned with the Campbells in the past.'

'Aye, good, Innis.'

Their talk went on for some time and Ross watched as Ilysa took it all in. He'd surprised, nay, shocked her by including her. Although she listened quietly, intently to their discussions, she asked a few questions because she did not know his family's history, or indeed much of her own. But once the topic moved to their preparations, she had much to offer.

If his men thought it strange to have her there, they did not say. Well, when he'd first suggested it to them, they raised no objections at all. Gillean would welcome her presence to avoid being the one to tell her what must be done and facing her onslaught of questions. It made more sense for her to be here.

Once Ross knew they had everything that they could impact under control, he reached out for his wife's hand. The men stood as she did and he led her from the chamber back towards the hall and the stairway up to their chambers. Before she lifted her foot to the first step, a loud rumbling echoed from her. She covered her stomach, but the noise repeated.

'Worry not,' she said. 'Gavina will check on me before she seeks her rest.' Ross took her hand and tugged her towards the other stairs—the one leading down to the kitchen.

'Come, I will take you to your chamber, but first I will find you something to eat.'

'My lord, nay.'

'Wait here.'

He ran down the steps and took the lantern there to light his way to Ronald's private cupboard. Finding a basket, he filled it with foodstuffs and a flagon of ale and returned to her. She had not moved.

When they reached the corridor where their chambers sat on opposite ends, he led her to his. He released her hand and waited for her reaction. Lifting the latch, he pushed his door open and wondered if she would enter.

She did.

Chapter Thirteen

As daylight flooded the chamber, Ilysa woke in a strange bed.

Naked in a strange bed.

An empty bed at that.

As she slid her hand across the bed, the warmth of the bedcovers revealed his recent departure. She lifted her head and looked around his chamber. It was larger than hers by half. His bed was as well. She could roll several times before reaching the edge.

They *had* rolled several times from one edge to the other.

But the passion they shared was not what had her smiling this morn. Nay, the cause of her happiness was the place that he had offered her in his clan. And in his house. Ilysa stretched and sighed as she guided her bad arm to her side.

'My lady!' Gavina said as she rushed into the chamber. 'He is waiting at table for ye to break ye fast.'

She dropped the bundle she carried over the chair there and helped Ilysa see to her needs and dress quickly. Gavina held out a gown she did not recognise. But her maid did not give her time to ask any questions as she helped fit the sleeve for her arm in place, gathered up the length of fabric and tossed it over Ilysa's head and down. With an efficiency she'd given up resisting, Gavina had her ready to leave his chamber within the shortest time she could have. As she took the last piece from her maid, Ilysa stared at it.

The kerchief.

'Make haste, my lady.'

She did not. She looked at the kerchief and wondered.

Could she? Could she put it aside as he'd asked her to do?

Oh, it was just a piece of cloth. It was…

More.

Her hand shook as she held it tighter.

'Would ye like me to place it for ye, my lady?' Gavina reached out to take it from her, but Ilysa shook her head.

'Mayhap just a ribbon to control them?'

She shoved the kerchief inside the curve of her sleeve to have if she needed it and raised her gaze to the woman. The approval she saw there nearly took her to her knees. The woman quickly grabbed a length of ribbon and wound it around Ilysa's head, catching most of her curls and holding them back from her face.

'Come along, Gavina. My lord waits at table.'

Excitement bubbled up within her. Anticipation of his reaction outweighed the anxiousness of what others might think. By the time she reached the archway to the hall, doubts assailed her and her steps faltered. But only until her husband saw her. If she'd hoped to make a discreet entrance, he ruined any chance of it by rising and striding quickly to her.

'Are you terrified, Wife?' he asked as he blocked the view of her with his height and his nearness. 'If you do not wish to do this, you must not.'

She was terrified. She'd never deliberately gone against conforming with what was expected of her. She'd never put herself in situations that drew attention to herself for it inevitably drew attention to her deformity and her shame.

Now, looking at his face, filled with concern for her, she knew she must. For him. To repay him for his every kindness. To show him how much she lo—

Ilysa smiled then, confident in this choice when she'd had so few before in her life. In reality, it was such a small action, but one that he wanted and she could give.

Would give.

Luckily, her stomach growled then, breaking the rising tension between them.

'Terrified, aye, but hungry—again,' she admitted.

'Well, come to the table,' he said, stepping away and holding out his hand. 'I can fix that.' As they walked, Ilysa waited for the whispers to begin.

And nothing happened.

A few called out greetings to her, but they arrived at the table with her unscathed. He led her to a chair and she realised what had bothered her last night at supper. She'd been seated at the opposite side of him to where she'd been before.

'You moved your seat?' she asked. As he settled next to her, he beckoned to the servants to begin. 'Is this not your place?' He sat and waited for their cups to be filled.

'I did. If you sit on this side of me...' he pointed to their positions '...'tis less likely a servant will jostle your arm.'

'Why? Why do you do these things?' The words came out as an emotional whisper. Her throat tightened.

'Can a man not treat his wife with respect?' She was going to point out the origin of their marriage—again—but she'd promised not to do that. 'Why did you do that?' He nodded at her hair, smiling as he did. 'Especially if you were terrified.'

'Because you asked.'

He stared at her as though stunned that she would fulfil a request from him, but in the blink of an eye, his expression changed into one that held a challenge within it.

'So, if I ask something of you, you will do it?'

Thankfully, the servants placed bowls of steaming porridge before them before she could say something witless. Or worse. She dipped into the thick mixture of oats and cream and scooped it into her mouth, fighting the usual reaction to such delicious tastes.

'You are teasing me, my lord.' She put the spoon down and faced him. The time for pretence was past. 'Your words have two meanings and my answer is aye to both of them.'

Much of the time they spoke, he jested as she did, adding a layer of meaning beneath the obvious. It was not an easy thing for her to do since she worried over his implications and intent. The other part causing her apprehension was her lack of experience at flirting like this.

Young women of her status usually practised their

wiles while being wooed by men intent on marrying
them. Instead Ilysa had spent that time praying at the
nunnery, speaking little if not addressed first and ignoring men and their antics. For flirting and wooing were
not for her. Her arm ached just then, reminding her of
her shame and exile.

'You smile when I tease you so. And you blush. I
cannot help that I like seeing the colour in your cheeks
when you do.' He leaned closer. 'When you arrived here
you were pale and you looked gaunt from your time at
the nunnery. I like that you seem happy and you enjoy
your food and that you smile.'

'I am happy,' she said. That was the truth.

'So, if I ask you to accompany me this morn, you
will leave your duties behind and do so?'

'Aye.' He laughed at her quick reply.

'Do you ride?'

'Some.' She winced and shook her head. 'Not much
at all in recent years. Mayhap I should stay behind or I
will slow you down?'

'Nay, speed is not necessary. I thought you should
see the scope of our holding here and understand what
we defend.'

'There is more?' She'd thought this castle and its
village and farmland further inland were the extent of
MacMillan lands.

'Aye,' he said, nodding to Dougal as he approached.
'Bring a cloak, for the autumn chill seems to be arriving in the air.'

They finished their meal and when she rose to go,
he grabbed her hand before she could leave.

'I am pleased, Ilysa. Truly,' he whispered as he

pressed her hand to his mouth. 'My thanks for your bravery.'

Ilysa almost flew up the stairs to her chamber to ready herself to accompany Ross from the castle. Gavina, bless her, could not even keep up with her and was pulling in deep, hurried breaths when they reached the chamber. When Ilysa pulled out her cloak that she'd worn at the nunnery, Gavina tsked at the sight of the threadbare garment.

But not even the poor condition of her cloak could diminish her joy as she sought out and found her husband in the yard astride a monstrous horse. She looked for the one she was supposed to ride when he held out his hand to her. He leaned over and took hold of her waist, lifting her in an effortless way and placing her in front of him on his mount.

Before she could object, question or speak, he touched his feet to the horse's sides and they were off.

The next hours passed in a blur as they travelled miles around Castle Sween, past the edges of the farm-lands and into the hills. He told her more about his family and his parents. Even though a dozen warriors rode with them, they seemed to disappear, leaving only the two of them.

The night that followed that magical day made her believe that she might have a place here and with him.

The next days of waking with him, working with him and watching him strive to defend his people were the best of her life. And more, they were beyond any imagining she ever had of her life. He took her ad-

vice seriously and never questioned her right to offer it
or to be part of any of the rather unusual discussions.
Each time it happened, Ilysa had to stop and wonder
if she'd been kidnapped by the fae and taken to some
other strange land.

As his men returned with news of a force of warriors
and ships building in the south, Ilysa understood that
the time was coming that would prove if they and their
preparations—including many of her suggestions—
were right or wrong. If they were enough or would fall
short. If his people, their people, would live or be destroyed.

Though their efforts bordered on frantic, the chores
and duties each day as they readied for battle brought
them closer together. With everyone in the keep and
village giving their best efforts, Ilysa had the hope that
it would work out. Her father would provide the support he'd promised and the MacMillans would defeat
their enemies.

And live happily ever after.

And she and Ross would live happily ever after, too.

'We are as ready as we can be,' Munro said.

Standing at Ross's side on the battlements of the
keep, his commander sounded confident, but not in an
arrogant manner. Dougal and Innis grunted their agreement.

'I almost wish…' Ross did not finish the words for
he truly did not want what he nearly said.

'I wish we were not sitting here idly without kenning
when we will defend ourselves.' Munro spoke Ross's

wish aloud. 'I would have us be the ones in control of this fight.'

'Aye,' Ross said. He caught the gaze of each man and nodded to them. 'As would we. But with our own men split between here and with Fergus—'

'I ken, Ross. 'Tis just that I would rather be making the Campbells pay rather than this delay.'

'As would I, but with word that they are now on the move, it makes more sense to remain behind the safety of the walls and deal with them when they arrive. As Fergus will at Castle Barron.'

'Our men return this night?' Dougal asked.

'Aye, Dougal. Once the sun sets,' Innis said.

'We will have a more complete view of their scheming and be ready for them.' Ross turned to go.

'The Lady is not here,' Innis said. Ross met his inquisitive stare and nodded. 'Is there a problem we should discuss?'

'Discuss, Innis? Nay, not discuss,' Ross said. 'We all realise that my wife's father is the biggest unknown in this endeavour. Her presence rather than her sister's made it clear that he plays his own game around whatever the Campbells are playing.'

For as much as he wanted it not to be so, Ilysa was a bigger part of this situation than he wished her to be. He had no doubt that she was a pawn, as was anyone connected to Iain MacDonnell, but her presence and her actions here made it difficult to discern her larger role.

The sly MacDonnell would not have sent her here, substituted her for the expected sister, without a purpose. Well, other than to vex him and make him play the fool. And though not the chieftain his uncle had been, Ross was no one's fool.

'But the Lady has proven herself trustworthy, has she not, Ross?' Dougal asked. 'Look at all she has accomplished here.'

Ross held up his hand to stop his friend. 'This is not about my wife. Her father's actions and goals are his and his alone.' He put his hand on his cousin's shoulder— Dougal had become Ilysa's biggest defender since he'd brought her here. 'But she is a part of the plan he is enacting. She plays a role that only he seems to understand.'

'And the MacDonnell warriors here now?' Munro asked.

'Continue to assign them duties outside the keep. Did they argue over sleeping in the village or notice our men? Any more trouble between them and ours?'

'Nay. They seem content to do whatever task is asked of them. And, other than the one time, things are calm,' Munro explained. 'The blacksmith is spoiling for a fight with one of them, though.' He shrugged.

Ross crossed his arms over his chest and shook his head. He knew what the trouble was—The MacDonnell warriors had the same disrespect for his wife that her father clearly had. Worse, one man had been arrogant enough to offer an insult of Ilysa in front of the blacksmith. The blacksmith whose daughter Ilysa had led to safety during the last attack.

'Keep them separate,' he said. 'When this is done, I will have a word with him as well. I hold back only to see this through, then he will pay.'

'If he lives through whatever comes our way,' Munro

said. The threat was clear and Ross had no intention of ordering differently.

As the others began to walk away, Dougal motioned for him to remain. His friend must have something else to discuss. Once the others were far enough away so their words could not be heard, Dougal spoke.

'Ross, do those you sent to Dunyvaig seek news about Ilysa?' Dougal asked.

'Aye. As do those I sent to Iona.' His friend startled, surprised by this.

'When? When did you begin searching for knowledge of her?' Dougal's reaction was interesting.

'The morn after she arrived. Once I learned the true identity of my bride but did not have enough knowledge of her. Two followed Eachann back to Dunyvaig and a few days later another went to Iona.'

'You sent a man to the nunnery?' his cousin scoffed.

'Nay. I took Elspeth's words to heart and sent a woman.'

Dougal stumbled back against the stone wall and shook his head, confirming to Ross that he'd been correct in doing that. Elspeth had always grumbled about not being taken seriously and not being allowed to do many of the things that men did. In her situation it was about fighting and defending herself, but when considering how best to approach the prioress and gain her assistance, it had seemed to Ross that a woman was perfect for the task.

'Hell, I would have sent Elspeth if she was still here,' he said. His sister would have been thrilled at such a request, but she was already at the abbey near her betrothed's home, awaiting their marriage.

'Has she, the woman you sent, returned? It has been weeks since your marriage.'

'Aye, she talked with the prioress and confirmed all that I kenned from rumours or from Ilysa's own words. And the holy mother told her that they'd had no warning or word from The MacDonnell until his men arrived in the night and took Ilysa from the nunnery's sleeping chamber. The others who shared it were terrified, but not harmed.'

'So, you believe her?'

'Aye, I do. In spite of her father—who I trust not at all—I think she is separate from all this.'

That seemed to calm whatever Dougal's concerns were and they continued to discuss some of the complaints from those who farmed outside the village.

A short time later, Dougal gazed over Ross's shoulder at something.

'Look,' Dougal said as he pointed south.

Ross turned to see a lone birlinn headed for their dock. It moved swiftly as the northerly winds carried it towards them. A banner, one identifying the vessel as belonging to The MacDonnell, blew wildly in the brisk winds.

'Interesting that he sends someone just before our own spies are due back. Come,' Ross said, already walking to the steps, 'let us greet our visitor.'

By the time he reached the gate, Munro stood watching his approach. Ross glanced around for any sign of Ilysa.

'The Lady is in the village with Morag,' his commander said.

'Morag?' Munro stopped and shook his head at Ross.

'Do not ask. I ken not. More than likely talking about the herbs and other things the old woman needs.'

Ross let it go, knowing that his wife would return to the keep once news of a visitor reached her. No messenger had arrived in advance, so Ross could not even guess at the identity of their visitor—be it The Mac-Donnell's kin or emissary or even himself. Guards lined up behind him, Munro stood on one side and Innis on the other.

As they watched, Ross glanced around, noticing the placement of his other men where they would not be recognised as the guards they were. He took nothing for granted when it involved his wife's father. Content that they were prepared, Ross stepped forward.

A small group climbed out of the birlinn and walked towards him. The tall, burly warriors separated, revealing a woman in their midst. Her hooded cloak hid most of her within it, but he caught a glimpse of eyes resembling Ilysa's as she came closer. One man stayed at her side as she walked to Ross and stopped there.

Ross knew the name before that man announced her.

'The MacDonnell's eldest daughter,' he said after a respectful but short bow. 'Lady Lilidh MacDonnell.'

The lady who should be his wife lowered herself gracefully into a curtsy and then rose and lifted her hood and let it drop on her shoulders.

'My lord,' she said. She met his gaze and then openly appraised him, from his head to his feet, pausing at his groin for several moments that pushed the bounds of propriety for an unmarried lady.

'Welcome to Castle Sween, my lady,' he said as he should. 'Your sister did not mention you were coming.'

'My father thought I should visit since she's sent no word of her condition.'

'I am certain she will be touched by your worry.'

'Where is my sister?' The lady pretended well, but he'd seen people like this before and her lack of real concern was as apparent to him as the castle next to him.

'My wife is seeing to her duties.' The undisguised shocked expression on her face answered one thing for him—they truly had thought he would put her aside or something worse. 'Come, you can wait inside until she returns.'

He held out his arm to her, as he should, and she accepted. He noticed a strange exchange of glances between Ilysa's sister and the man who'd stood next to her. The man dropped back a pace and followed them.

The lady was accomplished at polite chatter, for she did not stop for a moment as they made their way in through the gate. There was never a question that would force her to pause and give him a chance to speak. They approached the keep when he noticed the sounds behind them. Ross drew them to a stop and turned.

Ilysa rushed in with Gavina barely able to keep up with her. Her gown was covered by an apron which also hid her arm. A basket filled with some plants swung on her other arm with each step she took. Her face was bright, filled with the colour of exertion and laughter. And her hair, the pale blonde curls loose and blowing in the breeze, shone as the sun's light hit it.

Then, in the next moment, not even in the time it took to exhale, all of that was gone as she became a ghost of herself at the sight of her sister on his arm. But that was not the worst of it. Nay. For when the man who'd arrived with her sister stepped out into view, Ilysa stopped and stared at him as if she was seeing the dead.

The passing of time seemed to pause just then as he watched her sway on her feet and he feared she would fall. Only when he began to move did he remember her sister held his arm.

'My lord, what have you done to my sister?' The MacDonnell's eldest asked him in a cold, accusing tone. She let out a short burst of laughter that shocked him. 'You have made her no more than a servant here just as she was at the nunnery.'

The light that he loved in Ilysa's gaze, the smile that would curve her lips until he wanted to kiss them and the blush in her cheeks as she thought of them all disappeared and the nun who'd arrived just a month ago re-emerged in an instant.

The burning in his gut told him he would never see the woman he loved again.

Chapter Fourteen

She could do nothing but stand and stare at the sight before her. Her sister's presence, standing there at Ross's side, touching him, took her breath away. Tall and beautiful, she was the perfect lady for Ross. She should have been his.

Seeing her so unexpectedly shocked her. But not as much as seeing the man who stepped forward, making himself visible to her.

Graeme MacLean.

Once her betrothed. The man whose rejection ended with Ilysa's exile to Iona so that her presence would not lessen Lilidh's happiness when she was then betrothed to him. Now here he was, clearly a lapdog for her father and part of whatever her father planned. Worse though, his gaze was not filled with pity and disgust as it was when he saw her arm exposed. Nay, now disgust flashed across his brown eyes followed by something worse, something more insulting to her—relief.

Relief that he had not been forced to marry her as he thought he would be just over three years ago. Then, he raked her with a glance at her appearance, lingering on her uncovered hair that matched her sister's in colour.

At Lilidh's insulting words, Ilysa saw Ross stiffen and drop his arm. He took a step towards her and stopped, turning to speak to Gillean. The steward nodded and motioned for the others to follow him. When they did, Ross glared at everyone in the yard until they dispersed, leaving just the two of them staring across the distance at each other.

She needed to run to him. She wanted to run away. She wanted to retch or cry or fall to the ground. She wanted to hide.

Her newly claimed sense of confidence had proved false and deserted her at the sight of her sister and Graeme. Every bit of satisfaction and joy at becoming the woman she was now dissolved and dispersed into the winds. As Ross now strode to her, Gavina took her leave, lifting the basket from Ilysa's arm as she did so. Ilysa never even realised the woman had remained behind her until she whispered words and walked past. The servant paused near her lord to say something and then entered the keep.

When he reached her, he stood in silence just watching her. Finally, she knew she must speak to him, even if to beg his permission to remain elsewhere while Lilidh…and Graeme were in the keep.

'I beg you—'

'Do not beg me, Ilysa.' His gruffness surprised her as did the softness in his gaze. 'Whatever you wish, whatever you need, is yours.'

'I…' She reached up to tug her non-existent shawl, but he grabbed her hand first.

'Tell me who he is.' Ross slid his arm around her waist without letting go of the other, holding her up—holding her close—as he began to walk them towards the keep.

'I cannot, Ross. I cannot—' Her words choked off.

'Take a breath in slowly, love,' he ordered in that tone she could not ignore. 'Let it out now just as slowly.' And still they walked.

'Graeme MacLean,' she could finally whisper.

'Of the clan that sponsors the nunnery on Iona? The prioress is a MacLean, is she not?' She slipped then, but he held her up. Slowing their pace, he asked again, 'But I do not mean what clan he claims. Tell me who he is to you.'

The words, the question within them, were hard to hear and harder to answer, no matter that he softened his voice. He stopped them then, turning to the path that led to the kitchen entry that would keep her out of sight once they entered. When they reached it, he guided her past the doorway to a spot where they would not be seen or heard.

They stood in silence at first and Ilysa simply enjoyed a moment of peace in his embrace before she must reveal her shame to him. These last days, and even the ones before, had been filled with joy and companionship and a pleasure in life she'd not known before and the grief at their ending cut her deeply.

'Graeme was…we were betrothed.'

'When?'

'Just over three years ago,' she said.

'Did you love him?'

Of all the possible questions he could have asked, she'd never expected that one.

'Ilysa, did you love him?' His voice filled with something that sounded like jealousy, but that simply could not be.

'I had never met him. Lilidh had and she described him to me.'

'Oh, hell,' he whispered.

'Aye. She decided she wanted him and my father agreed.' It mattered not that their father had had other plans for Lilidh, ones that included her marrying someone much higher in rank. When she'd demanded it in the way she'd discovered would work on their father, he'd agreed.

'And the man involved?'

She took in a deep breath and let it out before even trying to say the rest. Turning to him, she leaned her head against him and attempted to find the words.

'What did he do, Ilysa?' Now menace filled his words. God forgive her, she liked hearing it.

'We were walking by the sea and he saw my arm.'

'There is more to this, Wife. Tell me now. I would ken the rest of it.'

'Lilidh was with us. I stumbled,' she said, remembering now the push from behind that sent her to the ground. 'He reached out to grab hold of me and my gown, my sleeve, tore and my arm…'

'Your arm fell out.' He breathed then. 'And you did not ken.'

'Nay. I cannot feel it most of the time, so I did not realise it was uncovered. He released me and I fell.' She lifted her head and stared off as she revealed the rest of it. 'When we returned to the keep, he told everyone he would not marry such a deformed woman. That he would not lie before his kin and the Almighty and accept my defect,' she whispered. 'That he could never touch a woman who was so...'

'Hush, love. Enough.' He stroked her hair then and she felt the tears falling on to her cheeks.

'Before that, my father had never mentioned my a... arm in public. And my family rarely spoke of it. But Graeme's actions forced him to break the betrothal and put me aside.' She stepped away and Ross released her. Dashing away the trail of tears, she cleared her throat. 'Sending me to Iona was a gift, even if neither my father nor I kenned it at the time.'

With a shaking hand, she tugged off her apron, smoothed her gown and adjusted the position of that arm.

'Where are you going?' He grabbed her shoulders and turned her back to him.

'There are guests,' she said. She shook and lowered her head. 'I do not want to...'

'You are Lady MacMillan, wife of the chieftain. You do not do anything you do not wish to,' he said. 'Do not waste your strength or efforts on them, Ilysa. Let Gillean see to them.'

The need to hide overwhelmed her now. On the morrow, she would see to them with a fresh attitude. For now, she only wanted to get away.

'I would seek my chambers, my lord,' she said.

He started to say something, thought better of it and just nodded at her, allowing her to enter the kitchen and go her own way.

'Come to mine later?' he asked as she took her first step away from him.

'I think I will be too restless this night, my lord. I will see you on the morrow.'

He started at her words and looked as if she'd slapped him with her admission, but he did not require her to come to his chamber or to say anything else. If he could acquiesce so easily in the matter, why did her heart feel like it was breaking open in her chest as she walked away?

Ross punched the thick wooden door of the storage room as he walked by and the crunching of the wood and the pain in his fist felt good somehow. It was not what, who, he wanted to introduce to his fist, but it would have to do for now. If he began punching the man who deserved it, he would not stop with one blow and then he would have to answer for killing The Mac-Donnell's man.

Nay, as chieftain he could not simply avenge his wife's honour as he wished to do. Not when her own father had allowed it to happen.

One or two servants approached, saw his face and backed away without saying a word. His temper rarely got out of his control, but it was escaping its bounds now. To hear her describe what had happened, to hear the shame in her voice as she spoke of the man's public rejection of her—he wanted to tear Graeme MacLean and Iain MacDonnell to pieces.

But so much, too much, depended on their support.

In this moment, he wished he was not chieftain. He burned to strike down the men who'd shamed and harmed Ilysa. It mattered not to him that it had happened before she was his, before he loved her.

Because she was his and he would not let them undo the hard-won victories she'd made in these last weeks. He would not allow them to drain the joy from her. He would not stand by and watch as they broke her down into the scared, empty woman they'd exiled to a cold, damp nunnery on a windswept island far away from home.

For now, he would see hospitality extended to them while he saw to his duties. But when his duty was done, when his clan was safe, they would be made to answer for what they'd done.

Ross approached the hall the next morning, unsure of whom or what he would find at table. Nay, that was not the truth. The truth was he only wondered if Ilysa would be there. He arrived to an empty table, but several of the elders took their seats a short time later. Munro brought a message. Dougal joined him and then Lilidh and her guards entered the hall, claiming the attention of everyone else. As she drew closer, he stood and waited for her to sit. Instead of the chair where Gillean tried to direct her, she walked to Ross and sat in the one closest to him.

In Ilysa's seat.

Facing the situation—that he would have to speak to her as they ate—Ross was surprised when Ilysa walked into the hall. He fought to keep the disappointment from his face as he took in her appearance.

The coif and veils were back, covering most of her face and all of her hair. Her gown was one he had not seen, most likely one in the trunks that arrived with her, ones she usually avoided in favour of her practical work gowns. Ross stopped her sister's aimless chatter with a word and waited for Ilysa. The fear in her gaze as she watched him sickened him.

'Good day, my lady,' he said, trying to make her smile. 'I am glad you are here.'

'Good morn, my lord,' she replied. Her voice was quiet and even and then she realised where her sister sat. 'Good day, Lilidh.'

'Do you always keep your husband waiting, Ilysa?' her sister asked. Missing her own rudeness as she accused her sister of the same, she continued, unaware that everyone within hearing was taken aback by it. 'At least you are dressed as you should be. I did not recognise you in the yard when I saw you. Father would be shocked to see you thusly.'

'My lady?' Ross stepped behind Lilidh and began to ease the chair back. 'This is my wife's chair. You need to move from it now.' It was worth seeing the woman sputter in disbelief and the tiniest of smiles brighten Ilysa's face.

'I am a guest here,' she argued.

'But she is my wife,' he repeated.

With the chair pulled back from the table, it took little effort to lift her to stand. He used her surprise against her, walking her to an open chair halfway down the table. Ross returned and held out his hand to Ilysa and helped her to sit.

When her cup was filled and a bowl of porridge placed before both of them, he let himself relax against the back of his chair. His fingers itched to pull the coif off. He only let it remain because he understood she would be horrified now to be without it. All it had taken was for her sister to remind her with insults of her *shame*—an injury to her arm that she had no part in and could do nothing about—and Ilysa had changed back to The MacDonnell's daughter rather than The MacMillan's wife.

'Do you have more to see to in the village or are the preparations in place?'

'A bit more work with Morag,' Ilysa said. She barely touched the steaming bowl before her. One that she had emptied every morning. He'd noticed. 'But, by day's end, it should be complete.'

'Will you show me through the castle, Ilysa? We have much to talk about,' her sister called out from her place.

Before Ilysa could speak, Ross reached under the table and placed his hand on her leg to stop her.

'I fear that your sister cannot, Lady Lilidh, for she has duties she must attend to.'

'My lord,' Ilysa whispered. He pressed his hand on her leg. 'I will have time.'

'Nay, Wife, you will not.'

'Would you rather she wandered freely to see what she would see?'

He had not thought about that. He'd only been thinking about saving Ilysa from Lilidh's company...and insults.

'Take Dougal with you,' he said. Dougal could be charming and distracting when he wished to be.

'I will be well, my lord.'

'Ilysa,' he growled. 'Keep your time with her short. Turn away from her harsh words.'

'Have you spent time with my sister, then?' Ilysa said. The first hint of a smile crossed her face. 'Your suggestions speak of familiarity.'

'I am familiar with bullies and cowards,' he said. 'They behave the same whether man or woman.' He leaned in towards her, staring at her mouth and fighting the urge to kiss her now. Which would only add to her unease. 'Gird your loins, Ilysa. Harden your heart against her cruelty.'

To avoid kissing her or tearing off the coif and more, Ross lifted his hand from her leg and leaned back. He turned and met the gaze of his sister by marriage and nodded.

'My wife will have time after all, Lady Lilidh.' He stood then. 'But do not take advantage of her softheartedness, for she does have duties to see to and she answers to me if she does not fulfil them.' He tried to sound menacing and to infuse his words with an implied threat. From her narrowing gaze, Ross guessed she understood he was not taken in by her.

'Dougal?' he said. His friend stood and waited for his orders. 'Accompany the ladies.'

After a whispered farewell to Ilysa, he walked away, seeking out Gillean's chamber. Dougal caught up with him before he'd taken three strides. Grabbed by his arm, Ross stopped and waited for Dougal's objection.

'Why do you not go with them yourself?' The question was impudent, but not unexpected.

'Three reasons, my friend.' He placed his hand on the man's shoulder and pulled him in. 'The first—if I must be in Lilidh's presence or that of the man who accompanied her here, I will kill someone.' Dougal nodded.

'The second is that I am chieftain here and can make someone else do it. And it would be better if someone else carried out this task.' Dougal chuckled and nodded again, accepting the truth of it.

'And the third?' Ross dropped his arm. Dougal waited on his words.

'The third reason is that I must go and find Father Liam and arrange for a novena to be prayed in thanks to the Almighty for not giving me *that* woman as wife.'

Dougal laughed aloud now, full and hearty, drawing everyone's attention. Ross made his escape then, not truly seeking the priest, but he added this to his growing list of why he would be grateful for the wife he'd received, even if she was not the one he chose.

Chapter Fifteen

By the time that supper was being served in the hall, Ilysa was completely exhausted in a way that long days of hard work, little food and lots of prayer had never done. Every word her sister spoke insulted someone or something.

Lilidh feigned anger at how she said Ross was belittling and shaming Ilysa by making her work among the people and—God have mercy!—out in the village, too. Then when Ilysa defended him, her sister attacked Ilysa's words, trying to prove she was seeing some regard from him that did not exist.

Dougal took pity on her and led, almost forcibly, her sister away to show her the improvements to the barn at the edge of the village. Mayhap because it was not so personal, he could dodge the arrows she let fly? No matter his reason, Ilysa could have kissed the man for his bravery. Unfortunately, Lilidh was not a believer in being among the people one ruled over, so the respite was over too quickly and she reappeared before Ilysa, wanting to see more inside the keep.

The only thing that made this tolerable was the absence of Graeme.

Ilysa thought that was her sister's intention, but Graeme could not be found when they were leaving the hall. Dougal, after that exchange with her husband, took control and refused to wait upon his appearance.

Now, hours later, all Ilysa wanted to do was find a quiet, dark place and hide there until her sister left. Or until her sister decided to finally reveal the true reason for her visit here…now. Why would their father send her when they were on the brink of war with the Campbells?

The answer was obvious to anyone who had only heard the rumours about her father and did not know him personally—for his own purpose. And until that purpose was made known, she feared that Lilidh would remain here, stirring up trouble.

Through the day, Ilysa tried to cajole the knowledge from her sister. She asked her own questions of her, especially as Lilidh seemed to seek out details about certain aspects of Ross's wealth and position. She'd asked about the surrounding clans and the distances to their holdings. And more. But she always seemed to find a way to ask that would seem like innocent curiosity if one did not know her sister or their father.

Ilysa made her way through the busy kitchen and climbed the steps leading to the main floor. More than anything she wanted to get to her chambers unnoticed. And, other than speaking to Ronald with a request for food to be sent to her, she made it there and collapsed in her chair. Needing to loosen the uncomfortable headdress, she waited for the servant to arrive before doing that.

* * *

It was dark inside and out when next she woke.

The growl of her stomach sounded terribly loud in the empty chamber, reminding her that, no matter the hours that had passed, she'd not eaten since early this morning.

'I thought I was feeding you regularly, Wife.' The disembodied voice came from the darkest corner of her chamber and she stared into it, searching for him. 'Ronald had orders to make certain of it.'

He struck a flint and lit the lantern on her table. The light shone across the chamber and after shifting in the chair, she noticed a tray on the table and a small metal pot sitting in the midst of the almost burned-out fire. Well, Ronald or whomever he'd sent had tried.

'It would seem that he obeys your orders, my lord,' she said.

'And it seems you remain skilled at falling asleep in your chair.' He came to her and she fought the urge to jump into his embrace. 'How long have you been sitting there?'

His gaze narrowed and she recognised that expression and the target of his disdain. The worst thing was that a piece of clothing that had been so unnoticed by her for three years now weighed so heavily on her. But she understood it meant more than a piece of linen and a veil between them.

At first, she wanted to tug it off, but she waited, closing her eyes until he did it. Though not without pausing the tiniest part of a moment first—the pause that always gave her the chance, the permission, to refuse.

He'd mastered the art of removing the covering that offended him with only a tug and a slide of his hand.

'Why are you here?'

She wanted it to be between them as it had been before her sister arrived. She did not want to question how much she wanted him and wanted to please him. But her sister's arrival served to remind her that the world outside always came crashing back in.

'I will not allow this, Ilysa.' He reached down and took hold of her shoulders. 'I will not allow you to leave me even while you still live in my keep.'

'I am not leaving you,' she argued.

'The moment you saw her on my arm and those memories lived once more within you, you began to step back.' Without warning then, he reached down and lifted her in his arms. 'I will not allow it, Ilysa.'

He crossed the chamber to her door, lifted the latch and carried her out into the corridor. She was watching his face, awed that he cared enough to take this step, and did not see her sister standing there, mouth agape as she watched them, until the last moment.

'Sleep well, Lady Lilidh,' Ross said to her as they passed her on the way to his chamber.

She wanted to laugh at the shock on her sister's face, but she leaned her face against his chest as he carried her into his room and placed her there on his large chair. Without a word, he left, returning quickly with the supper tray and metal pot.

'I would not have your sister tell others that I starved you,' he said.

'I do not believe my sister will get the wrong notion of what you were planning, my lord.'

'Damn it, Ilysa! If you continue to refuse to use my name, I will have to find a suitable punishment for that sin of disobedience.'

In spite of the melancholia that had filled her at facing her shame and her past, Ilysa smiled at his irritation. He'd come to her chamber. He'd brought her here. Somehow, she did not think it only to attain satisfaction for his physical needs.

'First, eat. Your stomach growls so loudly, I can hear nothing over its noise.'

Once she lifted the lid, she could not stop herself from eating every spoonful of the stew. Ross sat at the table after circling the chamber and handed her bread already broken in small chunks to sop up the thick sauce. Soon, too soon for her liking, the pot was empty and the bread consumed.

'Do you hear the sounds you make when you enjoy the food you eat?' He stared at her mouth.

'Sometimes, it tastes so delicious, I cannot stop it. After three years of bland food and always being on the edge of hunger, I find it impossible not to appreciate the taste or the plentiful amount of it.'

'You moan that same way when you eat as when my mouth is on your flesh and I am pleasuring you.'

Her body ignited at his words. Her flesh, especially the place between her legs, seemed to remember and crave every flick of his tongue or pull of his mouth as he tasted and touched her in that indecent way. Now, her skin felt tight and hot. The corner of his wicked mouth curved up—he knew well what he was doing to her with just his words.

'The last time I had my mouth on you there—' his

gaze centred on the place that throbbed with need '—you let out this low growling sound that made my cock even harder.'

She squeezed her legs together and the tightness made the aching even more pleasurable.

'Let me hear it now, wife of mine,' he whispered, not moving towards her or doing anything…yet. 'Let me hear the sound of your arousal.'

The sound erupted from deep within her, a moan as his words provoked a response in her body that she did not expect. She felt the thrill of anticipation fill her and shuddered at it. Then, she…growled.

He moved *then*, sliding out of the chair on to his knees and crawling towards her. Stalking her. Wanting her. Her body shook with the power of her arousal as he reached her side. Grabbing the bottom of her chair, he pulled it around until she faced him there. On his knees before her. She waited, panting and needy, for him to lift her gown. Her feet edged out from under it, giving him leave. Instead, he knelt up and slid his hands into her hair, pulling her closer.

He kissed her. Once. Twice. Thrice. Each one longer and more intimate, touching his tongue to hers and making her want more. Then, he slowly released her and sat back on his heels. His hard flesh tented the cloth of his plaid and she wanted to reach for him.

'I want you, Ilysa,' he whispered.

'Have me.' She waited for him to take her.

'I want more than your body. I want you as my wife. I want no more space or doubts or secrets between us.'

A shiver of warning raced through her at his demand.

Something dark threatened them. Something she could not control. Something coming soon.

'I know you live in fear of being humiliated. By having your deformity exposed and shamed, as your sister and Graeme did.' He pushed up to stand and drew her to her feet before him. 'But I want you to trust me and know that would not happen to you. As my wife, I have cherished and cared for you. I *will* protect you, from your enemies, from those who would denigrate you. For this—' He pointed at her arm. 'Or for your hair or any other shortcoming you fear will be uncovered by that she-wolf you call sister or by your father.'

'Ross…' What could she say? 'What is it you want from me?'

'The truth.'

'You ken more than anyone else alive,' she said.

'Tell me how it came to be.' He stepped back and watched her.

'Here? Now?' Frowning, she reached up and touched the sleeve that held her lifeless arm. 'You have seen it.'

'I saw your arm only that first night in your bath when there was so much else I wanted to see. I paid little heed to its appearance then. Your wear the sleeve that makes it more comfortable for you, for us, but hides it from my sight. Other times the lamps are low or we join in the darkness with only the shadows of the fire around us.' At her request. To ease her embarrassment.

He reached out and rubbed his hand down that arm. She felt only the way the cloth of the sleeve pulled on her shoulder and nothing on the flesh itself.

'Why ask me to show you?'

'Because he has seen it.' Ilysa blinked in surprise.

His words were calm, but there was a seething anger just below the surface of them.

'This is about jealousy? Over...*him*?'

'This is about secrets that can be used against me, against us. If an enemy holds knowledge that I do not, it is dangerous, Ilysa.' He let out a loud breath. 'I know your father is playing a larger game here. You being substituted as my bride was no accident.'

'Certainly, it was not,' she said. 'I just do not ken why.'

'Because he kens one of my secrets and plans to use you against me.'

Silence reigned then as the import of his words sank into her thoughts.

'How can he do that? Use me against you?' she asked. 'I am only a MacDonnell in a sea of MacMillans. I have no friends here. I have only what you give me. How could I be used against you?'

'You could tell him the names of every soul who lives here, every place in the keep and castle, even how many warriors we have and if we could survive a prolonged siege.'

'Oh.'

'If your father was my true enemy and not The Campbell and his get, he'd have placed the perfect spy here at Castle Sween.'

'But I am as much prisoner here as I was on Iona or even while at home. Everyone watches me. I have left the keep and village only once and it was on your horse.' She could not help it that the memories of that special day and the repercussions flooded her thoughts. 'If I was his spy, how could I share this knowledge with him?' She gasped and closed her eyes as the answer, or answers, to her question became obvious, even to her.

Brother Kevin, who'd disappeared when Ross was injured.

Lilidh, who'd arrived uninvited, but full of questions.

Even Graeme would have his usefulness in observing and getting reports from the other MacDonnell warriors already here since neither she nor her sister could approach or converse with them openly as a man could.

Opening her eyes, she met the gaze of the man who stood to lose the most because she was unwittingly doing her father's underhand work for him.

In spite of not seeing it before. In spite of never wanting to help him carry out his backstabbing plans. In spite of all that, she was her father's weapon of betrayal.

'You think I do this for him? You think I would help him after everything we…?' She could not finish that. Ilysa saw the truth in his eyes.

'I did suspect exactly that at first,' he admitted.

Ilysa sank on to the chair at his words. His respectful, kind even, acceptance of her that first day. Then, he withdrew from her, keeping his distance, but always watching. She'd noted someone always kept close to her those days, whether in the keep or village. Had Gavina been her gaoler, chosen by her husband to see and hear everything that happened around or with her?

'And now? What do you believe now?'

'I have struggled with the knowledge of how your father works, but I do not believe you willingly help him.'

'What happened to change your mind on it?'

He smiled then, his expression losing its hardness, as he answered her.

'I discovered that I liked you more than I should have.' He shrugged. 'And that was your father's plan all along, Ilysa. Making me like you enough to trust you. Worse, I fell in love with you in spite of kenning the risks of doing so.'

He crouched down before her again.

'You, my love, are my Trojan Horse.'

Chapter Sixteen

Ross knew, as an educated woman, his wife would know of the ancient Greek story of a gift given while hiding the enemy within it. The Trojans had accepted the gift, a huge wooden horse to honour the goddess Athena for desecration of her temple.

That gift had led to Troy's destruction.

As Iain MacDonnell had hoped his frightened, innocent, maimed daughter would lead to Ross and the MacMillans' destruction because he was unfit, too soft, to be chieftain.

'I do not understand.' He hated to see the turmoil showing on her face as she heard the truth. 'How am I dangerous to you?'

'Though 'tis not widely known, my uncle did not wish me to succeed him as chieftain. 'Twas why he pursued marriage—and begetting heirs—with such singlemindedness of purpose.'

'But you are his closest male kin.'

'The son of his brother whom he despised as being too weak to take the high seat from him.' He stood up and retrieved the pitcher of ale and two cups. 'He swore to me he would have a male child to keep me from it.'

'But he did not.'

'Nay, he killed a wife in his efforts, but there was no son.' Ross could remember the sight of Sorcha, pale and ill, lying in the bed, as her lifeblood and that of her unborn child poured out of her. 'He was searching for another bride when the Campbells attacked.'

'You spoke of my sister as a possible bride for him?'

'Aye, but there was some disagreement that ended that discussion.' Was that the reason behind The Mac-Donnell's actions? Had his uncle insulted Ilysa's father in some way? He would never know.

'I do not understand, Ross,' she said. 'Why? Why would you not be considered as his heir?'

'He considered my lack of ruthlessness and brutality a weakness for one who would command after him.' Ross stared off, not able to look at her. 'His method was to instil fear and use it.'

'Like my father.'

'Aye.' There was more, and he would tell her because he wanted her trust. He wanted her love. 'But, the schism between my uncle and I went deeper than that.' He stood then and walked to the hearth. After stirring the remaining embers, he tossed in more wood and stoked it. 'My uncle and I did not agree on who our allies and enemies were. And that some of our elders sided with me made it worse.'

'How does this make me your Trojan Horse?'

'Your father sent you to me and waited to see what happened when he insulted my honour and that of my clan with his deception. If I'd responded as my uncle would have—or as he would have—you'd be imprisoned below, beaten or worse, for being the one who'd lied and carried out the ruse.' He shook his head and smiled. 'So, when you lived and thrived even, your father kenned he was right about me.'

He turned back to the hearth and watched as the flames caught, building into a respectable fire. He did not hear her approach. She slid her arm around his waist and leaned her head against his back.

'Why did you not respond like my father or your uncle would? Most men would have,' she said.

'I hated the sight of the fear in your eyes when I approached you. When you showed some sign of boldness and then crumpled to the floor waiting for my fists to land, it sickened me.'

'So, you are a lesser man because you stay your hand and do not punish those who have committed no insult against you?'

'Your father, thanks to at least Brother Kevin, kens that I do not react in anger. I think he waited for me to strike you down so he could raise his might against me and mine. When I accepted you, and his gold, instead of raging and threatening, he discovered my weakness. And the daughter he thought worthless and used as a way to test and taunt me yet lives. Worse, I have discovered her value and raised no complaints about having her as my wife.'

He turned, drawing her around until he could wrap her in his embrace. It felt right to hold her.

'You put your kin and kith before your own safety and benefit, Ross. You stayed your hand to ready your people for the danger they face. To protect them. To save them. What better chieftain can you be but one who answers first to his people?'

He leaned down and rested his cheek against her hair.

'I have one more confession, love,' he whispered. 'I kept you because I wanted you. I saw the glimmer of intelligence and wit and willingness to work and kindness and I wanted you.'

'And now that you have met my sister, you've realised that I saved you from her?' He held her and laughed.

'Did Dougal tell you that?' She shook her head. 'Aye, I forgot to mention your sense of merriment. I kept you for that, too—for your ability to make me laugh.'

She stepped back out of his embrace and the serious expression made him allow her to move away. He knew what she was doing. She was going to show herself to him in a way she'd not done before. She would gift him with herself.

Ilysa walked over in front of the hearth and faced him. She released her grip on her shawl and tossed it towards the bed. With shaking fingers, she untied the sleeve and pulled it down. He reached out to help, but she shook her head. Her next target was the ties of her gown which he only now realised were on the front of it rather than the back. Another practical accommodation that made her less reliant on others to dress. Pushing the edges over her shoulders, she let it fall and stepped out of it.

Whether she knew it or not, the shift hid little from his sight since the flames outlined her figure. Her bad arm hung at her side as she loosened the ribbon that held the flimsy fabric in place. He knew every inch of her body, including what she would show him now, but this would be of her own choice. She would expose her ultimate weakness to him, trusting him not to reject her. Though he had seen her arm that first night as he'd washed her, the sight of her lovely breasts and the darker shadow of the delights at the junction of her thighs had truly held his attention.

And the sounds of arousal that she'd uttered had distracted him and made him want to rush his task to completion.

'Tell me how…' He moved again until he was only inches from her, shifting to her left side.

'An accident.' Her voice quivered and somehow he knew it was not the truth, or at least not the full truth.

'Was your father involved?' Her gaze flitted to him for a moment before she stared away. 'Bastard,' he whispered under his breath. She'd heard him for she sucked in a breath that sounded like a sob. 'Steady on now, my love,' he said. She inhaled and let it out slowly and with a nod she explained.

'I had about ten years when he gifted my sister with a horse. It was a beautiful thing, full of life, and she had an easy disposition.' A smile lightened her face as she thought on the horse. 'I loved the horse as though she was mine. My sister was content with me taking care of her because she did not wish to be "mired in the horse's muck" as she'd say.'

'Knowing Lilidh now, that does not surprise me.'

'One day, I rode the horse out along the sea. It was…a feeling I cannot even describe to you.'

'Joy?'

'Ah, aye. Joy.' A sigh escaped from her. 'I returned

to the stables to find everyone and everything in an up-roar over Lilidh's missing horse.'

'You'd left without permission?'

'Aye. I was not permitted to leave the keep alone then. My father was furious—first at thinking the horse had somehow been stolen and then at my boldness for taking the horse on my own.'

Now he had to gird his loins as he listened to her words.

'He grabbed my arm and wrenched me from the horse, throwing me to the ground. He'd used so much force he'd pulled my arm free from the shoulder.' She swallowed again and again, but Ross just waited. 'He yelled out insults and threats at me, raging about my disobedience. The horse was young and his ranting ter-rified her. She shifted and reared up and landed on my shoulder.'

He could see that she was remembering every mo-ment of it again as she told him. He did not want her to suffer. It had been wrong of him to force her to tell him.

'Ilysa, pray, stop,' he said. 'I should not have asked you to speak of it.'

'I want you to understand,' she said. 'I do not wish Graeme and my sister and others in my family to have knowledge you do not.' As she lifted her hand to give the final tug on the ribbon, *she* reassured *him*. 'It does not pain me now. Well, sometimes when bad storms are rolling in, it aches in some few places. But mostly, I can't feel it.'

A moment later, she stood before him and, though much tempted to look on her beauty, he instead looked on that part of her she thought her disgrace. Ross stepped closer, careful not to move his hands towards her. He saw the tears gathering in her eyes and he wanted to kiss them away, but she was not ready for that. Not yet.

Because her arm bone was not in the shoulder joint when the horse's hooves had landed on her, it would never fit back into place. So, her arm hung lower and back from where it should. Scars crossed the area, thick, rough patches of skin that had not healed well. Even now, even with the light illuminating it, her arm was not the worst he'd seen. Truly, most injuries that could compare to hers involved men suffering them in battle and were far more disfiguring. Ross moved his gaze lower where the bone below her elbow was uneven and her arm appeared to be turned in towards her body in an awkward position.

'And this?' he asked. 'Did the horse do that as well?'

'Nay, that was another accident about two years later.'

'Another accident that seems like a purposeful act?' A light nod was her reply. 'Your father again, damn his soul?'

'My sister.'

'Sister?'

'I was sitting on a bench at supper and Lilidh lost her bearings and fell on to me. I usually made certain to keep my arm tucked next to me when I sat, but it was not. She landed on it. The cracking sound was the only way I kenned it had broken.

'You just growled, Husband.' He didn't realise what he'd done, but she laughed. She laughed. In spite of her revelations to him, she laughed.

'I did?'

'Aye.'

'I do not like your family, Ilysa. I want Lilidh gone. And that man gone. And your father's men gone.'

'Even as you speak, you growl.' She reached out and touched his chest. 'The wounds are years old and I have learned to live past it, Ross.'

'I wish I could change it, heal it, for you. Or at least avenge you.'

'What good would that do? For you or your clan or even for me? Worry not over it.'

Those were not the words he wanted to hear. She deserved vengeance. He took the chance then of reaching out and touching her arm. From the damaged shoulder down past her elbow and following the curved bone to her hand, he used a gentle touch. Even with the softest caress, she did not react to it.

'So, nothing?' he asked. At the shake of her head, he placed his mouth on her skin and kissed her shoulder. 'Nothing?' Another shake. He followed the same path his finger had traced, lifting her hand and holding her arm steady until she did shiver. 'Ah! There?'

''Tis the strangest thing,' she said. 'My skin, my arm, does not feel your touch or your mouth, but my body kens the excitement of your kisses and aches for them.'

'Just tell me what you want, my love. If I cannot give you pleasure on your arm, tell me where you wish it.' He kissed her shoulder once more, finding the place where sensation began and biting it gently.

'Here.' She pointed to the curve of her neck, a spot where he'd left a love mark on previous nights. He pressed his mouth there, suckling the sensitive skin until her body arched.

'And here,' she whispered as she touched the tight tip of her breast. One of his favourite places to taste, he pulled the aroused, rose-coloured tip into his mouth and nipped at it with his teeth.

Her legs gave way and he caught her in his arms and carried her to their bed. As she leaned back, he placed her arm to the side carefully and then waited for her next request.

The woman who had been confident and bold in their pleasure before her sister arrived was reappearing now. The one who demanded his attention and who revelled in their intimacies. As he waited, Ross loosened his belt, dropped his plaid and pulled the shirt over his head. He reached down and took his cock in hand, encircled it with his finger and thumb and stroked his growing length as she watched.

Her hips rose even as her head fell back. And the wondrous moan made him harder. Stepping closer, he eased her legs apart and hoped she would invite him in. Her legs shifted, exposing the place he wanted to be.

'Here,' she said, her voice husky with need now. Her hand slid down and she touched herself, stroking deep in the folds even as he stroked himself. 'Here.'

He fell to his knees, pulled her hips to the edge of the bed and gave her what she wanted.

It was some time before either of them could speak… or move.

When he did, Ross rolled to his back and eased away from her sleeping form. After the hours of exploring each other and trying out ways to drive each other mad with need and then satisfaction, he was too awake to sleep. He'd lost track of how many times they'd joined or touched or just held each other in the quiet of the night.

Now, he waited for the arrival of his spies, men who were overdue to return from Islay and from the east where Fergus now defended their kin. From messages sent and received, it did indeed seem that the Campbells had divided their forces to conquer and reclaim their ancestral lands.

Since the MacMillans were granted Sween and the surrounding lands by the King after Alexander Campbell massacred most of their clan, Ross was honour-bound to protect their claim—and his people. With Ilysa at his side, his clan would prosper and grow. In but a few days, they would make their stand, defend their place here and then he could finally get around to the life he'd never planned. With the wife he'd not expected.

And a love he'd never thought to find.

The servants who entered carrying trays and pitchers and buckets of water and more the next morning all gave their best efforts not to stare at the bed where his wife still slept. As soon as one noticed, all of them moved quietly and quickly and were gone before Ilysa even stirred.

'Good morn, my lord,' she said. She stretched out her body then, disappearing briefly under the bedcovers before pushing them away from her face.

He played servant to her, helping her with the clothes Gavina had brought earlier for her. Any hesitation seemed gone as they ate in a companionable silence. She did not make any noises of appreciation while tasting the porridge or other foods provided for them. After her unrestrained response last night, Ross knew he would never get out of the chamber if she did.

'What will you do today?' she asked. She placed her spoon in the empty bowl.

'We're finishing up the preparations in the village. And you?'

'Gillean assures me we have everything where it needs to be when…' She stopped and cleared her throat. 'The attack comes.'

'I do not want you to stray far from the keep now. If possible, stay within the walls.'

'But I need to see Morag,' she said. 'I want to move several of the older men and women inside…before the danger arrives.'

'And you may—from within the walls.' Ross stood. 'Sadly, I must ask you to keep your sister close to you, unless she is departing?'

'Sadly not,' she said. 'Will you order Graeme to remain within as well?' He leaned down and kissed her.

'As a chieftain extending hospitality, I must try to keep him safe.' He picked up his sword and dagger and placed them in the scabbard on his belt. 'If it was my decision alone, I would encourage him to ramble about in the village.'

Her laugh, a reluctant one, was a promising sign.

'Give me your vow that you will not allow your sister to ruin your good spirits.' He held out his hand to her and she took it, standing before him. 'I think that last night, with its truths shared, has put us back on a common path. Do not allow her, or him, or anyone to tell you that you have no place here. Or that I do not want you at my side.' He kissed her forehead and stepped back.

'I will obey, my lord. As a good wife does.' There it was—the humour was back in her tone.

'Gag and bind her if you must, to prevent her interference, Wife. But stay within.'

He left, seeking out Munro. The lateness of their men concerned him. They'd sent several out over a few days to seek the Campbells and to watch The MacDonnell—Ross did not trust either. He would not doubt that Iain MacDonnell was offering help with one hand while his other sought ways to undermine Ross's control.

Soon. Soon now 'twould be time to deal with both of them and he felt the surge of anticipation rushing through his veins.

Soon.

His spies returned later that day and the news they brought ruined any chance he'd thought he had with Ilysa. As much as he wanted to believe she was an innocent pawn of her father, his spies reported some damning news. Before he could confront her, the attack began.

Chapter Seventeen

Feelings ran high that day as word passed like a wild wind through the keep and village that their foes were coming. As Ross had asked, Ilysa remained within the walls and was able to ignore most of Lilidh's nips and jabs. Until her sister summoned Graeme to join them for the noon meal.

For the first time in her life, Ilysa lost her temper and left them sitting and staring after her. She almost faltered, but caught the supportive glances from the servants and those at table for her words, as angry and rude as they were. Sadly, Ross was not there to witness her new-found resolve.

Midday had passed when the call came that the attack was underway. She nodded at Gavina to gather their supplies and began to head below, as they'd planned and practised the last time. But in her gut she understood that this one was no warning—this would be to destroy them. To destroy everyone she'd come to care about. To kill Ross—the man, the husband, she loved.

Just before she reached the stairway leading to the kitchen, a guard, several of them, surrounded her.

'Have you come to help?' she asked. Ross must have assigned them to keep her from doing anything foolish—like leaving the keep. 'I have no need yet, but come along.' She took a step towards the doorway, but they did not move from her path.

'My lady,' one said. 'You must come with us.'

When Gavina tried to ask their purpose, one of them pushed her maid aside as another took hold of Ilysa's arm.

'What are you doing? Where are you taking me?' she asked. When the men would not slow or stop, she called over her shoulder to the woman. 'Gavina, we did not get the elderly into the keep yet! Send word!'

Though they were careful not to hurt her, they would not be talked out of their intent. 'I pray you, release me! There is much to do!'

With one in front, one pulling her along by her arm and the two more that followed, she could do nothing but acquiesce. They walked to her chamber and stopped. The man in front opened her door and stepped within. He pulled the door open and nodded to the others.

'Put her inside.'

With a push that had her almost losing her footing, the guard tossed her inside. Before she could ask another question or protest, the door slammed shut. Ilysa ran to it and tried to lift the latch to no avail.

'Why are you doing this?' she yelled. Banging on the door, she tried again. 'Let me out! We are under attack!'

She continued even as the sounds of battle grew louder outside. Rushing to the window, she opened one of the wooden shutters and peered out. Her chamber faced the north and the village. As she watched, people from the village were still running towards the gates… and safety. The warriors had formed as they planned, but from this height she could see that several villagers would not make it.

She had not seen to moving them into the keep as she'd planned to do this day. Now, they would be caught in the onslaught of the attack and be killed, whether by the enemy or simply being in the midst of it all. She must do something. They must not die because she'd failed in her duty.

Ilysa struggled to pull a stool over to the window and to open the other shutter. Climbing on the stool, she leaned out of the window as best she could to gain the attention of…someone. But the din of fighting, as Munro and others shouted orders, and the fierce noise of battle made it impossible for anyone to hear her.

She climbed down and ran to the door, banging until her hand could not and then kicking the wooden barrier to gain someone's attention. Finally, the latch was lifted and the door opened—the guard who had seized her first stepped inside even while holding the door so she could not get past. She could see another behind him.

'My lady, you must remain here.'

'Did my husband order this?' she demanded. Then, understanding time was critical if she wanted to save lives, she shook her head. 'I must get word to my husband.'

''Tis not possible, Lady.'

Seeing their hardened faces and the tension in their bodies as they now held swords, she knew they'd been given these orders and would not budge. Not without serious reasons—ones that would stand up when their commander demanded it. Only then did she recognise the one who'd stood back and not touched her.

'Angus? That is you!' she said. This young man was Morag's grandson for she'd seen him at his grandmother's cottage helping her with the heavier tasks. 'I must get word to my husband. There are still villagers who will not make it to the gates before they close. The elderly who I was supposed to bring inside. I pray you, tell him now.'

The guards, Angus and the others, glanced at each other and then away, clearly not willing to take such a message. She tried to come up with reasons they should help her, but the ever-increasing roar of battle scattered her wits. She slid to the floor and sobbed, knowing those lives would be on her soul.

'They will be slaughtered where they stand,' she cried.

A moment passed before she heard them whispering. Rubbing the tears from her eyes, she noticed the oldest guard was the one arguing with the others. Then, he nodded at Angus who ran down the corridor.

'I witnessed their chieftain's attack all those years ago. He was without mercy or control and slaughtered relentlessly, not caring if he killed man, woman or bairn,' he said.

The one in charge pulled the door closed quietly.

Then, Ilysa did the only thing she could while being kept here as the fighting raged outside—she prayed. It took less effort than she'd thought to climb up on her knees and begin the prayers she'd recited count-

less times over the last three years. Even lacking the prayer beads that aided her in keeping account of the routine of prayers, she continued. Time passed and still the fighting went on.

Had the children made it to safety? Did their preparations aid in the fight? Was Ross alive? With each new concern, she began another round of the prayers, beginning and ending with intercessions for the survival of those trying to protect themselves and for the innocents caught between enemies. And, she added a prayer for forgiveness—for her sins of failing those who needed her. Who would prevail this day? How many would die?

Would she ever have the chance to tell Ross of her love?

Ross was near the gates, about to call for closing them, when the guard approached. This attack was not a foray to test them. This one was to destroy them and his warriors fought knowing that. The young man called to him and he rushed closer. Munro was at his side before the guard could speak.

'You are supposed to be inside the keep,' Munro yelled in between directing others to where they were needed. 'With the Lady.' Ross clenched his jaws at the mention of her.

'My lord!' The guard pushed closer to be heard. 'The Lady sent me with a message for you.'

Munro held him back, fully aware of what information the spies had brought back—that his wife was a willing participant in her father's plans. That she had passed along knowledge of their preparations through Kevin and that her sister's arrival was a furtherance of her father's own designs on taking control of Castle Sween in spite of the Campbells' plans.

'Get back to your post!' Munro ordered, even as he repositioned himself between Ross and the gate.

'The Lady said there are some villagers left behind, my lord.' The guard struggled to stay close as waves of people ran through into the yard. 'She said the ones she had not brought in, my lord.'

Ross leaned his head back and cursed his anger to the sky. A sky filling with the black smoke of cottage and crops burning beyond the walls. The gate was moments away from closing. He did not want to think of her. It was bad enough that it was her suggestions that had already saved lives.

He did not want to do as she asked. But, hell, he, they, had implemented some of her tactics and, damn it, they'd worked.

He did not...

Want his people to die.

'I need four men,' he called out to Munro.

'Ross, the gate is closing!' Munro yelled back.

Ross started to run for the gate, knowing his commander would follow his orders. By the time he'd stepped out of the wall's protections, those men were at his back. Searching for a way to find the missing villagers, Ross led them down a path that would miss most of the fighting. They might have little chance to return un-accosted, but at least this one would get them to the far side of the village quicker than fighting their way through the Campbells.

Only as they reached the end of the path did they find the three—an old man and two women hiding behind a half-built wall. As they turned to return to the keep, they were attacked. One of his men was struck down from behind before they made it back to the path. Ross managed to kill the one who'd done it but, in focusing his attention on bringing along one of the women, he hadn't even felt the Campbell blade that slashed down his arm. Ignoring it, he hurried them along and only when the gate was in sight did he chance a look up at Ilysa's window.

Why did she send word to him? Why did she bother? What vexed him the most was that she'd played her part so well he had believed her story.

Screams from nearby had him running faster and calling out to those ahead of him. As he shoved the man and women behind him towards the guards protecting the gate, Ross turned to make a stand.

It was the last time he had the luxury of thinking about anything, or anyone, for a long time. He and Munro and his warriors used their opportunity of being outside the walls to force the Campbells back. And as he'd suspected, allowing his sword to speak for him felt so satisfying.

By the time full dark fell on Castle Sween, the Campbells left alive had fled. It took hours to clear away the worst of the destruction and to see to those who'd been wounded or died. And then hours more to see to the survivors among his clan.

The pale light of the rising sun met him as he finally returned to the keep. He'd washed most of the gore and blood off in a trough of water in the yard before entering and climbing the stairs to his chamber.

He nodded to the guard standing before her door as he fought a battle of another kind within himself. His first thought when they'd routed their enemies was to celebrate all their work with…her. Now, he could barely think of her without pain tearing through him. In spite of his welcoming in one who'd contributed to their near downfall, most of his people had survived.

As he reached his chamber and collapsed in the chair, he could only thank the Almighty that the results had not been worse. More Campbells had been killed this time and would lower the number of those able to fight against them again. That gave him some comfort in the midst of his grief over too many MacMillan deaths.

He heard the commotion in the corridor and knew that the guards were bringing Lady Lilidh to her sister's chambers. He would rather deal with both of them at the same time, while leaving the MacLean man down in the cell below. Ross would deal with him later and for different reasons now than he'd thought he would need to.

Ross opened the cupboard in the corner and found the stone jug stored there from his uncle's time. He pulled the stopper and swallowed several mouthfuls of the powerful *uisge beatha* his uncle had favoured. The burn of the first one was eased by his second pull on the jug. By the third swallow it did not even hit his stomach with the same searing punch as the first. But the warmth of it flooded his blood by the time he stoppered the jug and put it back. Some was good, but more than that might loosen his restraint. As he removed his bloody shirt and plaid and pulled on clean garments, he prepared to do what he'd advised Ilysa to—harden his heart.

Ilysa had slept little all night. Once she heard the cries of the fighting diminish, she'd moved from the floor to the chair.

When it was quiet outside, she dared a look out of the window. The sun was setting so she could not see very far, but she did see the bodies. Too many. Too many lay strewn in the yard and through the village which seemed to be the attack's main path.

She could see burned cottages and buildings in the village. The blackened hulls of several boats—whether Campbell or MacMillan she knew not—lay beached on the shore of the loch.

The one thing, the one person, she could not see was Ross. As she searched, the skies grew darker and she was unable to identify people, for they became shapes moving in the growing darkness. Hours ago, she'd given up waiting for word or for him and had sat in the chair, expecting someone to tell her why she'd been dragged here and left. Why she was locked in her chamber when she had never before been a prisoner.

As the sun rose, she heard heavy footsteps coming closer down the corridor. They stopped and she held her breath, hoping and praying that Ross was here. The steps moved on and, when she pressed her ear to the door, she heard Ross's chamber door slam shut. She raised her fist to bang on the door, but her hand was swollen and abraded from attempting to get out or get someone to come in. Her throat burned from screaming and crying and praying.

A short while later, another's screams echoed outside her chamber and it sounded like her sister's. She stood up and waited as a scuffle outside her door led to someone landing hard against the wood and then a spate of curses. A man's voice yelled them, so it was clear her sister had annoyed someone. When the door opened, her sister entered with help from the guards. Still cursing, but under his breath now, the guard involved rubbed his cheek as he turned to leave.

Lilidh, for her part in the uproar, gave a contemptuous glance at the door before walking over and climbing on Ilysa's bed. Stretching herself out, she let out a sigh.

'I did not sleep a wink all night, Sister,' she said.

'I should think not.' Ilysa's voice was rough and her throat hurt when she spoke.

Lilidh gifted her with a sharp look before rolling over several times *on Ilysa's bed.* Ilysa walked to the table and poured the last bit of ale into her cup. Taking a sip, she sat in her chair and leaned her head back.

'Where have you been, Lilidh?'

'I was put in a small chamber on the floor below this one. A guest chamber, but smaller than the one I'd been given on my arrival.' She rolled once more. 'Your bed is much more comfortable.'

Leaning up on her elbows, Lilidh finally paid heed to Ilysa, the chamber and mayhap the grim expression her sister wore. Or mayhap it was her swollen eyes that finally drew her sister's attention? Whatever caused it mattered not, but finally her sister, her self-centred sister, took notice of something that was not herself.

'What happened to you?' she asked. Sitting up on the bed and letting her feet dangle over the side, she squinted at Ilysa. 'You look terribly drawn, Sister. Did he finally beat you for disobedience?'

Before she could respond, *he* entered.

She drank in the sight of him—alive, terribly pale, forbidding and clenching his fists. Alive. Praise the Almighty, he was alive. Ilysa pushed out of the chair and ran to him, only stopping at the last possible moment because of the grimace he wore.

'Are you injured?' she whispered.

He did not answer her. Instead, his grimace turned into something else. An expression she'd not seen before on his face and wished she was not seeing it now.

Loathing.

Ilysa reeled back and nearly fell. She would have if he'd not grabbed her at the last moment. He set her aright and released her immediately as if touching her repelled him now.

'What have I done?'

The tension grew and when her sister opened her mouth to say something, he silenced her with his glare. Turning that steely look on her, he made the accusation she wished he had not.

'Nothing more than being your father's daughter.'

She shuddered at his words. She was not that except in name only. He had accepted that before this. His sister's laugh, inappropriate and harsh, sickened her.

'We are what we are, my lord,' Lilidh said.

'Ross, what has happened? You said on yester morn that—'

'That was before my men returned.'

'Your spies, my lord?' Lilidh asked.

'Your father underestimated me if he thought I would accept his deception without finding out more.' Ross stared at her now. 'So, aye, spies were sent just as he sent them here.' When his gaze moved between them and he crossed his arms over his chest, Ilysa's heart tore. He thought she was a spy for her father.

'Ross, I did not…' She stopped. That expression of loathing told her he would not believe her now.

She would have said more but Munro entered, along with a man she did not recognise. But Lilidh gasped at his entry.

'My lady,' Munro said quietly with a nod. Strange that the gruff commander was the only one showing her courtesy now. 'This is Gowan.'

'I thought your name was Seumas.' Lilidh gasped, establishing that she knew this man. And more than simply in passing, from her expression.

'Gowan,' Ross repeated. 'Tell them what you discovered in your time on Islay.' He walked away then, choosing to stare out of the window that remained open.

'The MacDonnell is not helping us for any alliance, my lord. As I told ye, he wants Sween and these lands.'

'Ross, we—' Ross held up his hand to stop Ilysa's words.

'Not now. Continue, Gowan.'

'Yer marriage is the first step,' the man said. He directed his words at Ross's back and would not meet her gaze. 'Pretending to help you, us, against The Campbell's plans was part of it.'

'Ross—'

'Lady, hold your tongue and let him have his say,' he ordered, without turning to face her.

'When do I have mine?'

He was in front of her in the time it took to exhale. So close and so tall, she needed to lean back to meet his gaze where pure fury stared back at her.

'Oh, Lady, you have had enough to say.' He forced the words out around clenched teeth. 'More than enough, I think.' He stepped back then and put half the chamber's distance between them. 'Go on, Gowan,' he said, turning back to the window.

Only as she looked back at the spy did she notice that Munro had moved closer as well. Was Ross angry enough to harm her? She'd always thought he would never, he'd promised he would never, but now? He'd lost faith in her. In them. He believed her part of her father's schemes. The desolate sound escaped before she could stop it.

'Lady? Are you ill?' Munro, not Ross, asked.

Ilysa stumbled back and sat down hard on the chair. Though Munro reached out to assist her, this time Ross did not bother. He remained as far away as he could get.

'Gowan.'

'Aye, m-m-my lord,' the man stuttered as he began. 'His plan was to send warriors here whom you thought were to defend us, but they were to wait until the attack and kill you. In the confusion of battle, there would be no way to tell if it were anyone but the Campbells who did it.'

'Ross!' she cried out. 'Nay, I would never help him harm you!' She stood then and rushed to his side. Even as he held her away, she would not quiet. 'I played no part in his deception or in his plan. You must believe me!' When she could not get him to look at her, she shook her head. 'You must believe me,' she whispered.

She walked away, looking at each one listening and trying to sort out the words that would convince him of her truth. The smug expression on her sister's face terrified Ilysa. There was so much more going on here than she'd been told or knew and her sister was at the heart of it. So, she waited for the worst, for surely it must be coming.

Chapter Eighteen

The *uisge beatha* had been a bad idea.

The strong brew rolled in his empty stomach and threatened to force its way back out. He'd heard all the man had to say on his return to Sween. Well, he'd heard most of it before walking out. Munro had told him the rest.

Yet she'd lain in his arms and lied in word and deed. As for his proclamation to her and his vows, none of them mattered to her. She was a player on the stage built and directed by her father.

Once she'd backed away, he nodded at his man. Before Gowan could begin again, she interrupted once more.

'Ross, think about this. If you are dead, I have no claim, no hold on this castle or these lands. They would go to your brother as your heir.'

The smile he showed her was not in mirth, but irony. He nodded to Gowan and turned back to the window.

'The Lady said—' Gowan continued '—Lady Lilidh, that is, said she taught Lady Ilysa what she needed to do so my lord would return to her bed. To get his heir on her.'

The only sound, above Ilysa's breathing, was a soft laugh from Lilidh. He would see to her later.

'An heir who would have claim,' Ross said. He measured his words carefully, not allowing his temper free. 'An heir who would need a guardian, a powerful one to hold on to it in these dangerous times. As my brother now does for our kin.' He did turn then to face her. He wanted to see her face when she tried to deny this. 'So, have you been successful in your endeavours? Are you breeding, Wife?'

It was worse than seeing the fear in her eyes that first time. No matter how many times he told himself he would not believe her the innocent she claimed to be, seeing her lose every bit of colour in her face and hearing her choke in distress cut him to the bone. And, damn her, she reached up and tugged her shawl tighter around her shoulder and bad arm as she did when afraid or worried. Now though, he pushed every feeling she'd brought about in these last weeks away and refused to relent into the softness that had led them to this.

The lack of ruthlessness that had him appealing to their enemy and accepting his agreement to an alliance. The lack of strategy that let their enemy close enough to harm them all. The attempts to rule his clan with a lighter grasp than his uncle.

In the end, his uncle had been correct. And his clan had paid a steep price for it, even if he was still alive.

It would not happen again.

'Answer me. Are you with child?'

'A child?'

As she stood there, her eyes darting back and forth across the chambers, tugging on her shawl and shaking her head, he thought she resembled a frightened animal when caught in a predator's sights. Her breathing became erratic as she sucked in big gulps of air and let little out. Shudders racked her body and for a moment he thought she would faint.

'Carrying a child? I do not ken. Is it possible?'

'Come now, Sister,' Lilidh said, speaking for the first time since his arrival in the chamber. 'You can tell him now.'

'Tell him what, Lilidh?' The shuddering made her voice shake. 'I…'

'We spoke of how it would happen. You were to take his seed as often—' Ross did not realise he'd crossed the chamber and taken her by the throat until Munro shook him to let go. The lady coughed and then smiled at him and tempted death whether she knew it or not. 'Ilysa told me her courses had ended a fortnight before she returned home from the nunnery.'

He could not calculate the days or weeks or the timing of when it could have happened. He knew only that Ilysa had lain with no other man since her arrival here and that she had been innocent *in that way* when they wed. So, any child was his. Where that thought had given him joy and hope when he'd considered their future together a short time ago, now it caused the stabbing pain of bitterness in his gut.

'Sit down before you fall down, Ilysa.' His rough tone startled her, but she sat. He turned away, not wanting to look on her or speak more.

There was more that Gowan could tell them, having

shared the bed of not only Lilidh's maid but also of the lady herself—that was part of the 'more' that Ross had already heard. Ross motioned for him to leave. A guard arrived just as Gowan left and Munro walked to him, to get whatever message he brought. Ross looked away from Ilysa and waited for whatever news was coming.

There was so much to do this day—bury the dead, find the others who'd spied on them, decide what to do about the daughters of The MacDonnell. Oh, he knew what he must do about them, but the doing of it needed planning.

And there was Fergus to worry over. He'd sent word to his brother, but no messengers had returned yet with news of their sister's arrival from the abbey or the situation at Castle Barron. Munro called his name and drew him over with a tilt of his head.

'Calum Campbell has sent word.'

'He survived, then?' Ross had hoped the father or son, or both, would have perished in the battles—it would have made things easier. 'What news?' He leaned down so the guard's words would not be overheard by the women. Munro asked a few questions and waited on Ross's further instructions.

'So, the son yet lives as does his father,' Ross said.

'He asks to meet under sign of truce,' Munro said.

'He lost,' Ross said. 'What can there be to discuss?'

'His dead and injured, my lord,' the guard said. 'He mentioned wanting his dead.'

That was not such an unusual request—to collect the dead for burial or to see to it where they fell. The Church required it of warring clans—one thing they could demand since they could not stop the clans from fighting each other. Father Liam had shriven his men before the attack and had blessed their dead before nightfall.

'Very well,' he said.

'You do not trust him, do you, Ross?' Munro asked as the guard stepped away.

'Nay, but I will hear what he has to say. Tell Dougal and get some men to accompany me.'

'I should go.'

'Nay. I want you here should anything go wrong.' Ross closed his eyes and shook his head. 'If anything goes wrong, the castle is prepared for a siege. Pull all the warriors inside and close the gates, even against a supposed ally. Open them only to my brother.'

'And the Lady? Ladies?'

'She could be carrying my heir, so keep her safe until her condition is kenned.'

'You believe that she-devil over your wife?' Ross truly did not know what he believed and did not wish to speak of it. 'Even kenning that Gowan thought she boasted of things not true to make her seem more important?'

Ross pushed away any doubts in his path right now, for the security of those who depended on him.

'Send word back I will be there at midday and make the arrangements.'

Munro could be counted on to prepare for all contingencies and to choose those who would go with him. Once he left, Ross turned back to the women. Damn her, Ilysa looked so small and vulnerable in that chair. She sank deeply into the cushions and watched him with suspicion as he approached.

'I have matters to see to,' he said. 'Arrangements will be made to move you to a place where you can wait until we learn...if your plan succeeded. Your sister will accompany you there.'

He looked over to find her sitting with her eyes closed as she clutched the damn edge of that damned woollen wrap around her shoulders as if it would save her.

'I do not stand with my father, Ross.' Her voice was so low he barely could make out her words. He did not answer her. She sighed. 'What will happen now?'

'If you are carrying, then I will have an unexpected heir from my unwanted wife. And you will be sent back to the nunnery on Iona until the bairn's birth.'

'And the child?' Her voice weakened with each question and, damn him, he noticed.

'If there is one, I will see to raising the child and you will go wherever you wish after the birth.' He forced the words out in the harshest tone he could manage. Cruelty like this was not in his nature, but it seemed the only thing Iain MacDonnell's offspring understood. He finished it. 'If there is no child, you will be set aside and returned to your father. He probably has other plans in mind for you.'

She recoiled from his words as though he'd struck her. He turned and left, but not before hearing the sound of Lilidh's taunting soft laughter and then Ilysa's gagging and retching. The battle to walk away was a fierce one within himself, yet one he won. As he passed the guards waiting in the corridor, he faltered.

'Send for Gavina,' he said. 'Tell her to see to her Lady.'

Angry at his concession, angry at his inability to ignore her discomfort and angry at everything, he strode down to break his own fast before seeking out Munro.

There was nothing left in her belly to expel. She'd not eaten at all since... Well, since whenever she'd eaten last. No matter that, her body continued to heave until only bile came forth. She remained there, kneeling next to the chamber pot, and still trying to sort it all out. Just when she thought it might end, her stomach seized and she was forced low once more.

Gavina did not arrive as a meek servant would. Nay, she entered like an avenging angel, shoving the door open and letting it slam against the wall. The guard tried to stop her. That did not work. Ilysa would have smiled if she had not felt so wretched.

'My lady, ye look horrid,' the maid said. 'Come now, get off the floor.' Gavina reached over to help her up when the next wave struck. Her reassuring hand holding Ilysa's head up and smoothing her hair back eased the discomfort of it all. When her body paused, Gavina stepped away and came back with a cup and a cloth. 'Rinse yer mouth out and wipe yer face with this.'

A short time later, Ilysa finally let Gavina help her to her feet. But when they turned around, Lilidh still lounged on the bed and showed no sign of giving up her comfortable place. And Ilysa had not the strength to argue.

'The chair, Gavina,' she said.

'Here now, Lady,' the maid said to her sister. 'Ye get off that bed or I will see it done.' Whether Gavina was jesting or not, her sister moved faster than Ilysa thought possible and Gavina led her to it. 'Ye have not slept, have ye, my lady?'

'Nay.'

'Not with the battle or whatever is between ye and yer husband.' The woman managed to get her shawl, shoes and stockings off and manoeuvre her on to the bed before Ilysa knew what was happening. 'No wonder yer stomach is rebelling.'

'Her stomach is rebelling because she is breeding,' Lilidh said, interrupting them.

'Is it true, my lady? A bairn?' Gavina stared and then smiled. 'Yer husband must be happy.'

'I ken not,' Ilysa admitted. 'I have not always had regular courses.' The tears threatened then. 'And happy my husband is not.'

'Aye, that can happen many times. But ye have not bled since ye arrived here.'

'As I said,' her sister added.

'My lady,' Gavina whispered, after glancing over her shoulder at Lilidh. 'May I?'

Ilysa was too exhausted and empty in body, heart and soul to listen to or deal with her sister. She nodded.

Gavina strode to the door, called in one of the guards and gave him instructions. If the man was going to argue, he looked across the chamber at her and then nodded. Without another word, he entered, took Lilidh by the arm and tugged her from the chamber.

'Have a care now, Gavina. You should not anger your lord,' Ilysa warned.

'He is the one who summoned me here, so I would not worry over that, my lady.' Gavina tossed another blanket, thick and warm, over her and Ilysa felt the need to sleep pulling her down.

Mayhap she would wake and discover that she'd had a days-long nightmare and none of it had happened after all? Mayhap she'd dreamt the turmoil and it would be gone?

Sounds and colours and faces filled her dreams, but a growing darkness kept her from a meaningful rest.

When she opened her eyes, it was to confusion. Lilidh sat in one chair, obviously not kept away for long, glaring openly at Gavina who sat in the other. Her maid sewed some garment while her sister continued doing naught but staring at the servant.

'How long have I slept?' she said, drawing their attention.

'A few hours, my lady,' Gavina said. Putting her sewing to the side, the maid gathered a few items before approaching the bed. 'How do ye fare?'

Ilysa lay quietly without moving for a few moments and noticed there was no pain or need to empty her belly. The worst of her exhaustion had been eased by the sleep, though she felt as though she needed another full night of it.

'I am better, Gavina.'

'My lady, if ye would take a sip or two of this concoction, ye may recover even faster.'

Sister Agnes had created a number of potions and tinctures to treat this or that for the residents of Iona. After having taken several of them, Ilysa was now prepared for the worst and was pleased when it tasted delicious.

''Twill ease yer stomach ills, my lady. Only a bit of it until we see if it works for ye.'

The woman took the cup and helped her to sit up, watching her closely as she did so. Once she was up and the bedcovers and blankets were sorted and smoothed, Gavina held out a crust of bread.

'If ye feel the need for something, this should be easiest on yer belly.'

The snorts and loud sighs across the chamber reminded Ilysa that her sister was there and made it clear she yet had things to say. Though she might be somewhat recovered from the bout of stomach distress, she knew she did not have the patience to deal with her sister.

With steadfast determination, Lilidh continued to offer guttural commentary on anything and everything Ilysa's maid offered or asked and on any of her sister's answers or comments. Just when she was about to ask Gavina to throw her out once more, a clamour grew outside under her window.

'What is happening, Gavina?'

The servant walked to the window and looked out, leaning against the frame to watch. 'Yer husband, my lady. He is leaving the keep.' The woman continued observing for a few more moments. 'And now he is riding out of the gate.'

Struggling to the edge of the bed, Ilysa pushed herself free of the layers of blankets and sheets and made her way to the window. The day was bright and the glare of the sun hurt her eyes. Holding her hand over her brow to block some of it, she saw Ross leading a group of eight or nine others on horseback down through the village. The gates closed behind them and Munro called out to the guards from the walkway high on the parapets of the keep.

'Where could he be going now? It cannot be safe yet.'

Her question was not meant to be answered by anyone in this chamber and yet her sister's silence bothered her more than her taunts. When Ilysa turned to look at her and saw the smug expression of someone who knew more than they were saying, she grew worried. She'd seen this expression before and knew Lilidh was challenging her to ask her what she knew.

With Gavina present, Ilysa would discover nothing. Her sister's shrewdness and guile had served her well and she would not expose her plans, or their father's, before it suited her. As her servant placed the shawl around her shoulders and adjusted it as she liked, Ilysa said the one thing guaranteed to get the woman out of the chamber.

'Gavina, I find I am hungry.'

'I will get ye something to eat,' the maid said. 'Have ye need of anything else, my lady?' The need to escape from Lilidh's presence was clear in the haste with which Gavina left the chamber without waiting for her sister to answer.

Ilysa remained at the window, watching Ross until the group disappeared from sight some distance north of the village. Gathering her wits, for she would need them to do battle with her sister, she walked to the empty chair and sat. Finally ready for this battle, she spoke first.

'That morning at Dunyvaig, you begged so prettily for my forgiveness, Lilidh. If you had not betrayed me before that, and apparently since, I might have believed your words.' Ilysa wanted to smile at Lilidh's reaction to finding out that her younger sister was not the complete fool she thought. 'Ross was correct in one thing he said—*you* are our father's daughter.'

'Father believes you are *not* his,' Lilidh sneered. 'He did not think a daughter of his would be as weak as you.'

'As appealing as that would be to me, our mother would not have lived to birth another bairn of his if he thought she'd been unfaithful.' Ilysa walked over to stare out of the window. 'So, what now?'

'Now, Sister?'

'Now that Ross has survived and I am in disgrace.'

'Has he?' Lilidh's attempt at innocence failed and Ilysa heard the mocking tone. She must discover the rest of it, even if seeming the fool was how she had to act.

'The battle is over, Sister. He stood here alive and well.'

'And where is he now, *Sister*?' Lilidh stood then and walked to the edge of the chamber, circling in a leisurely manner until Ilysa turned to face her. 'He has left the safety of the castle to meet with The Campbell's son. And anything could happen outside the walls.'

The warriors her father had sent. They were outside the walls.

'Why would Father kill him before an heir was a certainty, Lilidh?'

'You never asked why Graeme accompanied me here,' her sister said. 'Were you not curious?' Surprised by her sister's change of topic, she shook her head.

'Truly, I was not. I never wanted, never want, to see that man again.' Her sister made a noise that was like a soft huff and a chuckle together. 'You do not believe me? After what happened, what he did and what you did, why would I?' Lilidh stopped and laughed. She laughed loud and long and then rubbed her hands together.

'Well, sister of mine, prepare to see much, much more of the man than you have before. Graeme Mac-Lean will be your new husband and guardian, if or when you carry a child.'

She could not help it—her hand slid down over her flat belly as if she would feel something to tell her she was carrying…or not.

'I do not think I am with child, Lilidh. This plan falls apart without a child.'

Lilidh walked to her and placed her own hand over Ilysa's, sliding it over her belly as if seeking life within her womb.

'You will be. Before you step foot out of this chamber again, you will be. If not by the filthy MacMillan's seed, then Graeme will see the deed done. And no matter which, Father will claim this castle and MacMillan lands in your child's name.'

Ilysa reeled back, falling hard against the wall at this revelation.

'Nay!' she yelled. All she received in response was one raised brow. 'I will not consent to such a thing.'

'You are more pitiful than ever,' her sister accused. 'He stood here and told you he would put you aside. What kind of woman are you that you even concern yourself with his welfare when he cares not what happens to you?'

'But you have wanted Graeme for years,' she argued. 'He chose you when you made certain he saw my…arm.'

Lilidh laughed and waved her hand. 'He is and has always been a means to an end, Sister. A means to an end. Once you were gone, I saw his true nature—'

'You mean you could not manipulate him as easily as others?'

'I recognised his weak nature and understood he was better as a tool in my hand than a husband in my bed.'

Ilysa could think about all that later. At this moment, all she knew was that she loved Ross and would do what she could to protect him from her father's nefarious plan.

'And you? What do you gain from playing your part in this scheme if you do not want Graeme?' She regained her footing and put herself in front of Lilidh so her sister could not avoid her. 'What has Father promised you?'

'I will choose my own husband!' she shouted. 'I will not lie beneath a fool or elderly noble while he slavers over me, taking his ease on me.' She gathered her control and cleared her throat. 'I will be able to choose whom I marry.'

Now it was Ilysa's turn to laugh. And she did, no matter her sister's reddening face and anger over being mocked.

'Come now, Sister,' she said. 'You understand Father better than anyone. He raised you in his own image when Mother produced no sons and when none of his lemans could give him one from the wrong side of the blanket to claim.' She shook her head. 'Now? Now you ignore the truth of this? He will give you to anyone if his needs are met and his desire for power and wealth is fed.'

For a moment, just one single moment, Ilysa thought her words might have affected her sister. That she might have made her see the truth of their father's nature— that no one was safe from him.

What she did not expect was Lilidh's reaction. Nothing could have prepared her for her sister to attack her.

With a scream, Lilidh launched herself at Ilysa, knocking her off her feet and to the floor. With her good arm caught between them, she could do nothing to cushion the fall or the blows that followed. Try as she might, Ilysa could not leverage herself to push her sister off or to pull her arm free. Pain burst in her face as Lilidh's fist struck her jaw. Then, in the next moment, her sister was lifted off her and pushed aside.

'My lady!' Gavina cried out. 'Here, Angus, help the Lady up.' Together the two lifted her to her feet and Gavina loosened her shawl and set the sleeve holding her arm to rights. 'We should check to see if ye've been injured anywhere, my lady.'

Only then did she realise that her sister was heading towards the door. The open door.

'Angus, my sister...' The guard reacted quickly and with his height and strength subdued Lilidh with little effort. 'My husband gave me permission to bind and gag her if need be and I think it does.'

As the other guard entered, Ilysa knew she must get to Munro with the news Lilidh had told her. Ross was riding into an ambush and his commander must help him. She did not hesitate then, running as best she could down the corridor and the stairs to the main floor. The guards realised she had slipped out and called out as they gave chase. She made it out into the yard before others grabbed hold of her.

Chapter Nineteen

'Munro!' she screamed, searching for the man where last she'd seen him. 'Munro! Your chieftain needs you now!' Her words shocked the guards who took hold of her and those in the yard who turned to her as she continued to shout. 'To The MacMillan!' she cried.

'Lady, return to your chamber now.' Munro reached her and nodded to the guards.

'Munro, Ross is going to be ambushed. The Mac-Donnell warriors lie in wait for him. They will kill him,' she explained. The commander nodded again to the guards who began to pull her back towards the keep. When she screamed out his name, he approached her.

'Lady, do not make this worse. Most have not heard about your treachery. Ross wanted to allow you your dignity.'

'My dignity matters not, Munro. You heard my sister—'

'Aye, I heard *from my own man* of your sister's part in this. And yours, Lady,' he said in hushed tones so others did not hear.

'My sister told me the plot did not end with yesterday's battle. The Campbells might be defeated here, but my father is not.' Ilysa fought the guards' hold of her, struggling to remain to speak to Munro. 'His life is in danger. Now, Munro. Seek your lord now where he meets with The Campbell's son!'

Munro frowned and shook his head and watched as she was dragged back inside. Frantic to find a way to help Ross, she only realised the guards drew to a stop when Gavina blocked their path.

'My lady,' she said. 'Come along.'

How was she to do that? The guards were ordered to… The guards released her and she turned to find a large gathering of those who worked in the keep blocking their way. Angus and Gavina stood closest to her.

'Go get the commander, Angus,' Gavina said. 'We will speak to him, my lady.'

With Gavina holding on to her arm, Ilysa returned outside where Munro stood, hands fisted on his hips, with Angus watching them walk to him.

'Ye must listen to the Lady, Munro,' Gavina called out.

More people gathered around them now and she recognised the villagers she'd helped, the servants from the keep and others of Ross's kin. The grumbling became louder until Munro shouted them down.

'Your chieftain ordered her held in her chambers,' he said. 'I follow his orders.'

'She saved my daughter and the others,' the blacksmith said.

'She showed us how to get to safety,' called out one of the villagers.

'The Lady got help for me after the last attack,' said one of the older men.

Ilysa could only watch as one after another of them took her part, defending her to the commander.

'If she says Ross is in danger, then he is, Munro. I stake my honour on it.' Innis winked at her after speaking and luckily Gavina held on to her arm or she might have fallen over at that.

'I beg you, Munro. Just send some men to him now,' Ilysa said. 'If I am wrong, then nothing has been lost.'

Munro's gaze moved across the crowd and she saw the exact moment he gave in. He turned and whistled as he crossed the yard to the stables, calling out orders as he did so. Soon, mounted with a dozen warriors at his back, he led them out of the now-open gate in the same direction where Ross had headed.

She could only pray they reached him in time.

'My lady,' Angus said. 'I must return ye to yer chamber now.'

'Could I wait in the chapel, Angus? With my sister in my chamber, I fear what I might do to her if…if…' She could not finish the words.

The poor young man could not answer. He'd already violated his orders for her and would need to answer for it when Ross returned and calm was restored. Now, she asked for more leniency than was his to give.

'I will take the Lady there,' a voice said from behind her. She turned to find Innis at her back. Relief shone on Angus's face as he nodded to the elder. Standing away, he allowed Innis to walk with her.

Usually, the chapel was a separate building whether small or as large as a church. Here, it was within and tucked into the corner of the foundation of the keep itself. As the castle was built on a huge promontory of rocks that jutted out from the land towards the loch, adjustments were made in the size and breadth of some chambers on that lower floor. Just such adjustments had the chapel shaped as roughly a triangle to fit into the rocks supporting it.

She'd found the small chapel by accident while lost in the lower floor of the keep during her first week here at Castle Sween. She'd been searching for the chamber used by the healer and was drawn by the strange patterns of light on the floor in front of its door. The small windows cut high in the stone wall and filled with costly glass allowed the sun's light in and broke it into intricate designs as the sun moved. She'd never encountered the healer—her cousin—until the day he'd disappeared, but this place had been her favourite in the entire keep.

Innis opened the door and Ilysa entered. Father Liam was elsewhere which meant she had the quiet place to herself.

'I will remain here, Innis,' she said. 'Tell Angus to come for me when…'

'Aye, my lady,' Innis said. His footsteps slowed at the door as she sat on one of the stone benches.

'That was brave of you,' he said. 'To go up against Munro.'

'To save Ross? Not brave at all. Self-serving at best,' she admitted.

'How so?' He canted his head, waiting on her words.

'I could not live, kenning that I was part of what killed him.' He nodded and left her then.

She searched within the sleeve holding her arm and

tugged the veil she kept there free. Placing it over her hair, she slid to her knees and began the recitation that brought her peace.

She remained there for some time, until the moving shadows of light and dark across the floor told her that the sun would set soon.

And still there was no word on Ross.

'Damn it, Ross. Did she have to be right?' Munro asked, surveying the cost, in lives, of the fight that had nearly seen Ross's own end.

They'd made it to the place where Calum had asked to meet when it happened. The attackers did not bother to hide their identities for they'd expected no one to be left alive when they were finished with their task.

Not Campbells. MacDonnells.

No discussion under flag of truce, but an ambush meant to kill them all. The only thing that had turned the fight into a victory for them was Munro's arrival with more men. Two of his warriors were dead and several others severely wounded when his commander crashed through the brush, screaming out their battle cry. Then, no quarter was asked or given, and the fighting continued until every MacDonnell lay dead or dying.

Now, when they could pause to examine what had happened, Ross did not wish to. Munro looked no happier about doing it either. After sending men out to search for any sign of Campbells or more MacDonnells, Ross gathered the others for the ride back to the castle.

She'd saved him even after he'd turned from her.

She'd chosen him above her family.

She'd risked all to spare his life.

As they rode back, Ross slowed his horse and waited for Munro to reach his side.

'What happened?' he asked his commander. All Munro had told him when he arrived was that she was the one who'd warned him of the coming trap and sent him to Ross. With few words as was his manner, his commander told him the rest. 'How did she learn of the treachery?'

'Her sister.'

Ross said words under his breath that no one need hear. 'And you believed her?'

Munro shrugged. 'Not at first. She gave no proof and what she said about her father's plans was nothing different from what her sister had said. And what Gowan had told us. When I pointed that out to her, she insisted taking your life was her father's true plan.'

'So, if you did not believe her and she told you nothing you did not already ken, why did you come?'

'They stood for her.'

'They?' Ross waited. When Munro did not reply, he asked again, 'Who stood for the Lady?'

'All of them. Her people. Those in the village she'd helped. Those in the keep who serve her. Everyone who has ever talked to her or walked by her it seemed.' Munro let out a breath. 'Innis.'

His enemy wife had taken his people from him. When he wasn't looking, she'd stolen their hearts even while stealing his. But, they had not rejected her. Nay, they believed her and stood for her, against him, even while for him.

If he had thought himself a better chieftain than his

uncle, different though better, this had proved him so wrong. Worse, he had indeed believed her sister over her.

And she'd sent Munro to save his pitiful arse.

The closer they got to Sween, the more he understood how he'd failed her. He'd not trusted her even when she'd begged him to. Now, he must clean up the pieces of this debacle and make the true villain pay the price.

The MacDonnell's minions must pay as well. The sister he'd escaped marrying and the man who'd destroyed Ilysa in a way that haunted her even now. That man must pay as well.

The silhouette of Castle Sween could be seen as they followed the curve of the road.

The one fact he could not ignore was that he had to pay, too. He'd promised Ilysa he was different from her father and his own uncle and, when he'd needed to stand by his word, he'd failed her and failed her badly.

Unforgivably even.

And try as he might to come up with a way to keep her at his side and in his heart, he'd broken her heart and her trust and he suspected he could not repair those.

It was past sunset by the time they arrived back and it took another hour to take care of those dead and injured, and send orders to put Lilidh MacDonnell below with the MacLean man and more. All the while he considered what he would say to his wife. And how he could repair the damage between them—if, indeed, it could be repaired. The one issue he did not want to address was what he would do if there was no hope for them.

Ross climbed the steps to her chamber, each one

more difficult than the last. He reached the doorway and lifted the latch. Her chamber, her bed, were empty. He stepped inside and glanced around, hoping she was in the corner.

She was not.

A burst of hope sent him running to his chamber. That was dashed when he found it empty as well.

Where could she be?

One person would know. Running down the steps, he searched for Gavina and ignored the disgruntled, disrespectful even, glances and sounds as he passed by servants and warriors. No one seemed happy for his safe return. It was worse when he asked for Gavina's whereabouts. One man sent him up to the second floor, another directed him back down to the kitchens and a third sent him to his own chamber. Only when he tired of being sent here and there did he raise his voice and demand Gavina's presence and the servant mysteriously appeared.

He wanted to ask her so many questions, yet the only one he could give voice to was a simple one. 'Is she well?'

Gavina harrumphed, tapped her foot and narrowed her gaze as she stared him down. 'Nay, my lord. I would not describe the way ye left the Lady as *well.*' She crossed her arms over her ample chest. 'The Lady could keep nothing down and then that…that…her sister attacked her.'

'She did what?' Ross nearly yelled that question. Munro had not told him that part.

'Luckily, Angus and I heard the commotion and dragged her away before she could do serious harm.'

'Where is she, Gavina?' He rubbed his eyes and squeezed the bridge of his nose tightly as the pain grew. 'Just tell me where.'

'In the chapel, my lord,' the maid said. 'She has been there for hours. Would not come away. Would not seek the comfort of her chambers. Would not accept anything.'

'I will do what I can to make it right with her, Gavina.'

'You had better, my lord. You had better.'

As he walked down to the chapel, a place he'd not visited in a long time, he tried to sort out what he could say to her. By the time he turned into the corridor that led to the chapel, he was no closer to knowing what to say than he had been hours ago.

Chapter Twenty

Ross passed by two guards near the door of the chapel and sent them off with a nod. He wanted no witnesses and no one to overhear the conversation he would have with his wife. He stood there for a short while yet, searching for the words to say, and when he reached out to lift the latch, he still was uncertain.

He entered and closed the door with his foot. Taking a few paces in, he did not see her. Was this another useless chase of Gavina's to make her well-made point yet again? Ilysa's gasp behind him alerted him to her presence. He did not turn immediately, but waited a moment to gather his wits. Then he faced her.

Neither spoke at first. He drank in the sight of her, noticing the bruise on her jaw and the way she clenched the edge of the shawl. Her wide-eyed stare hurt, for in it he recognised surprise, fear and confusion. When he stepped closer, she stepped away and it felt like a dagger in his gut.

He'd done this. He'd turned the woman he'd said he loved back into the fearful, hesitant, insecure bride who'd arrived all those weeks ago. Now, she could not trust him. Not trust him to do what he'd promised. Not trust him to mean what he said. Not to be the man worthy of her love.

'They did not attack you?' Her words were rough and pained.

'Aye, they did.' He remained still, not moving. 'But Munro arrived in time to save my life.'

'I am glad.' Her voice was a whisper.

Still searching for the words, he turned and walked to the small altar near the wall and watched as the candle's light flickered from his approach. Father Liam always kept one burning and had someone light one if he was unable. But who it was he knew not, for he had not…

'I have not been here since my mother's death,' he said. 'They were not married here all those years ago. Their vows were exchanged on our family's lands in the north. In the chapel there, not outside as most do. But she was laid to rest from his place.' She watched him closely as he spoke. 'We are not like them.'

She did take a step away from the wall.

'They loved each other for years before their marriage, though many were against it.' He waited.

'Why?'

'He was the chieftain's son and she was from the village. Many expected him to marry higher. His father did.' He smiled then, thinking on his parents. 'He and my uncle were twins. Although he did not fight to gain control over the clan when their father passed, he did fight my uncle and their father for the marriage.'

Ross let out his breath as he walked up to the altar

and circled it. Leaning his fists on the cool, stone surface, he watched her across it.

'They loved each other when they married,' he repeated.

'Not like us.'

'Nay. So many differences between them and us.' He shook his head. 'Yet, you are like her in many ways. You have her spirit. Her kind heart. Her resilience.'

She took another step closer and he opened his hands, placing the palms down on the altar.

'I have wronged you, Ilysa. Grievously wronged you and harmed you with my arrogance and lack of trust.' He could see the light of the candle reflected in the tears gathering in her eyes. *'Mea culpa. Mea culpa. Mea maxima culpa,'* he whispered.

None of this was her doing and he wanted her to know that he held himself guilty for the damage done between them. She would recognise those words. He only hoped...

'None of this was your doing and I will not hold you to promises made by your father or words given under duress. I would only ask that you remain here at Castle Sween until the business between him and me is done.'

'What do you mean?' She reached the altar and placed her hand there.

''Tis not over yet. More battles are to be fought. Though the meeting with Calum was a ruse, he and his men are on their way even now to join with his father against my brother and our allies. I would take you back to the nunnery, but I could not guarantee your father would not have you plucked out in the dark of night again.'

'Ross, I—' she said.

'You are free to do as you please. I have sent your sister and that bastard MacLean to another holding for now, so you will not encounter them. For now, rest and gain your strength back.'

He saw the dark shadows of strain under her eyes. The last days had taken a hard toll on her. He nodded and turned and realised he'd given her no sense of comfort or a plan forward.

'Once the Campbells are defeated, I will see to an annulment.'

'An annulment? But we have…' That she could still blush at any reference to their physical relationship was a wonder to him.

'I will find a way, Ilysa. There are always church officials willing to assist if there is gold to be had. Then, you can live where you wish, marry as you want or not, and I will make a settlement on you, so you never have to do what you do not wish to do.' He left then, but not before turning back at the door to look upon her one last time. 'I am sorry for not trusting you.'

'And if there is a bairn?'

The words stopped him. Images of her ripened body carrying his child filled his thoughts. He'd taunted her with threats when her sister had raised the possibility of such a thing. But the truth was…

'If there is a bairn, we will speak of it when you ken. Have no fear that I will force the child from you, Ilysa.'

He walked then, before he could demand or order or plead for her forgiveness. Seeing her condition, he was certain that would do more harm than good. Listening as he walked, his footsteps made the only sounds along the corridor. Ross waited on some indication from her of distress and, hearing none, he returned to his chamber.

Mea culpa. Mea culpa. Mea maxima culpa.
Through my fault. Through my fault. Through my most grievous fault.

Ilysa stood where she was and waited for the sound of his paces to disappear before sitting back down on the bench where she'd been in the back corner of the chapel. There she could lean against the wall and a conveniently placed tapestry that kept the worst of the stone's chill from her.

At first, she thought his words would bruise her heart even more than it was bruised now. He had finally accepted his guilt in not believing her. In questioning her word and her love for him.

And it gave her some measure of relief and comfort.

Although, now she knew she would not be his wife for long. He was giving her up. Giving up his claim on her body, heart and soul. A sad laugh burst from her. As if it was as simple as declaring it so. Worse, he did not even realise why he was doing it. In the long hours of prayer for his safe return, she'd had enough time to contemplate the truth of Ross MacMillan as a man, a husband and a chieftain.

The one thing she knew for certain was that they did have love between them. Just as it tempered her judgement of him and the wrongs done her, it steered his actions in all things. Their last night of joy had given her insight into the reasons behind his actions and had made it possible for her to understand him. Even if he did not understand himself.

But he was correct about one thing—she needed time to recover from the terrible strain of the last days and the pain of her broken heart. And the constant dangers around them. And the damage done by her sister's plotting with their father.

A long sigh escaped her then. Her entire body ached, from the lack of sleep and sitting in that chair, then sitting or kneeling here on the stone bench or floor. Added to those aches were the ones from landing on the floor of her chamber under her sister and the blows Lilidh had managed to inflict before being pulled off.

For now, Ilysa would see to her own needs so that she could think more clearly and decide whether she would allow him his way. She made her way along the empty corridor, up the stairs and through the quiet main hall. As she was walking to the steps leading to her chambers, she spied Morag in the corner.

Some pallets had been arranged in a small area and Morag tended to some of the warriors who'd been injured, though she knew not if it happened during the battle or the ambush. She'd rushed through here so quickly this morn, trying to get to Munro, that she'd not seen them.

'My lady,' the woman said, beginning to rise to her feet from the low stool on which she sat.

'Morag, do not,' she said. She shook her head at the others there who tried to do the same thing. 'Tend to those who need it.' Ilysa examined the supplies strewn around the pallets to see if anything was missing. 'Have you need of anything? I can help, if you—'

'Nay, my lady,' Morag said with a laugh. 'As I told

yer husband, with yer own injuries, the last thing ye should be doing is seeing to others.'

Ross had already spoken to her? Shocked by this revelation, Ilysa frowned at the wise old woman. Morag's knowing glance and raised brow tempted her to question her more.

'See to yerself, my lady.' Morag smiled gently then and nodded. The woman was exactly the person she needed to speak to about so many things. Things she did not understand. Things about…possibilities.

'Would you find me on the morrow? If you have time? I would speak to you about…some matters.'

'Womanly matters?' The woman's tone was teasing, as though she reminded Ilysa of their previous excuse for Morag's presence in the keep. 'Aye, my lady. I will seek you out.'

Ilysa nodded and turned, exhaustion filling every part of her as she headed for the stairs.

'My lady?' Ilysa faced the healer before she walked away. 'I sent a concoction to yer chambers that will aid you in sleeping and help the pain.'

She barely made it to her chamber and removed her gown and shoes before climbing up on to the bed. Closing her eyes, all she could see was Ross, standing across from her, separated by the altar. Falling into sleep's embrace, his words echoed in her head and in her heart.

Mea culpa. Mea culpa. Mea maxima culpa.

Through my own fault. Through my own fault. Through my most grievous fault.

She'd forgiven him before his return to the castle. Before he'd sought her out and proclaimed his guilt.

Forgiving, the prioress had taught, was the easiest

part of dealing with a transgression by another against you. The forgetting was the difficult part.

Ilysa thought the holy woman had one thing wrong—it was not the forgiving or forgetting that was the hardest. In Ilysa's opinion, the effort it took to make things right again was the real battle.

That would begin on the morrow.

Other than the strange and enlightening conversation with Morag, and after more than twelve hours of undisturbed sleep, Ilysa felt that she had somehow flown back in time to the first week after her arrival here. She and Ross moved about and around each other in what felt like a well-planned dance to avoid each other. They spoke to the same people—farmers, villagers, servants—but never at the same time or in sight of one another.

Word had arrived from Ross's sister that the abbey where she had been lodged had been attacked, probably as Calum made his way east to join his father, which was worrying until they learned she was safe and would join Fergus. With rumblings from Islay, Ross made the decision to remain at Castle Sween to head off any other problems.

If she did encounter Ross unexpectedly, they acted as if they were polite strangers. Even if she remembered every single thing they'd done together every time she saw him, she stuttered her way through the inevitable blush and escaped.

If that reaction had been only hers, she could have convinced herself that she was daft, but the hunger in his gaze during those encounters told her the truth—

desire still burned brightly between them. Their passion had been the honesty between them and she, and her body, missed the intimacy and pleasure they'd shared.

Morag's explanation later had assuaged her of any concerns about her possible condition. Morag was certain that Ilysa did not carry a bairn within her.

It was probably for the best since a bairn would complicate the situation more than it was. No child meant Ross could seek an annulment without doubts. And, truth be told, she had never once considered that having a child, or marriage, was in her future.

The letters exchanged with the prioress had given her some comfort. An invitation to return gave her a choice about where to go from here. Once matters had been settled, the nun had written, she was welcome to stay with them on Iona.

Now, almost a week after they'd exchanged any words between them, matters had not been settled. And as Ross grew more and more polite every time they met, Ilysa grew more and more impatient.

To say her piece. To truly settle matters. To make him see the truth.

So, before another attack or distraction and before he could be called away, Ilysa prayed that something would happen to force his hand.

Chapter Twenty-One

'This is worse than when she arrived here.'

Ross ignored Dougal, for he'd said the same thing at least ten times just this morn. They were gathered in Gillean's chamber to discuss sending supplies to Castle Barron when his friend repeated the words as though none had heard them before.

But they had. Indeed, he'd heard them more than the others witnessing the exchange. At least Munro could be depended on to stay out of his privy business involving his wife.

'Mayhap you just need to ask her to stay?' his commander said. So much for Munro remaining out of the fray.

Ross turned to his steward and waited for his opinion, for everyone seemed wont to share theirs with him. Gillean shook his head and busied himself trying to locate a parchment he suddenly needed. Wise man. Ross directed the discussion back to the matter at hand and he might have been successful if not for the unexpected arrival of their priest.

'I would speak to you,' Father Liam said. Only as he came in did he see the others there. 'Oh, if you are busy, it can wait.'

'Nay, not busy, Father. Join us,' Ross said. Anything to escape the intention of the two here to force his thoughts to…her. 'What is it?'

The priest held up a piece of parchment as he entered. From the way he remained close to the door, Ross had the feeling the priest stood there to be able to escape quickly once he delivered his news.

'The prioress at the Iona nunnery has written to me so that there is no mistake in the arrangements, my lord.' The man looked ready to burst into flames for he began sweating and his face grew red. 'I was unaware, so I thought it best to ask you, my lord.'

'Arrangements?' Dougal asked before Ross could.

'For the Lady's move to Iona.' Father Liam looked from Ross to Dougal and then to Munro and to Gillean as silence filled the space around them. 'Is the Lady moving back to the nunnery?'

The strained silence continued for no one, not even Ross, could come up with an answer. Oh, he'd offered her the chance to go wherever she wanted, but he'd hoped…he'd wanted more time…he did not want her to go. Suddenly the other men listening all stared in different directions as they waited for him to explain to their priest the unusual offer he'd made to his wife.

'Ross.'

'Dougal,' he ground out. 'Do not—'

'Ross.' Munro this time.

'Nay, both of you,' he said, shaking his head at them. 'I thank you for bringing this to my attention, Father.'

Ross stood and the priest backed out of the chamber and was gone.

'Get out.' None of them moved at all. 'I said get out.'

Though they glanced at each other, none of the three dared meet his glare as they got up and walked out of the chamber. The door had been closed only for a few moments when it opened and Munro came back in. Before Ross could speak, Munro placed his knuckles on the table where Ross sat and leaned down.

'You and the Lady are perfect for each other. You could not have found a better bride if you'd chosen her.' He shook his head. 'But, if you let her slip from your grasp or chase her away, you are a bigger fool than your uncle ever was.'

'I told her—'

'You gave her choices without ever telling her which you wanted. Without telling her how much you want her at your side.' Munro stood up. 'Without telling her that her place is here, with you.'

'You do not understand,' Ross said.

'I understand strategy and yours is a poor one,' he said. 'Do not be daft. Go to her. Tell her. Work this out here, now, for if she leaves, she is not coming back.'

Something swirled in his commander's words. Something personal that sounded like a profound loss. All Ross knew was that he needed to find Ilysa and sort this out before any more time passed. He rose from his chair as Munro pulled the door open for him.

After the way he had betrayed her faith in him, he had no right to ask her to stay, no matter that he needed her to remain. He had given up that right when he'd turned his back on her pleas. How could he now go to her and ask her to stay?

'The Lady walked into the village a short time ago. She should be returning soon.'

In that moment, he only knew he must. He must risk the possibility of her rejection or he would lose her for ever.

Ross almost knocked over the two men standing outside the door who'd been trying hard to overhear the conversation as he raced through the hall and out into the yard. He searched and saw her just as she came in through the gate, with Gavina at her side. He knew the moment she saw him, but she did not stop and instead met him in the centre of the open space.

When they did stop just a few paces away from each other, he could only stare at her. He'd not been able to do that in these last days since they seemed to be avoiding each other. For his part, he wanted to give her a chance to think on what he'd told her. But, as Munro had correctly determined, Ross had not told her the truth in his heart.

'Father Liam said you are moving to Iona.' He cared not who heard him. They would all know soon enough if she left him.

'I am considering it,' she said. 'You gave me that choice, my lord.' Her chin jutted out and he loved that she did not simply acquiesce.

'Aye, I did, Wife,' he said. As he crossed his arms over his chest, he heard the gathering crowd whispering. This was his chance now to make her stay. 'I owed you that choice, but that does not mean I want you to leave.'

'I will not stay where I am not trusted.' She turned

slightly and shook her head. 'I will not remain married to a man who does not trust me.'

The crowd shifted around them and it seemed that they mostly lined up behind her, supporting her as she spoke.

'I am not my father, my lord, and I will not be judged by his actions.' Whispers of *aye* and *not her father* echoed around them and she nodded at him. 'You said you accepted me. But when I needed you to believe me, over my sister's or anyone else's lies, you did not. I begged you—' Her voice broke then and she glanced away.

'I failed you, Ilysa. I want the chance to try again. To regain your trust,' he said. He took a step closer, so he did not have to yell his words. 'I want you to stay. Here. With me.'

'With us!' someone shouted. Laughter erupted. When it quieted, he did what he needed to do—he begged her.

'You are the wife I choose,' he said in front of everyone. 'I cannot promise you I will not fail you again, but I can swear that I will work every moment of our lives to be worthy of your trust again.' She met his gaze then as tears streamed down her cheeks. 'Can you, will you, give me that chance, Ilysa? Will you stay at my side?'

He held his hand out to her and stopped breathing. Everything hung on this single moment of time. On her decision. On whether or not she could believe his words when he had not believed hers. Utter silence surrounded them in a place filled with many people and so much activity. And still, she stared at his hand.

Any hope he had that he could convince her to stay and give him the chance to make it right with her began

to fade. She did not move for so long Ross was certain
of her answer. It felt like a year had passed before she
did reach out and take his hand. He pulled her into his
arms and held her tightly, afraid she would change her
mind if he let go.

'I love you, Wife,' he whispered to her as she lifted
her face to him. 'I love you.'

'And I love you, Husband. And I will stay.'

He kissed her openly, before their people, claiming
her. As he released her, he saw the priest there on the
steps of the keep watching them.

'Father Liam!' he called out. Without releasing Ilysa,
he walked her to the steps. 'Would you hear our vows?'
Before the priest could reply, Ilysa did.

'Ross, we are already married.'

'But I want to say the words to you. To make the
promises to you. So that there can be no doubt of my
sincerity or intentions or of the identity of the woman
I claim.'

'If you wish,' she said.

Ross turned her to face him. 'Do you want to do this?
Make a new beginning? Pledge ourselves freely?' She
searched his face as though deciding. 'If you do not,
say nay now.'

'Do you promise…?' She stopped and shook her
head.

'Do I promise?'

He leaned closer to listen to her words. Words she
did not wish everyone to hear. When she made her
conditions clear, he grabbed her up in his arms and
spun around with her, laughing and offering a prayer
of thanks that he'd taken the step he needed to keep her

at his side. Ross set her on her feet and held her until she steadied. 'Aye, Ilysa, I promise!'

If his wife wanted a new consummation of these vows, he was more than willing to oblige.

'Father, you can begin.'

The vows took little time, but the other part took much, much longer.

Ilysa had no choice truly. When he'd begged her and understood how important trust would be in their marriage, she'd had to say aye. She understood what his words and his plea had cost him—as a proud man and as a chieftain. He'd acknowledged his sins against her and pledged to do better. She did not doubt his intentions, or his love. Better still, he'd agreed to what she wanted.

As she watched him sit on the new, very large and cushioned chair in her chamber, wearing only his tunic, her body grew hot. She crossed to him and he stood, tugging her shift off and his, leaving her naked before him. Sitting back down, he guided her legs around his and supported her body as he tugged her hips forward. She slid her knees around his hips and he smiled.

Taking a moment to position her damaged arm on the side of the chair, he slouched down a bit, bringing her hips closer while opening her to his body and his touch. His rampant flesh stood between them as he settled her on his thighs. Her own flesh was wet and throbbing, ready for his touch.

'Kneel up now, love,' he urged. 'Hold on to my shoulder.'

She listened and followed his instructions, knowing that in a moment, once he was confident that she was positioned comfortably, he would pleasure her. It would not take much to send her over the edge to satisfaction. Her whole body was tense, anticipating that first caress. That first glide of his fingers deep inside her. That first touch of his tongue or suckle of his mouth. She closed her eyes, enjoying the thrill of waiting for it to happen.

It was his fingers.

His knuckles rubbed along her cleft, pressing deeply as he had in the bath that first night. His thumb flicked, searching for its target, and she gasped when he found it. Her body arched and, in her position, it brought her breasts to his face.

'Come closer, lass. Give me a wee taste,' he whispered.

And she did. Twisting a bit, she placed the tip of one in front of his mouth and watched as he smiled. Then his wicked tongue teased the tip until it was a tight bud. For a moment the sensation was too intense, almost a painful pleasure, as he worried his teeth there. Then he pulled it into his mouth and used his tongue to circle it, faster and harder.

When he extended his fingers and plunged them deeply within her, she moaned out her release as her body tightened and tightened and then exploded in waves of pleasure and aching until she fell against him, weak from her release.

'Ready?' he whispered into her hair.

'Done.' The muffled word made him laugh.

He moved his hand from her flesh and lifted her body closer, placing his erect male flesh at the opening to her core. Inch by hard inch, he entered her so slowly, as she begged him to move faster. Then he did, filling her fully, and the friction of his size and the glide of his flesh brought on another climax almost immediately.

He surprised her, standing even while holding her against him securely. She lifted her head to see his path and he walked them over to her door.

'Hold on, my love.'

That was the only warning he gave as he proceeded to take her against the strong wooden door of her chamber. With his arms bracing her body, he thrust in hard and deep enough to hold her in place. Faster and faster, he plunged his flesh into hers until she screamed out her release. Leaning his head down on her shoulder, his breath hot and steamy against her neck, he thrust three more times and then spilled his seed deep within her.

Their panting breaths took a bit to slow down and she laughed as she spoke.

'We have a perfectly comfortable bed just there, Husband,' she said. 'The door?'

'We have used the bed, the chair, the floor, the tub and even the bench before. The door was untouched.'

'Not any longer,' she said. 'There are no virgins left here.'

'Speaking of that comfortable bed,' he whispered against her skin. 'Let us try that out.'

He was still hard and inside her as he carried her to the bed and sat her on the edge of the mattress. After easing his flesh from her, he moved around her and sat with his back on the headboard.

'Come, I am ready for the consummation you made me promise you,' he teased.

Ilysa examined him thoroughly, making her plans on where to touch him. His body, muscular and strong, with the thick curls on his belly leading down to his manhood, made her mouth water in anticipation.

'Take me, Wife,' he commanded.

And as the obedient, compliant wife that she was, she did.

He held her close that night. Once they had exhausted their every desire, she lay in his arms, her leg thrown across his, sleeping. Sleeping deeply.

She slept so soundly that she had never known he had in truth come to her the night after he woke from his injury. He'd climbed into her bed and held her the night through, leaving only when summoned by a servant. And she'd never realised it.

Now, as the soft knock came, he knew she would not wake.

Easing from her hold, he covered her with the blankets and slid off the bed to find out who broke into their privacy. Pulling his shirt over his head, he padded to the door and lifted the latch quietly.

'My lord...' the guard nodded '...Munro said ye should see this.'

Taking the small, folded packet of parchment, he went to the window and used the faint light of the sun to read the message.

'Who is it from?' Ilysa asked. Surprised that she was awake, he read it once more, still not able to believe the words there.

'Fergus.'

He walked to the bed and held it out to her. Gathering his garments as she read it, he prepared to leave her much sooner than he'd hoped.

'Will you go?' she asked, now sliding from the bed and tugging her shift on.

'I must be ready, if he sends word.'

'This is not good.'

'Nay, not good at all.'

'Do what you must, Ross. I will be here waiting for you.'

'Promise?' He took the hand she offered and kissed it.

'I promise,' she whispered in a voice filled with love.

And she was there, waiting for his return, every time his duties called him away.

As they'd promised.

* * * * *

Read on for a teaser of the next instalment of
the Highland Alliances collection
The Highlander's Tactical Marriage
by Jenni Fletcher

'Nay, Uncle, not him! You can't mean it. Anyone but him!'

Coira Barron staggered backwards, feeling as if she'd just been kicked in the stomach. Her nerves had been on edge ever since the summons from her uncle-in-law had arrived the day before, but the reason was even worse than any of the dire possibilities she'd imagined on the eight-hour ride to his fortress. So much worse that she was doing the unthinkable and arguing back. There was no way that such defiance was going to end well, but she couldn't seem to stop herself, the words pouring out of her mouth as if her tongue had a mind of its own. Fergus MacMillan was the last man in Scotland she ever wanted to set eyes on again, let alone marry!

'Please, Uncle, I beg you.'

She shook her head so violently that one of her own dark braids, having already escaped from her veil, hit her in the face. Out of the corner of her eye, she could see various members of Brody's household muttering with disapproval, not that there was anything new about that, only there *was* something different about it this time, a gloating undercurrent that sent icy-cold shivers rattling down her spine. She knew the only reason they still accepted her was because of her son, Gregor, but their antipathy had never been quite so obvious or overwhelming before.

'You'll do as you're told.' Brody MacWhinnie, the fearsome head of his clan, had a voice as cold as the granite outcrop his hall was built on.

'But he must hate me after what I did!'

'Pah.' Brody's shrug implied that whatever her prospective bridegroom might think of her personally was of little importance. 'That was a long time ago.'

'I still doubt he's forgotten,' Coira retorted, before bending her head, sensing she'd gone too far as Brody's pale eyes flashed. Briefly, she thought about prostrating herself on the floor and imploring him to reconsider. Honestly, if he wanted her to crawl around the entire hall on her hands and knees then she was prepared to do it, but hard experience had taught her that Brody MacWhinnie viewed the world from one, and only one, perspective. His own. And once he'd made up his mind, there was absolutely nothing anyone could do to change it, least of all a woman.

'Forgive me, uncle.' She strove to sound suitably meek and dutiful, the two qualities she knew he valued most in the female sex. 'You just caught me by surprise, that's all, and my understanding is only feeble, not like a man's.' She gritted her teeth, peeking up through her lashes to see if the words were having any effect. 'Perhaps you could explain to me why I need to marry at all?'

'Because of the threat from the Campbells! The Mac-Millans and the MacWhinnies need to stand together.'

'But we can still do that! Surely a marriage isn't necessary? Let me defend Castle Barron!'

'What do *you* know of battle strategy?' Brody's lip curled scornfully. 'It was one thing to let you look after the place for your son while we had peace, but things are different now. Alexander Campbell intends to reclaim all the territory he lost twenty years ago, which means we have to be ready to defend ourselves. This is war and Fergus MacMillan is one of the fiercest warriors in the Highlands. If anyone can hold Castle Barron against the Campbells then it's him. I don't want their army getting anywhere near my lands.'

So that was the truth of it, Coira thought, dropping her eyes so that Brody couldn't see them narrowing with contempt. The head of the MacWhinnie clan didn't want the inconvenience of fighting Alexander Campbell or his son Calum himself. Far better to get a MacMillan to do it for him, and if that meant sacrificing her in marriage to a man who despised her then so be it.

If you enjoyed this story look out for the next
instalments of the Highland Alliances collection

The Highlander's Tactical Marriage
by Jenni Fletcher
The Highlander's Stolen Bride
by Madeline Martin
Coming soon!

And while you're waiting for the next books
why not check out Terri Brisbin's
A Highland Feuding miniseries?

Stolen by the Highlander
The Highlander's Runaway Bride
Kidnapped by the Highland Rogue
Claiming His Highland Bride
A Healer for the Highlander
The Highlander's Inconvenient Bride